T0285698

PEDRO AND MARQUES TAKE STOCK

PEDRO
AND
MARQUES
TAKE
STOCK

A PICARESQUE NOVEL

JOSÉ
FALERO

Translated by Julia Sanches

ASTRA HOUSE
NEW YORK

First published in Brazil in 2020, by editora todavia, São Paulo.
Published in agreement with Casanovas & Lynch Literary Agency.

For information about permission to reproduce selections from this book,
please contact permissions@astrahouse.com.

Astra House
A Division of Astra Publishing House
astrahouse.com
Printed in the United States of America

Library of Congress Cataloging-in-Publication Data
Names: Falero, José, 1987– author. | Sanches, Julia, translator.
Title: Pedro and Marques take stock : a picaresque novel /
José Falero ; translated by Julia Sanches.
Other titles: Supridores. English
Description: First edition. | New York : Astra House, [2023] | Summary:
"Pedro and Marques Take Stock is a modern picaresque novel and a vivid
satire on social mobility set in the favelas of Brazil, telling the
story of two supermarket stock clerks whose lives are upturned when
their small-time marijuana business takes off"— Provided by publisher.
Identifiers: LCCN 2023008869 (print) | LCCN 2023008870 (ebook) |
ISBN 9781662601231 (hardcover) | ISBN 9781662601248 (ebook)
Subjects: LCSH: Poor—Brazil—Porto Alegre (Rio Grande do Sul)—Fiction. |
Marginality, Social—Brazil—Porto Alegre (Rio Grande do Sul)—Fiction. |
LCGFT: Picaresque fiction. | Novels.
Classification: LCC PQ9698.416.A46 S8713 2023 (print) |
LCC PQ9698.416.A46 (ebook) | DDC 869.3/5—dc23/eng/20230227
LC record available at https://lccn.loc.gov/2023008869
LC ebook record available at https://lccn.loc.gov/2023008870

First edition
10 9 8 7 6 5 4 3 2 1

Design by Richard Oriolo
The text is set in Sabon LTStd Roman.
The titles are set in Frutiger LTStd Ultra Black.

For Dalva Maria Soares, who came late.
I love you, Preta.

CONTENTS

PEDRO AND MARQUES TAKE STOCK

AN UNPLEASANT
MATTER

Really, tchê? That's outrageous!"

The cell phone Sr. Geraldo was talking into hadn't been designed for giant hands like his. It'd taken him no fewer than five attempts to dial his boss's number, which just goes to show how hard he found it to press a single one of those tiny buttons. Now that he had Sr. Amauri on the line, it was as if Sr. Geraldo couldn't believe he was being heard on the phone; he made a point of shouting every word.

"Anyway, I didn't call for the gossip," he explained, then chuckled. "The truth is I rang to see if you had time to meet for lunch today and talk about . . . Uh . . . Let's call it an unpleasant matter."

Every last thing, from his casual tone of voice to the indirectness of his question, had been meticulously planned. Sr. Geraldo even rehearsed the sentence three or four times so he could have an idea of how it sounded. He knew better than anyone that Sr. Amauri, as supervisor of the Fênix supermarket chain, was always buried under a mountain of problems and never had a minute to spare, which is why he didn't take kindly to last-minute invitations like this one, even when they came from his most competent and dedicated manager, which is exactly what Sr. Geraldo was, and despite them being on friendly terms.

Sure enough, the supervisor was annoyed. He got straight to the point:

"Geraldo, about the issue at your store. Whatever it is, you have the autonomy to handle it on your own. In fact, you don't only have the autonomy, but it's also your duty to try to handle it on your own. After all, you're the manager, are you not?"

"Yes, of course I am, but . . ." Sr. Geraldo cleared his throat, hesitant and disheartened. Even though he'd expected the boss to kick up a fuss, he hadn't counted on him objecting so strongly. "Now look, tchê, if you've got to know, I'm not proud, not at all proud, of what I'm about to tell you." He then said, improvising, "But I think you'll understand. Or at least I hope you'll understand. The thing is, I simply have no idea how to solve this problem. There. That's all." And in a sudden burst of inspiration, he added: "You were a manager once, Amauri. I wonder if, back in the day, you never, never ever found yourself in the position I'm in now, without any idea what to do."

"Yeah . . . Sometimes . . . I suppose I did, now and then . . ." Sr. Amauri grudgingly admitted, unsure of how to rebut Sr. Geraldo's insinuation without seeming arrogant. "But," he insisted, "can you really not figure it out on your own? Must we really meet to talk it over?"

"Come on, tchê, I wouldn't have called if I didn't think it was a big deal."

The supervisor smacked his lips on the other end of the line.

"Alright. So be it. Same restaurant as last time? Can you be there in half an hour?"

"Yes, of course. Wonderful. That's just perfect," the manager said, savoring that small victory. "Thanks. I guess I'll see you soon. Bye."

He left the cell phone on a corner of his desk, leaned back in his chair, lit a cigarette, and gazed around his small office. The space, crammed full of things that never seemed to find their right place, looked more like a depot than it did the management of a supermarket. All those years stuffed in that room . . . Sr. Geraldo hated it. Yet as he gazed around him now, he felt something special. It's not that he didn't hate the space anymore; quite the contrary. He could have easily summoned up the usual rage. All he had to do was focus on the many annoyances contained in those four walls. Still, his current troubles had reminded him of everything the room represented, small and depot-like as it was: a good job, stability, a hard-earned position . . . He wondered if it would be his much longer, then sighed. He'd been sighing a lot lately.

He was a stocky man, prone to obesity, with a full nose and large eyes that were constantly wide open. There was something coarse and vulgar about him: although his hair was grayish and impeccably styled, and his face smooth and beardless, he didn't seem sophisticated. His low, booming voice and warm affect, at once a little ironic and intimidating, made it difficult to tell apart when he was kidding from when he was being serious. Most people would be hard-pressed to believe there was more to Sr. Geraldo than met the eye. He was a boorish, unattractive man who dressed in clothes that appeared elegant; that is, a man who used to be poor but had made his way up in the world with painstaking honesty. The staff loved him because he never gave them a hard time when they slipped up, or demanded too much, or played the tyrant—among other qualities any employee with a bit of sense could appreciate. At the same time, he had no patience for idleness or for people who did everything in their power to do nothing. He hated shirkers. To set an example, he helped out with several of the supermarket's manual tasks, spilling buckets and buckets of sweat, working just as hard as his most dedicated employees, even though he was the manager and under no obligation whatsoever to be doing that kind of work.

After smoking, he left the supermarket in the hands of Paulo, his assistant manager and second-in-command, and left for the meeting. He reached the restaurant before Sr. Amauri, who walked in several minutes later in a pair of handsome, polished dress shoes—shoes Sr. Geraldo had given him on the occasion of his last birthday and then regretted the minute he saw Sr. Amauri try them on, realizing, a moment too late, how much better they'd have looked on his own two feet. They smiled while enthusiastically shaking hands and exchanging a couple of casual remarks. Then they called over the waiter and gave their orders. It didn't take long for the food to arrive, and it was clear when it got to their table that the two men were famished.

"How's the back holding up, Geraldo?" Sr. Amauri asked out of the blue, after loudly ingesting a half-chewed lump of meat. A look of curiosity and concern flitted across his red, equine face.

Sr. Geraldo put down his knife and waved his hand like he was shooing away a fly.

"Forget about it. The doctor said the pain will ease up until it goes away, and I'm relying on it."

"I bet he told you to take it easy, though."

"He did. But you know what doctors are like."

"I know what you're like," Sr. Amauri retorted.

The manager rolled his eyes. He knew Sr. Amauri's spiel inside and out. It seemed they couldn't see one another without the supervisor going on about the damn thing. It was something of a ritual.

As expected, Sr. Amauri proceeded to chide him:

"You open the store in the morning, close up at night . . . You're the first one in and the last one out . . . You never rest. I'm not wrong, am I?" He shook his head. "You know you don't have to do all of it on your own. You could delegate to the assistant manager, like the other managers do. What's stopping you, tchê?"

"I like to keep an eye on things," Sr. Geraldo said between forkfuls, shrugging. "We've talked about it before, Amauri. We've also talked about you wearing those shoes in front of me."

Sr. Amauri failed to recognize the strategic non sequitur. Feinted, he smiled:

"You know, I didn't even have them on. I went home and changed before coming to the restaurant just to bug you."

A long silence ensued. Apparently both men thought they should finish their meal before broaching the subject they had come there to discuss. But before polishing off their food, the supervisor remembered to say:

"I may have to borrow some of your staff next week, Geraldo. Looks like everyone's decided to go to the beach this summer. It's mayhem: massive lines at the cash register, customers complaining around the clock . . ." He shook his head as if trying to chase away a bad memory. "Anyway. You can't imagine what a mess things are. I've been recruiting cashiers from our stores in the cities and sending them to branches up and down the coast: Cidreira, Pinhal, Quintão. It's only for two weeks or so. What do you say? Can you help a guy out?"

"Sure, no problem. I'm fully staffed," Sr. Geraldo said with pride. "Besides, it's been slow here. Probably for the same reason the beaches are so crowded. Porto Alegre's dead. I reckon I can loan you as many as three cashiers. Two weeks, you said?"

"Maybe more. It's so unusual, even for summer, that I don't know how long it'll go on. Not for certain, anyway."

They turned their attention back to the meal, lowering their eyes to their plates. They finished eating, then called over the waiter. No, thank you, they didn't want dessert, just coffee. Thanks. The flustered server disappeared with the dirty dishes and everything else, promising to bring their coffee soon. Sr. Amauri shifted in the chair and brought his hands together on the table, entwining his long fingers.

"Very well, then . . ." Smiling with cold, ceremonious ease, he narrowed his eyes. "I guess it's time we discussed the unpleasant matter you brought up earlier, whatever it is. I have to say, I'm curious." He checked his watch. "Curious and running a bit late, frankly. I need to go straight to the head office, see if I can figure out what happened with those unissued invoices. So? Go on, spill."

But Sr. Geraldo didn't answer. He glanced to the side, worrying the toothpick between his lips, as if scanning the tables around him for the right words.

Sr. Amauri narrowed his eyes even more. Was he seeing things, or had his friend's pride taken a blow? Sr. Amauri grew more and more intrigued as he waited. Finally, the wide eyes he knew so well became resolute.

"Alright, I'll get straight to the point. Because that's how I do things," the manager said, raising one of his hands in self-defense. "The issue is theft. Theft, theft, and more theft. Our stock is being ransacked—cookies, beverages, sweets, deodorant, everything—and I can't seem to get to the bottom of it. I don't know what to do. I've never seen anything like it. Damn it, Amauri, there's a thief on my staff!"

Sr. Amauri processed the information in silence. For a second, his equine features softened, as though the issue at hand weren't as serious as he'd imagined. Then, his face clouded over again. He was trying to gauge just how big the iceberg was beneath the information Sr. Geraldo had disclosed.

"Suspects?" he finally asked.

The manager was momentarily distracted, his tongue moving the toothpick from one corner of his mouth to the other.

"Hunh? Suspects? Well, yes, actually . . . I have a hunch it's the two stock clerks: Pedro and Marques."

"Then fire them," Sr. Amauri suggested, shrugging one shoulder in disdain. But as he said this, he realized that if things had been that simple, the manager wouldn't have called a meeting.

Sure enough, Sr. Geraldo shook his head.

"No, that's not the right way to go about it. I don't have proof. If it *is* them, they haven't left a single trace."

"A bad deed well done."

Two cups of coffee appeared on the table. They did so on their own, as if by magic, or at least that's how Sr. Geraldo and Sr. Amauri would remember it, so absorbed in conversation they didn't even register the light-footed waiter. They took two small, wistful sips of coffee. Then the supervisor said:

"If you suspect Pedro and Marques, then you need to stay on top of them. Have you checked the security footage?"

"I have, I have. Nothing. Neither of them seems to get up to much."

"Then let me ask you something, Geraldo: Why do you think they're the culprits?"

"Intuition," the manager said, lifting his cup of coffee and gazing at Sr. Amauri through the rising steam.

Though Sr. Amauri tried to contain himself, he couldn't help but laugh.

"Give me a break, tchê. Intuition? Last I heard, intuition is a gift exclusive to women."

"Come on, I mean it. I just don't like them. They're insubordinate. They don't take orders. They don't give a damn about the chain of command. They don't respect me. They're always wandering the aisles together, talking about God-knows-what." Just discussing the two stock clerks left Sr. Geraldo visibly flustered. "Anyway, that's it. You asked if I had suspects, didn't you? Well,

I don't trust them. They're the only member of staff I can imagine doing something like this. But I don't like flying blind either, Amauri. I can't justify firing Pedro and Marques when I don't have proof they're the ones behind all this."

"Sometimes it can't be helped, my friend. You've got to try. Everybody flies blind at some point in their lives. If you can't get to the bottom of things, as you said, why not fire them and see what happens?"

"Because Pedro and Marques . . . Setting aside the disciplinary issues . . . Pedro and Marques are the best stock clerks I have." Seeing how confused the supervisor looked, Sr. Geraldo shrugged and explained: "Maybe it's experience, I don't know. Both men have worked at other, bigger chains than ours. Are they insubordinate? Yes, definitely. But hard as it is to admit, they're better at their jobs than anyone else. They even remind me a bit of myself back when I was a stock clerk, the only difference being that I was disciplined. I toed the line. Believe me: It'd be a shame to let them go only to realize we'd made a mistake. It's the middle of summer, Amauri, you know how hard it is to hire new staff this time of year. Much less two workers as good as them."

Sr. Geraldo and Sr. Amauri paused to drink their coffee. Good coffee. Excellent coffee. So good in fact that the supervisor expressed his approval with a long, drawn-out "mmmmm."

"Damn, I'd forgotten how excellent the coffee is here," he remarked, then leaned forward slightly and picked up where they had left off, this time more quietly than before. "Look, Geraldo, I can't have any of our employees hearing this, but the fact of the matter is that our stores are extremely vulnerable to the issue you were just talking about. We can't always keep tabs on the staff, and they know the stores better than anyone. They know the blind spots, they know the security guards' routines . . . If they really want to steal from us, if they get it into their heads that they're going to steal from us, what's to stop them? It's virtually impossible to catch them red-handed. On top of that, Geraldo, you've heard the proverb, haven't you, about how one bad apple spoils the barrel? Well. A dishonest worker will always do his darnedest to corrupt an honest one. Always, without fail. The more friends he has, the better for him and the worse for us." He polished off his coffee with two final glugs, then checked his watch one more time, shocked to see how far the gold pointers had moved. "Damn, look at the time, tchê! I'm late . . . Right, let's be practical. What do you think: Are the security guards in your unit in on the scheme? Are they just looking the other way, or are they stealing too?"

The manager was shaking his head before Sr. Amauri had even finished.

"Frankly, Amauri, I haven't got a clue. I have no hard evidence. That's why I'm so worried. It's been two months since I started noticing our stock go missing, and even though it's gotten worse, I still don't have a single lead. It's like chasing a ghost! I inspect the staff lockers periodically: nothing. I inspect their backpacks when they leave: nothing. It's like things are vanishing into thin air!"

"Right . . ." Even as Sr. Amauri got up to leave, he looked deep in thought. "Very well . . . Here's what we're going to do: we'll scale up security at your store. I'll call a few of our other branches today and see if they can lend you a couple of guards. It's a temporary measure, of course. After that, we can figure out next steps. Sound good?"

Sr. Geraldo seemed to like the idea.

"Wonderful! When do you think you can get the guards to the store?"

"As early as tomorrow, most likely. I'll call you later today to confirm." Sr. Amauri checked his watch again. "Listen, Geraldo, I've got to run."

"Bye, Amauri. And thank you. I'll be waiting for your call."

"Bye. And get the bill, will you? I covered us last time. Don't worry, we're going to put an end to this nonsense."

They shook hands, then Sr. Amauri rushed out into the sunny day.

The manager treated himself to another cup of excellent coffee before heading back to the supermarket. "Don't worry, we're going to put an end to this nonsense." Sr. Amauri's words echoed comfortingly in his head. It sounded as if all of it—his good job, his stability, his hard-earned position—was still safe.

2

DREAMS OF
GETTING RICH

A sprawling region in the far east of Porto Alegre. One that still held traces of its distant rural past, even as it underwent a slow process of urbanization. A region where you could watch the Atlantic Forest slowly go up in smoke while following the devastating effects of the civilizational metastasis that had sailed to Brazil more than five hundred years ago. A region crowded with hills over which Estrada João de Oliveira Remião snaked up and down, up and down, zigzagging like a massive roller coaster. This is how you might describe Lomba do Pinheiro, one of the largest districts of Porto Alegre.

Not far from the border between the cities of Porto Alegre and Viamão, Estrada João de Oliveira branched off from Avenida Bento Gonçalves and rolled out the first of its many slopes, threatening to make the sky its destination. Which isn't to say that Lomba do Pinheiro was Paradise. Quite the opposite, actually: a long way from the city center, abandoned to its own fate outside the reach of public power, Lomba do Pinheiro had a reputation as a lawless place, where even the most blood-curdling deeds surprised no one. Unfortunately, this reputation was not far from the truth. The district was made up of dozens of neighborhoods, all growing unplanned on the side of the road, spilling chaotically down the steep incline, all bordering some green thicket. Two of the neighborhoods were Vila Viçosa and Vila Nova São Carlos. Isolated in their insignificance, in the heart of Lomba do Pinheiro, Viçosa and Nova São Carlos were inseparable from one another, like Siamese twins.

The foundation of Vila Viçosa dated to the mid-1970s, when a few dozen families had bought a piece of land from a man called Rafael da Silva Filho. Not long after, in the early 1980s, a woman by the name of Julitha Áurea Bastos sold several adjoining plots to the Municipal Department of Housing, which in turn used them to resettle the men and women who had been displaced from Vila São Carlos to make way for a new bus terminal, at the other end of the city. Which is how another neighborhood was founded next to the burgeoning Viçosa: Vila Nova São Carlos.

Even though these two neighborhoods sprung up like this— with all the requisite paperwork filed with the appropriate authorities, something few other communities in Lomba do Pinheiro could say for themselves—it was through a series of tactless deforestations, illegal incursions, and defiant occupations that, in the following decade, Vila Viçosa and Vila Nova São Carlos expanded into a single massive development on the western edge of Estrada João de Oliveira Remião. No one had any idea where one neighborhood ended and the other began. However, since they were both founded on the crests of two separate hills and spilled toward each other down opposite sides, it was safe to assume that the border was somewhere near the bottom, in the valley between the two slopes—a valley that, incidentally, in 2015 or so, would come to informally be known as Vila Sapo.

It was there, in that narrow strip of land between Vila Viçosa and Vila Nova São Carlos, in the future belly of Vila Sapo, that Pedro woke up and went to bed, day in and day out, for as long as he could remember.

Difficult as it was, Pedro somehow managed to shake off the urge to play hooky that Monday, February 2, 2009. When he finally left for work, convinced nothing would make this day different from any other, the blazing sun fell on his shoulders, which were shaped like a clothes hanger, and made his backpack feel even more cumbersome. The bright light burned his eyes. He scowled up at the vast blue sky and stuffed a cheap cigarette between his chapped lips. He took a couple of steps and ran through the usual checklist to make sure he hadn't forgotten anything, which is when he patted his jean pocket and saw that his lighter was missing.

"Fuck!" he said, turning back to the front door he had just finished locking. It hadn't been easy, and nor would it be easy to unlock it. Even though the whole thing had been on the fritz for a while, in the past week or so the door had reached an infuriating state of disrepair.

Like any self-respecting poor man, Pedro was used to things being less than perfect; like any self-hating poor man, he also believed he deserved better. Now and then, as he took stock of the world around him, he was shocked at just how much of it got on his nerves: the crowded buses, his dirty clothes and cheap cigarettes, never having enough blankets to keep warm in the winter or fans to stay cool in the summer, the reek of sewage in the patio, the rats, cockroaches, spiders, termites, fleas, ticks, and geckos infesting his house. "Nothing is perfect," the saying went. The problem was that nothing in Pedro's life was even remotely tolerable.

Pedro sighed and slid his key into the broken lock, at the edge of what little patience he had left. When he gave his wrist a sharp turn, instead of the usual resistance, he heard a metallic click. But

Pedro's habit of never trusting good luck, long since become second nature, prevented him from assuming the locking mechanism had worked. Sure enough, as he carefully slid out his key—tortured by that millisecond of suspense—the lock's cylinder came right out with it, wrongfully extracted from the only place where it had a purpose. Then there was a second click just like the first, and several pieces tumbled out of the hole the cylinder had left in the door, dashing any hope of the lock being salvaged. The pieces were so small Pedro could barely see them. They spilled across the floor, some of them vanishing from sight.

No one would have guessed from the blank look on Pedro's face that his body was shot through with an electric rage. Standing under the lean-to, Pedro swallowed the four-letter word wriggling up his throat and relaxed his hand, which had instinctively closed into a fist to pummel the door. "Cool down . . ." he thought and then wondered if it really made more sense for him to keep his cool than it did to lose it completely. "You win some, you lose some . . ." he argued. Incidentally, what he had "lost" wasn't so much the busted door lock or the likelihood of ever fixing it or the money they didn't have for a new one. No, what he had "lost" was the lighter, which was still inside the house. Pedro was a veteran smoker of tobacco and weed, making fire essential to his every day. How the fuck could he forget the lighter? He'd rather have walked out of the house without pants on! The key was still attached to the cylinder lock. He held it up at eye level and felt like crying. Why was his life such a joke?

Pedro's dingy house shared a dingy patio with six other equally dingy houses. He went up to a front door, knocked three times, and let himself in. The house was tiny, open-plan and surprisingly occupied by five people: Pedro's cousin, her husband, and their three boys. The chaos that reigned in those four walls made the space look all the smaller, and Pedro felt strangely uncomfortable, partly because he suspected his own house would be just as messy as soon as he no longer lived with his mother. The four men were the only ones home. Three boys sat elbow to elbow on a pile of twisted sheets on their parents' bed, playing video games and giggling while their father cooked lunch on the dirty stovetop and listened to music at a weekend volume. It smelled delicious, Pedro thought as he walked in. His cousin's husband, now a freelance motorcycle courier, used to work in a kitchen.

"What's up, Roberto?"

"Not much. Y'alright?"

"Yeah, chill." Pedro couldn't help smiling a little. He always got a kick out of seeing Roberto at the oven with his floral apron and wooden spoon, the Spice Girls blaring in the background. Roberto was tall and muscular, the kind of guy you'd expect to find destroying a punching bag, or something in that vein. "I need a favor," Pedro said, setting the cylinder lock on the table along with the key and other bits and pieces. "Will you give this to my ma if you see her? I don't know if she's gonna want to fix the damn thing or throw it out. Either way, make sure she gets it, yeah?"

"Sure thing," Roberto said, picking up the cylinder lock and studying it. "Sucks, huh?" He smiled after a while, no longer moved to assess the damage.

"Yeah, it fucking blows," Pedro agreed, casually lighting his cigarette on one of the burners. He blew out a mouthful of smoke. "I should bounce. I'm late for work. Again. Thanks, man."

"No problem, Pedro. I'll make sure your ma gets the lock."

Pedro walked out, closing the door behind him. He crossed the front patio, whose division from the street had become a mere suggestion after the wall fell two decades ago. Not the Berlin Wall, naturally, but the dingy wall around that dingy patio, the one Pedro's uncle had the good sense to tear down in the 1980s, for fear the wind would blow it onto someone.

It should go without saying that when Pedro left the patio, it wasn't for the sidewalk of Rua General Lima e Silva, or Rua Ramiro Barcelos, or any other semi-decent street in Porto Alegre. No, it was for the sidewalk of Rua Guaíba, a pitted asphalt road where some of the city's most stomach-turning behavior, off-color scandals, and cinematic shootings were staged.

As he dragged himself up Nova São Carlos to the bus stop, Pedro had a familiar thought: he had to figure out how to get rich. The issue had been on his mind a lot lately, and he was beginning to think he might not know peace unless he found a way to live his dream. His great-grandparents had been poor their whole lives; his grandparents had been poor their whole lives; his parents had been poor their whole lives. How long could it go on? If, as they said, all you needed to get rich—or at least live a life of dignity—was hard work and dedication, then where the hell had he gone wrong? Was it that he came from a long line of freeloaders? Did that explain all the blood, sweat, and tears he'd poured into this life of poverty? Generations and generations of slackers who deserved the humiliating conditions they'd been born into, and still lived in? No, of course not. His relatives had worked like dogs until the day they died. They belonged to the class of people who kept the country running, and the fact that they had always been poor meant something was broken . . . Their mistake had been to play by the rules . . . But that cycle of generational poverty would end there, with him: he was going to get rich. How? It didn't matter. Or did it? He heaved a long, afflicted sigh.

"Fuck this life! I'd rather be dead than keep living like this. Not sure I can even say what I'm doing is living; I'm surviving. I bust my ass just to take another breath. I'm a fucking factory working at full steam just to keep the goddamn lights on! That's it, I've got to get rich, no matter what it takes. I've got to find a way to do the stuff that makes life worth living, and it's not honest work that's gonna get me there."

HALFWAY UP THE hill, he glanced down an alley and saw three guys sitting on the wall, in the shade of an exposed-brick house. Even though they were pretty far, he recognized them straight away and headed toward them, blowing a coil of smoke through his nose and flicking away his cigarette butt. He was late for work and, if asked, couldn't have explained why he had gone down that alley instead of sticking to his commute. He was drawn to something he couldn't put his finger on. It was like there was some interesting yet long-forgotten thing he needed to do there.

He felt bad for those kids. Just as he felt bad for himself. There they were—three boys sitting in a back alley with rags for clothes and no shoes on, bumming around and talking shit, talking shit and bumming around, abandoned by their "kind mother." None of them had gone to school as far as he knew, and the education they were entitled to, had they been interested, was mediocre at best. At the end of the day, knowledge and education were consumer goods like, much everything else; they cost money, and money was something those kids didn't have. They'd need to settle for one of the two public schools in the area, Afonso Guerreiro Lima or Tereza Noronha de Carvalho, and Pedro, who has attended both, wasn't sure either of them was life-changing, no matter how hard the teachers tried. The thing that would make all the difference, not only in the lives of those boys, but in the lives of everyone, was money: money, period.

There was a direct correlation, thought Pedro, between a person's place in the world and how much money they had, and you didn't have to be a psychic to see what the future had in store for those kids, who couldn't even afford a pair of flip-flops. The day was silently approaching when they'd each have to choose between being a thug or a slave, if they wanted to survive. And their famously neglected public school system wasn't going to be the thing that saved them from that cruel fate.

"Yo yo yo, punks!" greeted Pedro.

The trio answered, in unison:

"Sup, Pedro?"

"Where y'all hiding the weed?" he asked, hopping on the wall and sitting beside them.

As far as Pedro was concerned, that was the most frequently asked question in the outskirts of Porto Alegre. It was as if weed were a beloved, popular friend; people always asked about it when it wasn't around. The truth is, almost no one considered weed a drug. Like alcohol and tobacco, weed was part of a group of substances generally overlooked by parents, who allowed their pre-teens to try it, or at least didn't go out of their way to stop them. Drugs, real drugs, were things like cocaine and harder.

"Nothing, not even shake, man," said one of the kids, clicking his tongue. "We looked everywhere this morning. Everybody's dry."

"Not even in Mangue?"

"Not even in Mangue."

"There's never any weed in Pinheiro, man. It's fucking bullshit!" one of the kids grumbled, indignant. "All anybody sells these days is rock and powder. I'd love to live in Rio. Or Sampa. I doubt folks there have trouble getting hold of weed. Traffic in those cities is the real deal. They'd never leave a dude hanging." He paused, then said: "Whatever fool decides to sell some good cannabis round here is gonna make mad money. There'd be no competition, cause dealers in these parts don't fuck with weed. No trouble with the pigs either, cause the pigs could give less of a shit about what goes on up here, at the end of the world. And they'd have no problem finding buyers, cause the place is crawling with potheads." He ticked off each advantage on his fingers as he spoke. "It'd be a killer business, man!" he concluded, then openly laughed.

Pedro said nothing, though he'd already given the idea some thought. The kid was right. It was an amazing opportunity. And it was no mystery why. To start, Brazil's economy was doing well (better than ever in fact, as news anchors never tired of saying on TV); people had more money in their pockets and were consuming things that, until recently, hadn't been meant for their eyes to see, just as they were consuming a certain substance that, until recently, hadn't been meant for their noses to snort.

Back in the day, Lomba do Pinheiro—and not only Lomba do Pinheiro but any neighborhood in Porto Alegre—was crawling with people who wanted to snort cocaine but were tapped out, or people who wanted to snort more cocaine than they snorted already but were tapped out; now all these folks had money. The coke business was more profitable than ever before, a reflection of the country's booming economy, a detail dealers hadn't failed to notice. There was also the small matter of the crack epidemic, which had produced legions of zombies as well as rivers of money. Taken in this context, weed wasn't as interesting commercially as it used to be. Only larger, better-organized outfits were still selling the stuff because they had wide distribution; in Lomba de Pinheiro, however, where a small gang operated in each neighborhood, no one was interested in marijuana, and pot-smokers had to travel great distances to get some, and often without success.

In the ensuing silence, Pedro allowed himself to entertain his resentment while gazing out at the majestic eucalyptus trees that loomed behind the jumble of shacks.

"How long y'all been up there?" he thought. "For as long as I can remember, you been standing there, huge and still, watching stuff go down. How many drug cartel deaths have you witnessed? After those people died, did anything happen? No. Nothing. Zip.

Am I right? A guy dies and twenty-four hours later he's been dead for a day, period. Life isn't worth a thing in these back alleys filled with misery, hate, and suffering; folks who kill don't care if they kill; folks who die don't care if they die. What about me—is my life worth anything? No, nothing. Not for now, anyway. For now. For now, I don't care if I die, cause, when all's said and done, I haven't been enjoying life, just trudging through it. The only way I'll care is if I start living a kick-ass life. But if I wanna live that kind of life someday, there's only one way to do it: I've got to forget the rules and put my shitty-ass life on the line."

3

THE STINGER OF
SELF-HATRED

As he sat on the impeccably made bed, listening to his wife sob and feeling like a fuck-up, Marques tried to take a deep breath, only to heave a powerful sigh, as though finally ridding himself of an evil spirit. He ran his hand down his face and stopped at his mouth, thumb and index fingers pinching his lips, as if this could somehow help him think. He was trying to find a noncombative way of making Angélica understand that he too had been shook by the news of the unexpected pregnancy. Very shook. Despite her malicious insinuation, however, it had never crossed his mind to "jump ship." He would stay by his wife's side for the rest of his life. Together they'd overcome this barrier and every barrier after, and he hoped never to ask her to give anything she wouldn't willingly give or do anything she wouldn't willingly do. Yet, in that moment, he felt neither noble nor virtuous. He knew that everything he had done—from his unswerving dedication to their marriage to deciding to shoulder the bulk of responsibilities, all for the sake of Angélica's well-being—was all part and parcel of a husband's duties. And it was more for his sake than hers, more to relieve his own remorse than out of kindness to her, that he felt the urge to console her, to hold her, to take back everything he'd said and apologize for slapping her hard across the face. But he did none of these things. He was scared. Terrified, actually. Terrified he would kick himself for being too soft. And the stinger of self-hatred zapped him for every loving word he didn't say, for every loving gesture he didn't make.

Angélica and Marques were more tired of offending one another than properly offended. They knew they were done arguing for the day. They also knew that the reason for their argument wasn't small change, or they'd already have made up and be fucking like rabbits. But that's not how things went. Though imminent, like thunder after a flash of lightning, their reconciliation would take the shape of warm words said as if nothing had happened, just as soon as one of them decided it was childish to stay quiet a minute longer. Both wanted desperately to rebuild their passion from the wreckage they had reduced it to; they were good at this sort of thing. But first they needed to exhaust the subject that had led to their disagreement and which they'd quickly digressed from, although they barely noticed: the new baby. In the end, it was Angélica who picked up where they had left off, after sighing several times.

"Alright, love, what's the plan?" she asked, with sudden determination. Angélica had bravely set herself one of the most quixotic tasks on earth: of not shedding another tear. She waited. She knew her husband well enough to understand what a good man he was inside. But she underestimated the strength of his pride, of his misogyny, and of his ignorance, strengths that narrowed the gateway between thought and expression. All Marques could do was slowly shake his head. He didn't even try moving his eyes from the middle-distance where they rested. This is when Angélica ran out of patience: "Damn it, Marques! Don't you see you're making things harder?"

Shocked out of his trance, Marques clicked his tongue and glared at his wife.

"How am I supposed to know what the plan is, Angélica?" he said, shrugging his shoulders and unfolding one of his arms, his open hand seeming to accuse the bedroom wall of posing an impossible question. "All we can do is pray for a miracle. Another kid . . . Christ! I've always wanted a crapload of kids. You know I fucking love kids. But it's one thing to want them and another to afford them . . . Well, at least we both have jobs."

"Right, yeah, totally!" his wife cut in. "Shit could be way, way, worse. Jesus, I don't even want to think about it. But the thing is," she laughed dryly, "the thing is, that doesn't make me feel any better, you know? We have a hard enough time trying to cobble together a decent life for Daniel (there's the milk, the daycare, the clothes, the shoes). Another kid? How are we supposed to manage with two of them . . ." She realized she was losing her composure and decided to stop, closing her mouth as well as her eyes.

"Know what I think? I think I gotta get to work. I'm already late as is." Marques stood up and grabbed his backpack from the bed. "We can talk some more later, okay?"

Angélica nodded emphatically.

"Damn it, Marques, I love you like crazy, you know," she said, voice shaking as tears rolled down her face again.

"I love you too," her husband replied.

She stood up to hug Marques, as the situation called for. It was a long, meaningful embrace. That minute, a light breeze blew in through the open window, sending the curtain into a slow, constant flutter. The light filtering through them cast yellowish waves on the bed, and the birds twittered outside, celebrating whatever it is birds celebrate. It could have been a magical moment, the kind where everything seems beautiful, like a scene out of a telenovela. *Could have.* Had it not been for a grating sound that weighed on both Marques and Angélica, tethering them to a reality that was anything but magical. The wood floor of the house, which had gone to rot years ago, groaned loudly, letting out a cry for help and threatening to cave in at any minute, while their son, Daniel, who more than anything was just another mouth to feed, ran this way and that with a big smile on his face, tuckering himself out. And sadly, due to their circumstances, they had to choose between fixing the floor and feeding their kid, since they definitely couldn't afford both—and where was the magic in that? Nothing, not even birdsong, can make total precarity seem magical.

They let go after a final squeeze, gripping each other's backs. Marques turned around and walked into the garishly furnished living room, where he said goodbye to Daniel, mussed his hair, kissed his forehead and, with a touch of sadness in his voice and an awkward smile on his lips, asked him to please stop running. Daniel did what he was told, then sat quietly on the couch. He watched his father as he left, shutting the door behind him. Though he'd noticed something was wrong, felt it even, it would be a long time before he had the words to describe the radioactive aura that envelops people when they are frustrated. His large, expressive eyes brimmed with curiosity as they lingered on the closed door, behind which that sweet man, that beloved man, that man who, unfortunately, needed something that lay beyond his childish comprehension, had disappeared.

Marques was a fitting representation of his generation: a young man of moderate stupidity saddled with responsibilities for which he was completely unprepared, carelessly stumbling through life with a mohawk and no ambition. Born and raised in Vila Campo da Turro in the Partenon district of Porto Alegre, Marques had seen all kinds of violence, and the friends he had in the area—childhood friends—had either become prostitutes, drug dealers, thieves, addicts, con artists, or else, like him, taken a job at the very base of the social pyramid. The heavy social pyramid. Around three years ago, with Angélica pregnant for the first time, Marques finally took her up on the offer to move into the house with the rotten floorboard, where she lived on her own, in Vila Lupicínio Rodrigues, in a district called Menino Deus.

Vila Lupicínio Rodrigues was the unwanted backyard of an important cultural center of the same name. The two places abutted one another, hard proof that the distance between culture and the poor is more than just physical. Rather than attend free events at the cultural center, the neighborhood residents chose to stay home and do nothing. It's like they knew, or suspected, that the events being held at that establishment weren't meant for them, which happened to be true. Instead they were attended by people from other parts of the city who drove there in their expensive cars. And as actors recited Shakespeare and Brecht on the stage of the Renascença, the cultural center's renowned theater, the neighborhood was the stage of real-life tragedies. Much like any place where poverty is widespread, there were people in Vila Lupicínio Rodrigues who also had nerves of steel, no blood in their veins, and no heart. One time, no one knows why, a military police officer decided to enter the neighborhood without backup, in full gear, and was shot to death. The man who killed him casually dragged the MP's body out of the neighborhood by the feet, leaving a trail of blood through the alleys. The authorities were never able to find out who had perpetrated the crime, much less catch him: even though it happened in the middle of the afternoon, no one saw anything, no one knew anything—or at least no one was willing to talk.

Marques's place of work—a branch of the Fênix supermarket chain managed by Sr. Geraldo—was on Rua General Jacinto

Osório, between Parque Farroupilha—better known as Parque Redenção—and Vila Planetário, not far from Vila Lupicínio Rodrigues. Marques was halfway to work when he finally admitted to himself that he was more to blame for their disagreement than his wife. He continued to walk, unhurried, ignoring everything that went on outside his head. His legs carried him to the supermarket; his mind returned time and time again to their argument, reliving it over and over. The more he thought about it—start to finish, blow by blow—the more the stinger of self-hatred zapped him; and the more the stinger of self-hatred zapped him, the more he felt the need to think about it—start to finish, blow by blow.

"I need to tell you something," Angélica had begun, cool and composed. "You're not gonna like it. But sit down, please."

Marques did what he was told, more curious than alarmed. Angélica sat down too, thighs pressed together, hands resting on her knees, back straight as a pin, in a posture that conveyed peace and quiet: rooted in fear, this strategy was used mostly by women who wanted to broach a difficult subject with their explosive husbands without things getting out of hand. Before she continued, she closed her eyes and heaved a self-encouraging sigh.

"Alright, love, I . . . Okay, here goes nothing: I think I'm pregnant. Scratch that: I know I'm pregnant."

Marques went cold. His first impulse was to stand up and cradle his head in his hands, but he stopped his arms and legs. Then he tried to hide his emotions. He fought to keep his blood from boiling. Knowing nothing good could come out of his mouth, he tried to stay quiet. But his tongue—*his tongue*! It's not half as easy to restrain that infernal whip as it is to restrain your arms and legs. The suffocating desire to make a snide remark, the *need* to say something hostile . . . His tongue got the better of him.

"Well, fuck. What d'you want me to do about it?"

The regret was immediate. Marques could hardly believe the words that had left his mouth. He felt angry and ashamed of himself. He had to take it back, and fast. God! He had to tell her he didn't know what he was talking about and ask for forgiveness right away. But his tongue—*his tongue*! His tongue was stronger than him and refused to cooperate, refused to beg for forgiveness. A mix of rage and disbelief swept across Angélica's face.

"What d'you mean 'what d'you want me to do about it'!" she shouted. "Aren't you the baby's dad, Marques? You think I knocked myself up all on my own?"

"Well maybe not all on your own, no. But there was that time we had a fight and you kicked me out, wasn't there? I spent all week on my ma's couch."

His tongue!

"You fucking asshole."

"What? It's true, ain't it?"

"What exactly are you implying? That I went round the neighborhood putting out? Go fuck yourself, for real. If that isn't some half-assed excuse to jump ship, then I don't know what it is."

"What d'you mean?"

"Don't try and pretend. You want out? Fine, we'll split, no hard feelings. But don't you dare come at me with that bullshit. I won't take it."

"Are you crazy? Who said anything about splitting?"

"You're the one who's crazy, Marques! I'm pregnant. It's yours and you're implying it isn't. What kind of bullshit is that?"

"That's not what I said."

"See, that's your problem, Marques. You never say things outright, you just insinuate. And that's some kind of chickenshit behavior. I guess it must run in the family. Your ma, that snake, hasn't got the guts to say she doesn't like me, so she hints at it instead, just like you do. I reckon—"

Angélica would've kept going if a hand hadn't suddenly struck her left cheek.

"Watch what you say about my ma! You hear? Watch what you fucking say about my ma!" Marques screamed, spraying saliva all over. He held his mouth to his wife's ear and gripped her by the hair.

That was the moment that hurt the most to remember. That was the moment that made him regret he couldn't travel back in time and do things differently; the moment when the stinger of self-hatred zapped him the hardest. "How could I be so stupid?" he asked himself as he waited at the pedestrian light to cross the stream of speeding cars flooding Avenida João Pessoa. Then he shivered, out of impatience and annoyance: what point was there in replaying the whole thing over and over in his head? What was the point of torturing himself like that? To summarize: he and Angélica had had a bad fight and then worked it out, end of story. She'd found it in herself to forgive him, and all he had to do now was forgive himself. He needed to forget about their quarrel. He needed to find peace.

It wasn't too hard wiping the argument from his mind. But not thinking about their second child, who was due before Marques had even had a chance to figure out how to bring up the first one . . . Just the thought of the unavoidable, devastating impact a second child would have on his life put a pit in his stomach. And knowing it was never Angélica's idea to have unprotected sex; knowing he always had to insist, and repeatedly, to convince his wife to dispense with the condom; this knowledge made the stinger of self-hatred zap him again.

When he reached the supermarket, his eyes were still turned inward, watching his own brain thinking, as Machado de Assis would have put it, but this time his thoughts were different, much more refreshing. What would his life be like if he'd had better luck? He'd be a lot happier if he had money, that much he knew for sure.

He might not have argued with Angélica. "You're pregnant, babe? That's awesome! Fuck it, let's celebrate." That night the two of them would've gone to a fine restaurant and enjoyed not only the food but the feeling of doing something singular, of having nothing to worry about, of living in the moment—and how lucky were they not to be another miserable couple in a plain, boring marriage? They'd have a car, of course, and as he drove them to an upscale motel, he'd ask Angélica to suck him off. He'd always wanted to do something crazy like that. They'd fuck all night long, then sleep until they were tired of being unconscious. When they woke up, they'd find other fun things to do to pass the time. Because they had a whole life of fun and happiness ahead of them, and when their time was up, they'd have no regrets . . .

No, no, no; what a ridiculous idea! Only millionaires could afford to live that way; Marques would've been satisfied with much less. For example, he'd be happy just to work four-hour days and bring home five thousand reais a month. That way he could play soccer with his friends in Vila Campo da Tuca, like the old days. On top of that, Daniel would need for nothing, and neither would the second kid they had on the way. Angélica wouldn't have to work at the pizzeria either. She could spend the rest of her life at home, looking after their children and watching TV . . . No; on second thought, that wasn't a good idea, either. She'd get fat. Unless she started going to the gym. And, with five thousand reais a month, Marques might even be able to afford a membership for his wife . . . Anyway.

Realizing it was time to clock in came as a bitter surprise. Time to snap out of it and get back to reality. A *harsh* reality. A *depressing* reality. A reality *near unbearable*. He gazed down, taking a good look at himself. He saw a man dressed in the same stained, mended, creased, and pathetic uniform God knows how many other poor bastards had worn before him. As he took in his uniform, he felt a deep sense of failure. At the end of the day, this is who he was: a man who wore those kinds of clothes to make a living; a man who would probably never know dignity; a man whose children would probably never know dignity. The stinger of self-hatred zapped him again.

4

MENTOR AND
DISCIPLE

A voracious reader, Pedro had developed—it hadn't been easy, but he'd done it—an enviable knack for reading on the bus without getting sick. The hard work had paid off. Once tedious, his endless commute now brought him unspeakable joy; it was the thing Pedro most looked forward to in his day, the moment he could "navigate other people's souls," as he frequently put it. But that day, he wasn't in a reading mood. After getting on the bus and settling into a corner, he started kicking around a recent idea he had, and let himself get carried away.

His mind was made up. He was going to leave behind his sad life as an upstanding, hard-working man, and do it by selling weed. This is how he would gain entry to the world of extravagant spending he had never set foot in or been invited to. As was to be expected, the plan came with certain risks, but he was up to the task. He'd be diligent and discreet. The plan had to work. Even if it didn't, what did he have to lose? Not even prison or death could be worse than his shitty little life.

Still, the thought that he could die or wind up behind bars troubled him, threatening to send him spiraling into a bottomless pit of self-doubt. Damn it! What if, he wondered, this reflection was the work of a cunning witch who was vying for his attention so she could cast a spell on him, drain his strength, poison him with fear, make him believe his plan was doomed to fail, persuade him to give up and accept the unacceptable: the mediocre life that had been forced on him the moment he opened his eyes. Though it took a lot of effort, he managed to banish the thought and drive away the vivid image of his body lying in a place that looked like the inside of a dark cell or a morgue slab. Because this moment, right now, was key—it was the moment he had to have faith. He had to dismiss the idea of failure and believe wholeheartedly in his ability to get things right; he needed to focus on the possibility of success; he couldn't entertain feelings of doubt or uncertainty, nor let his enthusiasm wane and give up on his plan, not for any reason. The second he set his mind to it, he felt a lion awaken inside him, capable of anything.

As always, Pedro got on the bus that stopped outside Júlio de Castilhos—referred to affectionately as Julinho—wound down the affluent street edging the public school, and steadily made its way toward the Fênix supermarket chain where he worked—the one managed by Sr. Geraldo. A few minutes later, in unassuming clothes, with a ripped backpack, messy hair, and an unshaven face, Pedro entered the supermarket with a stride so self-confident it bordered on arrogant. He pulled on his uniform in the locker room, which was on the second floor, then immediately sprinted down to the first floor, where he scanned the supermarket aisles for Marques. He couldn't wait to tell his friend about his plans.

"There you are, motherfucker! How's it going?"

"Alright, brother. You?"

"Alright."

Pedro and Marques were stock clerks. In other words, among the many things they did—unloading trucks, organizing the stockroom, mopping the floors—their main function was stocking shelves, hence why it made sense to call them stock clerks, or shelvers, as they were referred to by some. That said, the position stamped on their work cards—"support staff"—couldn't have been more ambiguous. They could have been labeled "pantologists" or "jacks-of-all-trades" and the outcome would have been the same: the supermarket could hold them responsible for all kinds of duties, leaving them no recourse to file a complaint for wrongful hiring.

Pedro had been at the store long before Marques started, and it was clear on Marques's first day, over a year ago, that they would become close friends. Moments before the two of them met all that time ago, Pedro, who was already on the afternoon shift, was helping the morning staff unload a truck near the stockroom.

"Y'all hear there's a new hire?"

"Yeah?" one of his colleagues said, surprised.

"Sr. Geraldo said he was gonna hire somebody to work afternoons with you, remember. Maybe it's him?"

"Maybe," Pedro agreed.

"Where he at?"

"I saw him on my way to the bathroom. They were taking him up to HR. He's probably still there. I bet you Ana shows up with him any minute to introduce us. You know how they do things here."

The men worked as they chatted, standing in what they spiritedly referred to as the "prayer chain." Which, of course, had nothing to do with religion. The prayer chain was just a tactical formation that allowed them to quickly and efficiently unload the trucks: the first person in the well-spaced chain stood in the back of the truck and picked up boxes, packages, and cases, then passed them one by one to the person positioned outside the truck, who then swung their arms in a single, pendular motion, catching the object mid-air and tossing it to the next person in line, and so on and so forth, until it reached the last associate, who then placed it on the dolly. Once the dolly was full, the stock was carted inside and shelved.

"Listen up, y'all. We've got to make sure the new guy doesn't sleep on the job," Pedro said. "Dude's gonna be a stock clerk like us, so he's better off knowing from day one that this j-o-b comes with a crapload of other responsibilities and get his ass over here pronto to help us unload this truck." As he spoke, Pedro became more and more convinced about the truth of what he was saying, and added: "You know what? I'm gonna go find the guy right now and tell him to come and give us a hand when he's done."

"I'm not sure that's a good idea, Pedro. The AM's gonna chew you out. He'll say training new employees is '*my* job, not yours.'"

"Whatever. The AM can suck it. Look at us, dude. Just look! We're beat, soaked to the bone. The sooner the new guy gets here, the better. Plus, if we had to rely on the AM for anything simple as this, we'd be screwed."

Pedro was right about that, as he would soon discover. On his way to meet the new hire, he spotted Paulo, the aforementioned assistant manager, flirting with one of the retail bakers, oblivious to anything and everything around him. "Fuck this shit," he thought, outraged.

Pedro went upstairs to HR, where he assumed the new hire would be. He knocked on the door and heard a woman's voice say, "Come in!" He went in. Before he had a chance to open his mouth, she started talking.

"Pedro! I'm so happy you're here," said Ana, whose job was to push papers. "You've made my day! Listen, things are crazy busy right now. Like crazy, crazy busy. How would you feel about introducing our new colleague to the rest of the team? Seeing as you know everyone and all." She turned to the new hire, who was sitting on the bench. Before Pedro could say anything, she blithely added: "Go with Pedro, Marques. He'll introduce you to your colleagues."

As Pedro walked down the steps with the new hire behind him, he started making conversation:

"So . . . Marques, is it? I'm Pedro. Ever work as a stock clerk before?"

"Yeah."

"So you know your job's stocking shelves, right?"

"Right."

"Here's the thing, though. At Fênix, we do a bit of everything, even mopping the floor." Pedro saw Marques's face fall and raised his hands, as if surrendering to an assault. "No, no. Now don't get me wrong, cuz. I'm not ordering you around or nothing. I'm not your boss. I'm an underling, like you. I just thought I should let you know how things work here. The AM will say the same later, but right now he's . . ." Pedro curled his lips and rolled his eyes. "Let's just say he's indisposed." Pedro felt it was time to move on to the important bit. He placed one hand on the new hire's shoulder, leaving the other free to gesticulate, which he did a lot whenever he had to explain something. "Listen up: today's Wednesday and on Wednesdays there's always mega discounts at the store. That means crowds of folks rushing to buy things and loads of stuff for us to do. So if you don't mind, I'm not gonna bother with what Ana said. I'll introduce you some other time. Instead, we're gonna unload the truck by the stockroom, cause it's hard work and we need your help. We need to finish unloading the fucker ASAP, cause while we ain't manning the shelves in the store, they're just getting emptier and emptier. You follow? On top of that, there's only two stock clerks on the afternoon shift: me and, now, you. The other three guys work mornings, and they're headed home soon. So we gotta hustle and unload the truck while they're still around to pitch in. Or we'll be the ones to pay for it."

After a second, Marques asked:

"If we're the only ones on in the afternoon, does that mean you used to stock shelves on your own, after the morning shifters clocked out?"

"Nah. Sr. Geraldo helps out too, even though he's the manager. The AM lends a hand as well sometimes. Everybody chips in round here. Just don't let them see you sitting on your hands, yeah? If it's a slow day and there ain't much going on at the registers, the boss will close down a couple of lines and have the girls restock shelves. See what I mean? So, like, keep that in mind. If one day you see there's no shelves to stock, that every one of them is full-up, then pretend to stock them, move stuff around or some shit, act like you're busy, cause otherwise they're gonna have you mop the floor or help the butcher organize the freezer or anything else that needs doing. Chilling is strictly prohibited."

"Right, but don't folks got somewhere they can sneak off to and rest a minute?" Marques asked, revealing his true nature.

Pedro's eyes twinkled.

"You know how things are: Slackers gonna slack and ain't nothing nobody can do about it. Sure, folks sneak off. In fact, I'm first in line, given the chance," Pedro quietly confided, laughing. "And I don't just sneak off to rest my dogs, either. I sneak off to have a bite to eat, on the quiet, if you catch my drift."

The new hire laughed.

"Yeah, yeah, I do!"

The two men had barely met and were already thrilled to discover they were cut from the same cloth: they wouldn't have to pretend to be anyone but themselves. Later that same day, after the morning-shift stock clerks had clocked out and the store had quieted down, Pedro and Marques snuck off with a box of chocolates and ate them in a corner of the locker room.

"Careful when you try this on your own, Marques," Pedro warned. "Tem dedo-de-seta adoidado, todos eles a fim de entregar os irmãos."

Marques didn't listen to samba much, and even though he missed the reference, he got the message loud and clear. *There's rats all over the place, itching to turn a brother in.*

"You'll find two-timing cocksuckers no matter where you go, that's for sure," he said. "What good does it do them to snitch on a brother? Fuck-all! If there was a prize for snitching, then maybe I'd understand. But there ain't: dudes snitch cause they're goddamned snakes. I know how it is."

"Dude, it makes me so fucking mad to have to hide out here like a rat, just so I can eat in peace . . . Everything in here belongs to us too. We own every last fucking product in this store. Did you know that?"

Marques was intrigued. He mumbled, a whole chocolate in his mouth:

"Hunh? How come?"

Pedro reflected for a moment. It wasn't normally a good idea for him to get into things with new associates, who often wound up thinking he had a screw loose. But he couldn't help himself. Finally, he propped one foot on the bench, hugged his knee, and said:

"Right, so, hear me out. Say you bump into me and I'm wearing a new shirt. You ask me where I got it and I tell you I made it. Bought the fabric, designed the pattern, cut it, sewed it together. I made the whole damn thing. On my own. Now my question for you is: would you believe me?"

Even though it was an unusual question, Marques replied:

"Yeah. I mean, why the hell not?"

"Cool. Now forget that. Instead, say you bump into me outside a new building. A skyscraper or whatever. You ask me what's up with that building, and I tell you I built it. On my own. I planned the building, laid every brick, prepped the concrete, painted it, etc. etc. Would you believe me then?"

"Nah, I wouldn't."

"Damn straight you wouldn't. See what I'm saying?"

Marques frowned and shook his head.

"It's simple, man! You can make a shirt on your own, but you can't make a whole building on your own."

"Right, yeah, I get that . . ."

"So . . ."

"I just don't get what that's got to do with the thing we were talking about before, when you said everything in the supermarket belongs to us too . . ."

"Cool it, man. I'm getting there. I just wanna make sure you've wrapped your head round this idea first, yeah? I need you to hold it in your mind while we're talking. So, does what I said to you make sense? Do you get that a guy can make a shirt on his own but not a whole building?"

"Yeah, I get it. I mean, it's obvious."

"Right, yeah. It's obvious. But people like to forget that, don't they? What we're talking about is limitations. Li-mi-ta-tions. People like to forget that mankind is limited. But these limitations are dead easy to demonstrate, right, and they're proof that some guys out there have way too much stuff. You follow? Some guys out there *own* way too many things. When you got too much money, when you own too many things, even though you ain't done nothing to deserve it, that means the guys who did the actual work don't have shit, and it's all your fault. Look, what I'm saying is there's limits to what a person can do on their own, Marques. Limits. And these limits, which vary from person to person, these limits *should* determine the best standard of living a person can have. See what I'm saying? Some dudes make shirts, others grow potatoes, others sweep streets, others teach math. Whatever: it's all work. When folks work, they contribute to society, yeah? When folks work, they produce, they bring into being shit that didn't used to exist, shit other people need. But everyone's got limits. For example, say our job is making shirts. Maybe I can make five shirts a day max, and maybe you can make six shirts a day, yeah? And if you make more shirts than I do, then your standard of living should be better than mine. Cause at the end of the day, your work contributes more to society than mine does, meaning you deserve a better standard of living."

"Right. Isn't that how things work?"

Pedro opened his eyes wide and dropped his jaw.

"What? Jesus Christ, man! What world you living in? Course that's not how things work!"

"How come?"

"Alright, now listen carefully. Say I'm making five shirts a day and you're making six: that shortfall should determine the difference between my standard of living and yours, no matter how small. Maybe you can afford some ham on your breakfast roll and I'm still eating fucking mortadella. Here's what I wanna know, though. How many shirts has a guy got to make to have the same standard of living as the dude who owns this whole supermarket chain? Hunh? You ever thought about that? How many fucking shirts, Marques? How much has a person got to work to deserve to live like that dude? Think about it, brother. Do the math. The guy who owns this supermarket chain's got tons of houses all over, in other countries too. All mansions, natch. Tons of cars. Tons of farms. Tons of expensive clothes. He can drop my salary and yours on a single meal, no biggie. He can give his wife jewelry that costs the same as your house. His money never runs out. If you counted, you'd see he probably makes millions off his stores, every month. Man, I can't even wrap my head round the kind of money the motherfucker *has*, let alone the money he's raking in. See what I'm saying? I swear, I can't make head or tail of it. This dude earns more in one month than you've earned your entire life. How is that even possible, Marques? Is he Superman or something? Has he got three nut sacks? Now do you see what I'm getting at?

"What I'm saying is there *should be* a causal relationship between these two things. There should be a direct correlation between how much you work and the money you take home. Like I said, everybody should have the standard of living they deserve, meaning, the highest standard of living available to them according to the amount of work they do. Now that's fair, right? And you're standing there telling me this kind of justice already exists, that that's how the world works! Fuck, man. If that's how shit works, then where's our money? You really think we work less than the dude who owns this chain? That man doesn't even work, Marques! Even if he did, there's no way he could work enough to deserve the fuck-tons of money he already has, while we're here working our asses off just to make *exactly* enough to stay alive and keep busting our asses. The right to open your mouth and say this thing belongs to me, in other words, the right to private property, should go hand in hand with your worth, and worth equals work. Your worth equals sweat and callouses. That's the only kind of worth there is. Work is the most honest metric in the world."

Marques looked pensive now. He'd finally managed to take in what Pedro was trying to show him. He felt a knot in his stomach. It frightened him—the sudden, clear-eyed realization that he'd never seen through the lame excuses he was fed about why some folks were rich and others poor. He confessed:

"Fuck. I never thought about it like that . . ." And yet, judging by how his face had darkened, something was still missing. He took his hand to his chin and rubbed it like a magic lamp. "Right, but, like, when they hired me, they showed me this video about the history of Fênix supermarket and stuff."

"Yeah, I know. I had to sit through that crap too."

"Yeah! So Fênix started as a small grocery store. Dude wasn't born rich. He opened his little store, knuckled down, and the place grew and just kept growing. So you're saying everything in that video's a lie? I don't see why I shouldn't believe it. That kind of stuff happens, brother. Think about it. Dude built the whole thing from the ground up."

"Is that right? He built it, did he? The whole empire, the dozens of stores and dozens of trucks carting products all over the country. The equipment too! You're saying he built every last bit of it, on his own? If you can believe that, then you ought to believe me when I say I built a whole-ass building on my own. Cause that's all Fênix is: a load of buildings, a load of trucks, a load of equipment, a load of products, a load of stuff. And you're telling me the owner built the whole fucking thing on his own?"

"No, no. Course he didn't build it all on his own. He hired a ton of people too. He didn't force none of them to work, though."

Pedro sighed, like a man forced to explain the obvious:

"Listen, Marques. From the moment Fênix supermarkets opened their first store, everybody who worked there and helped make it the empire it is today, every single person worked cause they had to. Look, I'm not saying Mr. Fênix is to blame. He didn't personally force them to work. But that doesn't mean they weren't forced. Que será será, compadre. That's just how the world was set up. *Set up*, yeah? You can bet your ass that the folks who set it up that way had millions . . ." Pedro rubbed together his thumb and index finger. ". . . millions of reasons for wanting the world to be set up just like it is. Think about it. If everybody who worked at Fênix supermarkets hadn't worked at Fênix supermarkets, what would they have done instead? Either starved to death, worked at another chain, or gotten another job. It doesn't matter. Their working conditions would be virtually the same; their wages would be virtually the same. And that's the bit that's forced on them: you either saddle yourself with a job—one of the few crappy jobs you're qualified to do—or you starve to death. You follow? Sure, Mr. Fênix didn't force any of those folks to work. But what difference does it make? They worked at his store cause they had to, and he took advantage of that. Now, dude's a millionaire. Billionaire, even.

"And you know what the scariest thing about all this is, Marques? For some reason, I don't know why, but for some reason folks think it's okay. Someone convinced them that this is just how the world works. Someone convinced them it's natural, like the wind or the rain. Someone convinced them the system wasn't rigged—it's been around forever. And I'll say it again: you best believe it wasn't some poor bastard like me or you that set shit up that way."

Marques looked more pensive than ever now.

"Hunh, you're right . . ."

"You can say that again, brother." Pedro loved talking about this kind of thing, and the more he spoke the more excited he became. The fact that his new friend didn't seem bored, a complete surprise to Pedro, only added to his enthusiasm. "Listen. I'm gonna walk you through how this shit works, step by step. That way you can see for yourself where the tragic flaw is," Pedro announced, eyes glinting. "Say you open your own business. Just like Mr. Fênix. A small grocery store. Here's the thing: so long as you're the only one working there, you deserve every cent of the profit you make. Now let me tell you why: it's only right for you to own everything you make with your own two hands. Everything, man. All the money you make with your hard work is rightfully yours, you've earned every last penny. Now, picture this. You start making two thousand reais a month from the store. You're the only fool busting ass in there, so there's nobody to split the money with, yeah? So far, so good. Now say you set aside a bit of cash every month until you save up ten grand. That's when stuff gets tricky. You decide to invest the money in the store. You buy a couple of ovens to make fresh bread. Sweet, now your business sells bread. Profits skyrocket, not just cause of the bread but cause your customer base has increased too. Tons of new customers start coming to your store. But these folks don't just want bread, they want a bit of everything. Here's the catch. Your business grew on account of that investment, yeah? So there's more work to do. Aside from all the stuff you did before, there's dough to make and bread to bake and ovens to clean and fuck knows what else. In a nutshell: You can't stay on top of all that work on your own no more. You can't do all the stuff you used to do *on top of* baking the bread. What now? You hire two bakers, one for mornings, one for afternoons, then go back to doing the stuff you'd been doing before.

"Now, listen carefully, Marques, cause this is where shit gets sinful. I just told you that people ought to own anything they make with their own two hands. Meaning that the right thing to do now is figure out how much more money the bakers are making for you and your business and give that money to them. Which isn't hard to do, at least not in this scenario. Bear with me. Pre-bread, you brought in two grand a month. Now you're bringing in, like, five grand a month, even though you're not working any harder than before. What this means is that the differential profit—three G give or take—doesn't belong to you. Why? Cause that money wasn't made by *your* two hands. Those three thousand reais were made by *their* hands. Like you, the bakers are entitled to everything they make too. It's only right.

"The problem, man, is that there's a huge gap between what *is* right and what the law *says* is right. The law says there's this little thing called 'minimum wage.' And that's where things get ugly. You pay each baker minimum wage, yeah? But who gets to decide what that minimum wage is, keeping in mind the real-world impact the bakers' work has on the money you been making? Who the fuck gets to decide? Any fool can tell there's something fishy going on. Wages are always way, way lower than the actual worth of a person's work. What does that mean for you? What that means is you're gonna pay the bakers chickenfeed, then pocket whatever's left of the three grand, even though you're working no harder than before. That's what some folks call being an 'entrepreneur.' You know what I like to call it, though? 'Lawful theft.' Yeah, 'lawful theft.' The reason I call it that is cause even though it's lawful, when you do things that way, you're pocketing money that doesn't belong to you, according to the logic of production. Which means you're stealing under the protection of the law."

It was clear from Marques's knit brow that he wasn't convinced.

"Everything you're saying makes sense, Pedro. For real. But get a load of this: When a dude saves up money to invest in his business, well, fuck, he expects to make that money back, and more, doesn't he? It's only logical. Otherwise, it wouldn't make sense to invest. Why grow the business if you have to fork over any extra money you make to your new employees? I think I'd keep my business small in that case; I'd not hire anybody and work at my little grocery store all on my own, cause that way I get to keep all the profit."

"Bingo! Except, if you do that, your business is always gonna be small and your store won't serve everybody in your neighborhood, leaving room for other folks to open their own stores. And that's cool, right, cause that way everybody gets to work for themselves, in peace, earning just what they deserve. But that's not how entrepreneurs think, is it? What entrepreneurs want is to work less and make more. Fuck, man, think about what you just said! You said you'd sooner not hire nobody than give your employees money that belongs to them more than it does to you. What you're saying is that if you can't get rich off other folks' labor, you're ready to write them off altogether. See what I mean? It's clear as day. All those entrepreneurs we put up on pedestals—cause, oh, won't you look at that! they're creating jobs!—ain't nothing but devils, parasites, deadbeats, good-for-nothing pieces of shit! And that's the truth. It's not for other people's sakes they're creating jobs, man. They're just taking advantage of the situation. Trying to make more money and work less. Entrepreneurship is just capitalist wizardry, Marques.

"This is how it goes: you save some money, buy some equipment, call up some workers, throw a black cloth over the whole thing, say the magic word, pull off the cloth, and voilà: You got yourself a dozen downtrodden, dog-tired, ticked-off, sad-ass workers; but it's your money and there's ten times, fifteen, twenty times more of it than there was before, and you didn't so much as lift a finger. Nice, isn't it?" Pedro laughed dryly. "Nah, dude. It ain't nice. We know better than anybody what goes on under the black cloth. And it ain't the least bit nice. It's frightening. Hopeless. Fucking dire. Don't you think? Fuck, man, you're a worker, ain't you? You know what I mean. You think I'm making this shit up? Don't we work our asses off? And for what? How do you feel about the crap we put up with every day? What about the blood, sweat, and tears we been spilling our whole lives, and that our parents spilled before us, and their parents before them—the blood, sweat, and tears that just make more money for those pathetic assholes who spend half the year on the beaches of Torres and the other half on the mountains of Gramado without a worry in the world, while we stay right where we are, wasting our lives doing fuck-all but work and sleep. How d'you feel about that, hunh?"

Pedro went quiet for a minute, then looked into his friend's eyes. He smiled and nodded. "Believe it, man. These chocolates we're eating now, they're ours too. You can eat them and not feel guilty. Cause these chocolates, and everything else in the store, were bought with the cash-product of my labor, your labor, and the labor of all the cleaners, butchers, and bakers who work here. You follow? The truth is that this empire, Marques, belongs to dozens of people, us included. I don't care how many documents there are that say Fênix belongs to one dude. A document ain't nothing but a piece of paper: you can write anything you want on it, even lies. But logic, man? Logic never fails. Only by thinking for yourself, with your own head, can you know who deserves what in this world; laws and documents aren't and ain't ever been the bearers of truth." Pedro seemed to have finished, but then added: "And in case there's any doubt left in your mind, let me say one last thing about saving up money as an investment, brother. First, if you save up ten thousand reais, then it's your right to spend ten thousand reais. That's it. You follow? *Ten thousand reais* and not one cent more. You can't save up ten grand, then hope it multiplies without your having to work for it. If the ten grand you saved becomes, say, fifty grand, that means somebody's fucking worked to make it happen. Aside from those ten thousand reais, which are yours, the rest of the money belongs to the guy doing the work, not you. Second, if you decide to invest those ten thousand reais in an oven, know that your honest-to-God, rightful ownership of that oven is temporary, cause once you hire those bakers and they start using that oven for their work, then it's their labor that's earned you back those ten stacks. Now lean in: wouldn't you find it weird if ten thousand reais suddenly turned into more and more money, like a load of cells reproducing on their own, without your working any harder? Course you would! Sure, it's nice to believe in that kind of magic. It's nice to believe that's just the way it is. But it isn't, man. A shitload of money entails a shitload of labor. The greatest sin in this world, the most shocking, lawful injustice under the sun, the mother of every social problem you can think of happens when you sever labor from money and funnel the cash-product of one man's labor into the pocket of some fool who's got jack-all to do with it. If you're sitting on a fortune that you haven't bust your ass to make, I guarantee you somebody has. That fortune ain't yours; it belongs to the sad fucker who put in the hours to make it happen."

The two went on to have many more conversations like that one, and Marques's admiration for Pedro only grew with time. Marques watched Pedro articulate his own outrage. Hearing him speak, it was like all the sorrow Marques felt as a poor man was justified. Still, even though he knew Pedro was the wisest, smartest person he'd ever talked to, he wasn't the least bit impressed when one afternoon Pedro referred to him as his "disciple."

"You know, you're the best disciple I ever had, Marques."

"Fuck you very much."

Pedro laughed.

"Whoa there, cuz. No reason to be offended. Even if I'm your mentor and you're my disciple, that don't make me any better than you. For real, just listen: if there was ten people left in the world, there'd be ten mentors and ten disciples. Anyone can be a mentor, Marques. Every person on this planet has a wealth of knowledge. I bet you know a ton of stuff I don't know. So much, in fact, that one of us would die before you finished telling me about it. It's not how much you know that makes you the mentor and the other guy the disciple. You become a mentor when, for whatever reason, you got something to teach that somebody else needs to learn."

"Right. So you think I *need* to listen to all the shit you say?"

"No. I don't think you need to. Sure I like it when you listen, but there ain't much I can do if you decide to stop. Loads of people out there could give a shit about what I've got to say. Not you, though. You listen. Meaning, you're the one who thinks you need to hear what I'm saying. Honest, I reckon I know why you think you need to listen."

"Why's that?"

"Well, I'm no psychologist or nothing, but I get the sense you beat yourself up a lot. That you go hard on yourself. You know you were given the short end of the stick, just like I know I was. Meanwhile, there's folks out there pissing away money. You see it, but don't understand why. So you buy into an idea that a lot of other folks buy into as well, even though it ain't true: meritocracy. And that hurts you. After all, if the folks throwing away money deserve the things they have, that means you, who don't have a pot to piss in, deserve not to have a pot to piss in. Which makes you feel like a failure. And that places a heavy-ass weight on your shoulders. You go through life asking yourself where you went wrong and what you done wrong. Then I open my stupid mouth and show you the world in another light. See what I'm saying? I give you a bad guy so you can direct your hatred where it belongs. I show you that you're not the bad guy in your own life. I show you that while you're trying to move up in the world, there's a load of snakes trying to keep you down and bury you neck-deep in shit, cause that way they don't have to get it on themselves. They're riding us, brother. That's what I show you. And it makes you feel better, Marques. Sure, you're still as dirt poor as ever, but at least you got less guilt and self-hatred on your shoulders. At least now you realize you're worth something. You're proud of yourself. You see that getting out of bed and facing up to a world that will kick the shit outta you till the day you die is a goddamn fucking miracle. That's why you need to hear what I got to say."

Marques couldn't agree more.

"Yeah, I guess you're right, as per uzh. But hold up: If I'm your disciple, then who's your mentor? I wanna know."

"I drink from many fountains, my man. I got a ton of mentors. Most of them died a long time ago, but I still get to navigate their souls through the writing they left behind. I'd say the dude that's most influenced my thinking is this German philosopher called Marx. All that stuff we been talking about is named after him. Marxism, it's called. Marx was the first dude to see the world the way I'm describing it to you: putting the worker first and the people who exploit our labor last."

"The guy was called Marques, like me?"

"No. Marx, with the letter x."

"Right . . . If none of this shit is new, then how come nobody's made it happen yet?"

"They've tried. It didn't work."

"It didn't work?"

"It didn't work."

"What do you mean? Why not?"

Pedro laughed.

"It didn't work cause most people still think it's too radical an idea. It didn't work cause it was ahead of its time. It didn't work cause nobody wants it to. Rich folks don't want a just world, and neither do poor folks. Believe me: Even the most hard-up bastards aren't into the idea of a just world when you tell them what it could look like. You know why? Cause in a just world, there are no rich people. There is no getting rich. We talked about this stuff the day we met. In a just world, your standard of living is tied to how much work you do. Remember what I said that time? There's a limit to how much anyone can do on their own. That limit is our maximum capacity for work, and it varies from person to person. A person's maximum capacity for work should never, ever be big enough to make them rich. It's impossible, yeah? You can't get rich when you're only profiting from your own work. The only way of accumulating wealth is to take advantage of a social mechanism, whether legal or illegal, that allows you to take possession of more money than you should be able to, according to your maximum capacity for labor. But if, on the one hand, it makes you richer than average, richer than you deserve to be, on the other, it makes other folks poorer than average, poorer than they deserve to be, because all the extra money in *your* pocket is money outta *their* pockets, much as they worked for that money and you didn't. Which is bullshit, yeah? But don't be fooled, brother! Don't think poor guys like us are nothing but a bunch of sad bastards. It doesn't take much to move up the social ladder. All we need is an opportunity. Poor folks hustle day in and day out, all so some bougie cocksucker can feather his nest. But you know what we want more than anything in the world? What we want is to *be* that bougie cocksucker. What we want is to get rich off of another man's labor. What we want, Marques, is to subject some other asshole to what we been subjected to all our lives . . ."

That minute, a strange look settled on Pedro's face. Marques would never forget it. It was as if he suddenly had a stomach cramp.

"What's up, Pedro?"

"The thing is, I do mean *we*, man. Me, too. Sometimes, when we talk like this, it can seem like I'm moralizing, like I'm trying to tell you what's right and what's wrong. Truth is, sometimes I am. But I shouldn't be. I know I shouldn't. I'm no better than anybody else. This shit's fucking complicated, dude! Maybe everything I been saying all this time is just a load of crap. It could be, y'know? Maybe it's a lot more complicated than I thought. Maybe one day some expert in this stuff, some Ph-fucking-D, will rock up and prove to me that A plus A equals B and I been wrong about all of it, about every single thing I've told you. It could happen. But listen, if there's one thing I know, one thing I know beyond a doubt, it's this: I want money. *I want money!* Don't kid yourself about me, brother. You thought I wanted to change the world? Yeah, right. You know, there was probably a time when I was naïve enough to think the world could be changed; I won't try and deny it. But I'm not interested anymore. When I look around and see just how unfair the world is, when I look around and realize nobody gives a shit about real justice, then I ask myself what the fuck I'm doing in this place. I didn't wanna end up here. I'm like Mephistopheles, right? Give me the choice and I'll pick the eternal void. But seeing as I am here and all, I ain't sitting on my hands. I want money.

"In fact, you know what all this reminds me of, Marques? It reminds me of when I was young. When we played games, there was always something nobody wanted to do. In soccer, nobody wanted to be goalie; in hide-'n'-seek, nobody wanted to be the seeker; in tag, nobody wanted to be it. The real world's no different. Most people think a just world is a bad idea. The world's got to have rich folks and poor folks in it: them's the breaks. Who am I to swim against the tide? Whatever, I can live with that. But there's one thing I won't stand for. I refuse to be the poor guy in this dumb game! I can't live like that, Marques. I'm poor and I been poor my whole life. But not a day goes by when I feel okay about it. Not a day goes by when I'm not trying to figure out how to make a shitload of money. I *will* make a shitload of money one of these days and I don't give a damn what I have to do to get there. If I have to steal, I'll steal; if I have to kill, I'll kill. I'm done with ethics, with morals, with laws, with right and wrong. Fuck all that! What I want is to get rich. What I want is money—a crapload of money. And another thing: I want it now. That's it, all I want. It's the only thing I ever think about. Write this down, Marques. I don't know how, man, but one of these days I won't have to buy toilet paper cause I'll be wiping my ass with hundred-real bills."

NOW, SEVERAL MONTHS after first making this prophecy, Pedro had decided it was time for his dreams to come true by selling weed in his neighborhood. Which is what he was explaining to Marques as the two of them stocked the shelves with boxes of cookies. Pedro laid out his plan in meticulous detail, gesticulating nonstop while revealing the amazing payoff that awaited them.

"Dealing drugs is just a game, man. Straight up," he said at one point, in the falsetto tone of someone sharing a widely known fact. "And I know the rules. Reckon I'd be a good player."

"It's not *just* a game," Marques rebutted. "It's a dangerous game."

"You're right. It is dangerous. But that just comes with the territory, as they say. Drug dealers can go to jail or be shot. Electricians can get electrocuted or fall. Motorcycle couriers can crash and lose a lung. Cabdrivers can be mugged or get murdered. I'm aware of the risks. I know what I'm getting into. Thing is, I'm sick of waiting, man. I been planning this shit for years. Enough is enough. It's time to put my plan into action: I'm gonna sell weed in my hood. It's time to go after the life I want. I'm done imagining what a better life could look like."

Marques raised his eyebrows.

"That's so weird, man. I was thinking the same thing today when I got to work."

"You were thinking you'd start dealing, too?"

"No. I was thinking what things would be like if my life was better. I was dreaming of a better life for myself, you know?"

"Yeah, I feel you. Everybody's always dreaming of a better life. It's what keeps us going, what makes us want to go on living. But listen: if we don't act now, we're gonna wake up one day and realize we're ninety years old and still dreaming, while our lives ain't changed one bit: they're still crappy as fuck."

"Yeah, man. No doubt."

5

OPERATION WITCHCRAFT

That day, Pedro and Marques went to the locker room during their break, like they always did. Alone, they dug into their banquet. There was ice-cold soda, a box of chocolates, a couple of candy bars, sandwich cookies, a large slice of savory pie, and several angel wings: all courtesy of Fênix supermarkets. As they stuffed themselves, Marques suddenly said:

"Okay, I want in."

"Hunh?" Pedro wasn't paying attention. His jaws went up and down, up and down. "In on what?"

"In on selling weed with you."

"Really? How come?"

"Angélica's pregnant."

Something—maybe it was Marques's curt, bland delivery, which expressed neither enthusiasm nor sorrow—confused Pedro. He couldn't figure out whether to congratulate Marques or commiserate with him. Unsure, he opted for the smile.

"Whoa! Congratulations, man!"

It was the wrong choice.

"Congratulations my ass!" Marques snapped; Pedro quickly hid his bared teeth. "Congratulations for what? It's gonna be fucking hell . . . if she's born, of course . . ."

"You all thinking of getting an abortion?"

"Far as I'm concerned, it's our best option. That's not what I told Angélica, though. Honest, we got into a huge fight this morning, so it's gonna be a while before I say anything that could send us back at each other's throats. If we get an abortion, the decision's got to come from her. If she says she wants one, I'm game. But what if she doesn't? All I know is I'm not mentioning it. I'm steering clear of that conversation. Anyway, maybe selling weed will finally make us some legit money, just like you were saying, man. Real money. If it does, well, damn, it'd make me happy as hell to raise another kid. I fucking love kids."

"Awesome, cuz. Let's do it. Hold up. Isn't your brother already mixed up in the Tuca trade? Why didn't you ever join him? Why hook up with me now?"

"Well, my brother's been in the slammer, right. He's been shot, killed folks . . . That shit ain't for me. I think your way of doing things is gonna be, like, lower key. You're smarter." Marques paused, drank from his glass of soda, then frowned and asked: "How come we're not selling rock and dust instead of weed? We'd make way more money that way. Besides, it doesn't matter if we're caught with a kilo of weed or a kilo of rock or dust: our asses still gonna get thrown in jail. If we're taking the risk, we may as well bring in more money, don't you think?"

"Here's the catch. We won't be running our own business if we sell rock or dust. Porto Alegre's fucking rough these days, you know that. The dudes slinging rock and dust are fighting for new turf, one block at a time, and they're ready to blow the head off any fool who tries to step in on them. Where does that leave us?

If we was to sell that shit, we'd have to join one of the cartels: the Balas na Cara, the Manos, whatever. So on top of having a boss, we'd have more trouble than we want. One minute we're at our corner, slinging grass, kicking back, next thing a rival cartel is blowing off our heads. No thanks, brother!"

"But that's the thing, man. If you go out in the rain, you gonna get wet."

"Hell no! If you want rain, then you can work for your brother. I don't like the rain and the only reason I'm in it is cause I got somewhere to be. That's what fucking umbrellas are for. Sure, I'm stepping into the rain, but I'm gonna make it to my destination as dry as possible. I mean it: you wanna start dealing together, that's cool, but I'm telling you now, we're not gonna be like other dudes that sell drugs. Look at your brother, man. Why you think he's always got problems? For guys like him, money don't cut it: they wanna go round armed to the teeth, they wanna kill, they wanna be feared, they wanna feel powerful. Whatever: to each his own. But the real gangster, that's me: my brains were made to think, not end up splattered on the floor. I want money, not trouble. But if trouble comes our way, we'll figure something out, do whatever needs doing. What we won't do is go looking for it. We're staying the hell away from bad blood, Marques. Got it? And that's why we're only selling weed. Ain't nobody ever start wars over weed. In my hood, nobody's selling grass right now, even though there's loads of dudes raring to get their hands on some. Speaking of, what's it like over in Lupicínio? Anybody sell weed out there?"

"Nah, just rock and dust."

"You on good terms with the boss?"

"Hell yeah, dude's my homeboy. We play pool together sometimes."

"Awesome! It's gonna be an easy ride, then. You'll sell weed there no problem."

Marques refilled his glass of soda and thought for a moment. Then, he asked:

"Where we getting the weed? You got any connects?"

"Nuh-uh," Pedro said, chewing on an angel wing. "But I got something else on my mind right now."

"What's that?"

"Our start-up capital. Money. Dinheiro. I don't know how we're gonna cover our first order."

"How much we need?"

"Dunno . . . One stack might be enough to get us started."

Pedro and Marques fell quiet and started racking their brains. The heat in the locker room was pretty unbearable, and the two men were sweating profusely. But they stuck it out, knowing it would be too dangerous for them to partake in the stolen candy and soda anywhere else, because "there's rats all over the place, itching to turn a brother in."

"I've got it!" Marques said, breaking the silence. "Operation Witchcraft!"

Pedro smacked his forehead.

"Man, of course! I can't believe I didn't think of that."

"Operation Witchcraft" was the code name for an undercover scheme Pedro and Marques had masterminded, and that they and several of the supermarket's other employees had dabbled in for some time. Pedro got the idea for the name from a book he'd been reading called *Tinker Tailor Soldier Spy*. People liked it because it sounded silly. Operation Witchcraft consisted in stealing items from the supermarket, either for their own consumption or for sale outside the store. The sizable thefts enabled by Operation Witchcraft were what drew Sr. Geraldo's attention to the growing discrepancies between the stock inventory and the actual stock.

For something so covert in nature, the scheme had become very popular. These days, nearly half the associates of that Fênix supermarket branch not only knew about Operation Witchcraft but actively took part in it. Employees across all departments were involved: security guards, butchers, bakers, green grocers, stock clerks, custodians, cashiers, baggers. Even Paulo, the assistant manager, dipped his finger in now and then, though he only stole the occasional rack of ribs or steak for grilling at a barbecue. The rest of the staff took a little of everything: sandwich cookies, deodorant, beverages, toys, you name it. The recent appearance of a mysterious tag had piqued the curiosity of the handful of employees who weren't involved in the conspiracy: the words "OPERATION WITCHCRAFT," written in pen, had started cropping up all over the supermarket.

"What's all this 'Operation Witchcraft' nonsense about?" asked some.

"I wonder who's been writing this shit," asked others.

Not even Marques and Pedro, the brains behind the operation, knew who was tagging the store. Then they started tagging, too; and they probably weren't the only ones influenced by that first act of rebellion either. It was said the inscription had even made it into the ladies' room.

Marques and Pedro returned to work after the break, their stomachs grumbling audibly from the surfeit of junk they had ingested. Could they make a thousand reais with Operation Witchcraft? They stocked deodorants in silence, puzzling over how to make it happen. It didn't seem possible.

Out on the street, beyond the supermarket doors, were the first signs of twilight. The blue sky darkened to the east and turned orange to the west. It was a busy time of day: hundreds of thousands of exhausted workers made their way home, vacating the higher-income neighborhoods and cluttering the poorer outskirts. Soon night would fall, and the supermarket would close; time was against them. Anxious as they were to put their long-term, get-rich plan into action, Pedro and Marques hadn't given any thought to slowly and methodically saving up the starting capital. As far as they were concerned, they needed to get hold of the money all at once—and they needed to do it today. What's more, they were moments from finding out that, starting tomorrow, Operation Witchcraft would no longer be viable.

"MARQUES, PEDRO, Y'ALL won't guess what happened," said Jorge, one of the security guards. Judging by his tone, whatever the news, it wasn't good. "Operation Witchcraft is done for, man. RIP," he told them.

"What? Why?" Marques asked.

"I just spoke with Seu Geraldo. He and Horse Face had lunch and decided to scale up our security. Then, a few minutes ago, Horse Face called to tell Seu Geraldo he's sending six guards from another store. Starting tomorrow they're gonna work here to help put a stop to the stealing. I'm telling you, man, it's over. Finito, kapoot."

Pedro seemed indifferent.

"Hmmm. Honestly, I'm not surprised. Been a long time coming, I reckon. We took Operation Witchcraft way too far. It was never meant to turn into what it did. Folks were hitting the stock hard. But don't worry. Tonight, me and Marques are gonna give it a baller send-off. Ain't that right, Marques?"

Marques nodded. Jorge asked:

"You lifting something today? What's on the menu?"

"That's the problem. Whatever we take needs to have a resale value of one grand."

"One grand?" Jorge seemed shocked. "Y'all crazy! You'd have to steal a truckload of stuff to make that kind of money. Unless . . ."

Pedro and Marques looked at Jorge with sudden hopefulness.

"Y'all given any thought to that fancy-ass whiskey?"

The two stock clerks were visibly disappointed.

"Natch, man," Marques answered. "It's the first thing we thought of. It's outta stock."

"Nah it ain't," Jorge said. "Some more came in the truck today. Ten units."

"What truck, dude? I didn't see no trucks come through today."

"What are you, blind? Course there were trucks. They just came earlier than usual. In the morning, before we clocked in. I saw the whiskey in the Graveyard."

The Graveyard was the part of the stockroom where they stored that type of beverage; it got its name from the large rat corpses that could often be found there.

"Fuck, yeah! Guess that's what we're hitting!" Pedro exclaimed. "If we take all ten bottles, it could just about get us a thou."

"What y'all need the money for, anyway?" Jorge asked.

"To buy weed to sell in our hoods."

Jorge smiled.

"Listen . . ." he warned. "This shit's no joke. You can't be fooling around. It's hot out there. No room for error. Fuck up and you get fucked."

It was Pedro's turn to smile.

"We're not morons. We know it's no joke, man. But the only reason those fools get locked up and killed is cause they're stupid."

"So, you think you're smart, huh? Riddle me this, then: How'd a guy as smart as you wind up working as a stock clerk?"

Pedro responded philosophically, as usual:

"Maybe the question you should be asking is: How'd a fucking stock clerk wind up this smart?"

Unlike Marques, Jorge had no patience for Pedro's antics. As far as he was concerned, everything that came out of Pedro's mouth was bunk.

"Nah, nah, nah, you can take that stunt and shove it. I got no time for your bullshit!"

The three men laughed, then Jorge took out a pen, tore off a corner of the shelf's price display, jotted down a number, and handed it to Pedro.

"If y'all really wanna sell weed, then call this number and ask for Fabrício. Just remember to tell him I'm the one who gave it to you, yeah?"

"Who is this dude?" Marques asked.

"Oh, just a five-o pal of mine," Jorge joked. "He's a dealer, smart-ass! Dude gets drugs from outside Brazil and distributes it all over PA. He's good people: I get a hundred big ones whenever I connect him with a new client. Who knows, dude might even give you a deal on your first order."

Some things have a funny way of working themselves out, of clearing every obstacle. From one minute to the next, raising starting capital had become a non-issue; they'd even found a supplier to boot. When fortune smiles down on you, it can feel as if you're finally on track; as if, from that moment on, things will always go your way. Night had already fallen by the time Marques walked across the store, which was still crowded with people, and stopped at register number six.

"Fabiana. Give me five grocery bags, will you?"

"Operation Witchcraft?" asked the discerning cashier.

"Maybe, maybe not," he answered. "Only time will tell."

Marques rushed to the large stockroom entrance, where a short teenager with a shaved, bulbous head stood with his hands in his pockets. The boy was close friends with Marques and Pedro, and his role at the supermarket—his sacrosanct first job—was to thanklessly bag groceries for several hours at a time. His name was Luan, and that's what everyone called him those days, though his friends used to call him Chokito, after the candy bar, an epithet that disappeared along with the pimples that once riddled his face.

"Listen up, Luan: it's going down right now," Marques said. "See Jorge over there at the other end of the store? He's gonna signal if anybody heads this way. So keep your eyes peeled, yeah? If he does, you gotta let me and Pedro know."

"Sure thing, man," the teenager said. "Just be fast."

To avoid two security cameras, Marques didn't use that stockroom entrance. Instead, he went up to the meat counter and ducked behind it, nodding at the butchers, who knew exactly what he was doing. Then he crossed the putrid room where the meat was deboned and walked down a dimly lit hall. At the end of the hall, he turned left. He was in the back of the stockroom now, where light was also scarce, and the only sound the echoing of Marques's footsteps. To avoid another couple of security cameras, Marques walked beneath the stairs to the locker room and squeezed between stacks and stacks of washing powder, which spat him out at the Graveyard entrance. He went in. That section of the stockroom was pitch-black: the light bulbs had burned out a long time ago and no one bothered changing them. Marques walked with his hands in front of him, careful not to bump into the cases of beer and pallets of soft drinks.

Pedro's hushed voice cut through the gloom.

"Marques! Over here." He'd already taken the bottles of whiskey out of their boxes. "C'mon! Let's get this over and done with."

The men placed the whiskey in the grocery bags Marques had brought, then headed up to the locker room.

In the back of the locker room was a tilting window. There was a special quirk to the window known only to the participants of Operation Witchcraft. For some reason, it was never mortared in place, which meant the window simply sat in the wall opening, wedged firmly enough that the wind couldn't dislodge it, no matter how strongly it blew, while also making it difficult to remove by hand. And that's exactly what Pedro did: he took out the window while Marques stood on his tiptoes, reaching for something on top of the lockers. Marques quickly found what he was looking for: a roll of clothesline stolen from the cleaning supplies aisle that the participants of Operation Witchcraft used regularly, though not for hanging clothes. Marques unwound the clothesline, threaded one end through the handles of the grocery bag with the bottles of whiskey, then leaned out of the large opening that had only moments ago held a window. Gripping the clotheslines in a U-shape, he carefully lowered the bags along the outer wall of the building, the pale moonlight the only witness to his actions. As soon as the bottles of whiskey softly alighted in the neighboring patio, Marques rolled up the clothesline and hid it on top of the lockers while Pedro wedged the window back in place.

"Done. Now let's change outta these clothes and bounce."

"Bounce? What do you mean? It's only eight o'clock . . ."

"We still need to sell the whiskey. The sooner we leave, the better. I don't wanna get home late, man."

"Right, cool. Let's get outta here."

They changed out of their uniforms, slipped on their backpacks, and went downstairs.

"It's all good, Luan. You can go now," Pedro said, tapping the shoulder of the bagger who'd stood guard at the entrance to the stockroom and giving Jorge a thumbs-up from the other end of the store.

There were a number of security measures in place at this Fênix supermarket branch. One of them was that the manager had to inspect the employees' backpacks before they could leave. Which is why Pedro and Marques knocked on the door of Sr. Geraldo's modest office space, the one that looked more like a makeshift depot than the management of a supermarket.

"Come in!" thundered the manager in a low, powerful voice.

The two men walked in.

"What's all this about?" Sr. Geraldo said the moment he saw his employees were not in uniform. "Leaving already?"

"That's right," said Pedro.

"But it isn't allowed! Haven't you read your contracts? They clearly say: 'one P.M. to nine-twenty P.M.'"

"It's just for today, Seu Geraldo. Besides, sometimes when it's busy and we clock in early to help out on the morning shift and then still stay till close, working longer than it says in our contracts. Isn't that right?"

"That's neither here nor there. You can't just do what you damn please, tchê!"

Though uncomfortable to some, these sorts of conversations didn't have much of an effect on Pedro and Marques. Pedro seemed to enjoy them, content to endlessly argue; Marques, on the other hand, had a short fuse and tended to get deeply frustrated. He was the one who interrupted Sr. Geraldo, just as the manager was about to start his spiel:

"Look, Sr. Geraldo, are you gonna check our backpacks or not?"

"But, Marques, your shift hasn't ended yet . . ."

"Right, so you ain't gonna check them? Cause we're leaving whether you check them or not."

Defeated, the manager frowned and inspected their backpacks while shaking his head.

"You can go," he grumbled, salvaging some of his authority.

The two men left the air-conditioned store for the heat of the streets, then turned right and walked along the sidewalk of Rua General Jacinto Osório. Just a few meters ahead, they turned right again and went through the open gates to Luciana de Abreu, the school that abutted the supermarket. The teachers had gone on strike last year, which meant there'd been no summer break and the students were still making up the classes they'd missed during that lengthy negotiation period.

"Do you go here?" asked a teacher in the lobby when she saw the two men. It was the first time they'd been caught entering the school. The lobby was usually deserted.

Pedro knew the powers of charm. He smiled and said, pretending to be shy:

"No, ma'am. We're not students. We're just on our way to speak with my sister. She goes here. It's important. I promise we won't be long."

"Alright. You can go in. Do you know what room she's in?"

"Sure do. Thank you, ma'am."

As soon as the woman left, they crossed the lobby into the back patio, which was always deserted at night, devoid of students, teachers, or any of the school's staff. The space was empty because the lights were off and the evening sessions didn't get recess or other outdoor activities. The two men casually advanced through the dark, skirting the large pavilion; back there, to the right, in a particularly dark corner by the outer wall of the supermarket, sat the five grocery bags they'd lowered with the clothesline, each of them holding two bottles of whiskey. They transferred the bottles to their backpacks and left.

Pedro and Marques needed to offload the whiskey, and their feet knew exactly where to take them. No discussion necessary. They simply walked to the nearest bus stop on Avenida João Pessoa and got on the first 346—São José bus they saw, direction Centro-bairro.

They were excited, like a couple of young, middle-class men fresh out of college trying to raise funds for a dating site, a veterinary clinic, or a law firm. Would they succeed in selling the whiskey for a thousand reais? Would that be enough to set them up? How should they price the weed? Would they make a lot of money? They couldn't wait to get started.

6

THREATENING
CIRCUMSTANCES

Elbows propped on the counter and face cradled in her hands, the woman flipped through one of those magazines where you can find everything you might want to know about celebrities. After skimming the text—purely for the sake of her conscience—she appraised the women's clothes and the men's muscles, all while sighing heavily. From time to time, someone would order another bottle of beer, or another shot of cachaça, or another loose cigarette. Only then, when she snapped out of that narcotic dream to serve someone at the bar, did she hear the conversation filling the establishment, mixing with the loud music and the dinging of the slot machine.

Another bus had just pulled into Vila Campo da Tuca, stopping right outside the bar. The woman only noticed because she was serving a customer. She gave a broad smile when she saw the two men get off, squeeze past a group of drunks, and enter the establishment.

"Marques, Pedro!"

"Sup, Catarina? Y'alright?"

"How's it going, sis?"

Catarina, Marques's older sister, wasn't surprised to see them. Lately, they had taken to visiting her bar every now and then, always around the same time. She had an idea what they wanted.

"Y'all got something for me?"

"Not just something, no," said Pedro. "We've got the motherload!"

"That right? Let's see it, then."

Pedro and Marques removed the bottles of whiskey from their backpacks one by one and set them on the counter.

"Here you go! Ten bottles of the good stuff."

"I can't afford it," Catarina warned them off the bat, shaking her head.

"What d'you mean, sis?" Marques complained. "We ain't even told you how much we want yet."

"Fine. How much y'all want?"

"A thousand."

"I can't afford it," the woman said impassively.

Pedro sighed.

"You can't afford it, hunh?"

"No, I can't. Most I can do is six hundred, and that's pushing it."

Marques grumbled.

"C'mon, you know it's worth more than that. Each bottle of this stuff goes for upwards of a thou in those flea traps downtown . . ."

Marques would've carried on had his sister not raised her hand to stop him.

"Listen, listen, listen, for fuck's sake! I'm not crazy or nothing. I know y'all are being fair. I'd make a thousand plus reais selling shots of this shit—"

"But . . ." Pedro presaged.

". . . but I can't afford to fork over a grand from one minute to the next. I got four kids, I got bills to pay. If I had that kind of money just lying around, that'd be a whole other story; but I don't. What I got is six hundred. That's how much I can pay you. And let's be honest, yeah? Six hundred is more than worth your time. Three hundred a piece, no sweat off your back . . . What more y'all want?"

"Thing is, we need a thousand. Any less than that, and it's no good to us."

Catarina raised her eyebrows and cocked her head.

"What y'all planning to do with that money?"

"We're gonna buy some weed to sell," Marques said, getting right to the point.

"Cool, just what we needed. Another dealer in the family," she joked.

"Yeah, whatever, sis. Don't go making a big deal outta this. Can you give us a grand for the whiskey or not?"

Catarina smiled. She loved it when her brother got riled up. It took her back to happier times, when the whole family lived together and she looked after her younger brothers and sisters. Marques, the youngest, had also been the most rebellious. Of all her siblings, she always thought Marques had the highest chance of becoming a criminal. Instead, it was the exact opposite. Marques was the only one of the lot who went looking for a job; all the others turned to robbery, with the exception of her brother, the career drug dealer. Either way, her little brother was about to set off on a life of crime . . . God protect him.

"Fucking hell! Didn't I just tell you I can't afford it? Are you deaf or something?"

"Fine, then. Let's bounce, Pedro. We can sell the whiskey at the club."

"Relax, Marques," Pedro said. He rested his hand on his shoulder as Marques got ready to pack up the bottles of whiskey. "Your sister's gonna hand over a thou. Don't sweat."

"I am, am I?" Catarina asked, intrigued. "I'm gonna just hand it over, hunh? How's that?"

"Here's the deal, beautiful: We're gonna pay you back four hundred. For real. Give us a grand now and we'll pay back four hundred soon as we've sold enough weed. It won't be no time at all. I give you my word, and my word . . ." Pedro held his hand like a gun, thumb and index fingers in the shape of an L, then pointed it at the woman's head. ". . . My word is a sure shot, yeah?" He winked at her and cocked his thumb as if it were a recoiled hammer. "What d'you say?"

"What do I say? I say somebody musta lied when they told you you were charming," Catarina said, poking fun at Pedro. "Wait here, asshole. I'll go get the money." She turned on her heels, then strode down the hall connecting the bar to the house where she and her husband lived with their four children. When she came back, she handed Pedro twenty crumpled fifty-real bills. "I need you to pay me back in a month at the latest. Okay?"

Pedro slid the money into his back pocket.

"You're the boss." Then he glanced at Marques, who still looked annoyed. "Let's have a cold one before we bounce. How about it, buddy?" Before Marques could answer, Pedro said: "Give us a couple of beers, Catarina."

"Good idea," said the woman. "It's the only way that stick is coming out of Marques's ass."

Marques clicked his tongue.

"Oh, fuck you, you just been wasting our time, playing hard to get, trying to get us to sweeten the deal . . ." he whispered low enough for her sister not to hear him. Catarina belonged to a small group of people toward whom Marques was too frightened to be openly disrespectful.

As Catarina placed their glasses on the counter and opened the bottle of beer, Pedro smiled:

"If what we want is for your fucking drag of a brother to cheer up, then we gotta do things right. You got any snow back there to perk us up?"

The woman sighed and rolled her eyes.

"Yeah, yeah, you fucking pest. I got some! Next thing I know, you'll be asking for some pussy." She turned around and vanished down the hall, then came back holding a rolled up ten-real note and three lines of coke on her ID card.

Marques held up his hand, palm out.

"Nah, man. I'm not in the mood."

His sister seethed.

"Well, guess I must be crazy then, hunh? Why the hell didn't you say you didn't want any, jerk-off? Why'd you let me head back there and fix up three lines?"

"C'mon, Marques. Don't start. Do a bump," Pedro said. "It'll help you relax."

"But I don't want any, dude! What're you gonna do, force me?"

"Brother, why you always so fucking tetchy?" Catarina asked. "Now take this shit and stick it up your nose." She put her ID card and the rolled-up note in front of her brother. "Go on. I mean it, Marques. Snort that shit right now!"

Catarina's sway over her brother was impressive. Marques wasn't Marques when he stood up—or tried to stand up—to his big sister.

"Fine, I'll do it. But only cause I want to," he said, finally giving in to Catarina.

Pedro started laughing.

"Cause he wants to!" he mocked. "You're gonna snort that blow cause if you don't, Catarina's gonna shove all of it—dust, straw, ID card and all—down your throat!"

Thirty minutes or so later, Pedro and Marques said goodbye to Catarina and climbed on the bus that would take them back to the center of Porto Alegre. Marques would get off outside Julinho and walk the rest of the way to Vila Lupicínio Rodrigues, while Pedro would take a second bus to Lomba do Pinheiro. The first leg of Pedro's commute ended outside the São Pedro Psychiatric Hospital, a bombed-out building that was creepier than the creepiest scenes in the creepiest horror movies, especially at that time of night.

Pedro was getting ready to leave the bus when Marques, who was sitting by the back door, said:

"Let's see if we can get that Fabrício dude on the phone tomorrow, yeah?"

They hadn't called him yet because neither Pedro nor Marques had any minutes left on their cell phones.

"Très bien!" said Pedro, who'd torn through several volumes of Hercule Poirot mysteries.

For some reason, that expression always rubbed Marques the wrong way.

"Très bien my ass, man!"

Later, as Pedro stood on the bus surrounded by other tired workers, he gazed out the window at the night and became lost in thought. As the vehicle rolled down Avenida Bento Gonçalves toward the easternmost part of the city, the landscape grew visibly poorer and more hostile. Now and then, when they stopped at a red light and a car idled beside them, Pedro would stare down at it and remember how much he'd wanted one as a young boy . . . The hopes and dreams of kids from poor families, he thought, are no different from those of kids from rich families; but unlike rich kids, as years passed and the poor kids got older and wiser, they buried their dreams one by one, after realizing it's hard enough to put food on the table, grueling enough to keep on their side of the class divide between them and the people who lived on the street. As a kid, Pedro hadn't only dreamed of having a car, but also of buying one for all his relatives. For some reason, he used to believe he'd be enormously wealthy when he grew up, and the way his life turned out was a resounding disappointment. He hadn't been able to buy his mother a house in the country, like he'd promised, nor travel to China, like he'd planned. Plenty of desires like those had never become anything more than that—desires. Later, even the desire itself had disappeared: once he realized that none of his dreams ever came true, Pedro simply stopped dreaming.

Right then, though, hope slowly awakened inside him and dusted off his old dreams. He saw himself behind the wheel of a car, in a decent house . . . Not that he was anywhere close to making those dreams, or any dream for that matter, come true. He had a long road ahead of him, he knew that. But in that moment, conscious of his own determination, he found himself believing he could do anything, just as he had believed a long time ago, before all the disappointment and heartbreak. Things could still go wrong, sure, they could. But if there was one thing he knew for certain it was this: he would do everything in his power to become rich, even if it meant abandoning his morals one by one, until none were left. Nothing and no one would stand in his way.

WHEN THE TWO men arrived at the supermarket the following Tuesday, February 3, 2009, the first thing they did was find someone with enough minutes on their phone who would let them make a short call. Jorge, the security guard who'd given them Fabrício's number the evening before, was walking past Pedro and Marques when he saw them ask an associate to borrow their cell phone.

"Y'all trying to get ahold of Fabrício?" he asked, stepping up to them and pulling his cell phone out of his pocket.

"That's right."

"Here. Use mine. Call collect."

Jorge had already clocked in and was on his way to a meeting where the six security guards from other Fênix supermarket branches would meet the security guards from their branch. Pedro and Marques still hadn't clocked in, so they grabbed Jorge's phone and went up to the locker room, where Pedro dialed 9090 and then the number on the piece of paper. He heard the usual collect-call tune, followed by the recorded message: "Collect call. After the tone, please state your name and the city you are calling from."

"What's up, Jorge?"

"It's not Jorge. This is his buddy, Pedro."

"Hmm . . ."

"I'm calling cause Jorge said you could hook us up."

"And is Jorge there?"

"Yeah, but he can't talk right now."

"How come?"

"Cause he's working. I'm a pal of his. We work together at the supermarket. That's where I'm calling from. I asked to borrow his phone. He said to call collect and—"

"Right . . . And what is it y'all want?"

"It's okay to just, like, say it on the phone?"

"Yeah."

"Cool. We want weed."

"There's a two-kilo minimum."

"And how much is a kilo?"

"Seven hundred. It's good stuff."

"If the stuff is legit good, then that's a great price. Here's the thing, though. I've got a thou, and that's all I can get my hands on right now. Could you front me four hundred for the two kilos? Or make an exception and sell me one kilo to start?"

"Right, well, you're a buddy of Jorge's, ain't you? I'll hold the four hundred for now. You can get it to me later."

"Cool, cool . . . We'll take two kilo, then. Do I come to you, or how does that work?"

"I'll find you."

"Right, okay. Can it be today?"

"Nah. I only do weed deliveries on Fridays; if it was rock or dust . . ."

"Got it. Next Friday, then?"

"Sure. Where?"

"You know the supermarket where we work?"

"Yeah."

"There's a square out front. Nine-thirty P.M."

"Listen, might be hard for me to get somebody over to you at a specific time. Our guy makes a ton of deliveries, and those deliveries take precedence."

"Okay. Right, that's gonna be a problem, though."

"How's that?"

"Cause I clock out at nine-twenty and don't live in the neighborhood. So I can't, like, wait around the square until late."

"I can send somebody to your place. Where d'you live?"

"I live in Pinheiro, but I don't want stuff delivered to my crib."

"Why not?"

"I wanna do this on the down-low. It's one thing if I get home with my work bag looking a bit heavier than usual; it's another if a guy comes up to my pad, hands me a package, counts a wad of cash, and leaves. The neighbors talk, man. And they know I'm not into pizza, if you catch my drift. What I'm saying is: the less attention I get, the better. The only folks who should know I'm selling are the ones buying. Which is why I can't have stuff delivered to my house."

"Yeah, alright, I get it. Look, I can tell my delivery guy to get the weed to you at nine-thirty, like you said. But I can't guarantee nothing. He might be late."

"How about this: If your guy ain't here by ten, I call you and we can discuss delaying the delivery or waiting awhile longer. That sound okay?"

"Yeah, that works. But gimme your number, in case I have to call."

"Cool." Pedro read out his cell-phone number. "We good?"

"Yeah. Two kilos of weed. Next Friday, nine-thirty P.M. The square outside the supermarket. Perfect. Be there with fourteen hundred."

"Hold up, hold up. Weren't you gonna front us four hundred?"

"Oh yeah, you're right. Then be there with a thou. Y'all have a month to pay me back, got it?"

Fabrício's voice didn't carry a hint of a threat, nor did it have to. The circumstances were threatening enough. Pedro might not know the man on the other end of the line, but he suspected he wouldn't send them flowers if they missed the deadline.

"Sure."

"Cool. Later, then."

Fabrício hung up. Pedro remained quiet and pensive as he tapped his knee with Jorge's phone.

Marques became impatient.

"So? What the fuck's up?"

"It's cool . . ." Pedro mumbled, eyes glazed over and fixed on the tile floor in the locker room. "We get the delivery next Friday. In the square out front, after clocking out. Two kilo. We're on the hook for four hundred, due in a month." He looked over at Marques and slowly said: "Listen, if something goes wrong and we can't pay him back, dude could have us killed."

Marques frowned, then stood facing his friend. He scanned his eyes for fear or hesitation, concerned Pedro's comment may be rooted in shallow ground. But his eyes held neither fear nor hesitation, only pure determination: a hard, nigh-indestructible determination; a cold, icy determination, like the surface of a frozen lake; and the thoughts behind his determination were probably icier still. A *grim* determination! No, Pedro wasn't scared, and he wasn't hesitant either. His words, Marques concluded, were a warning, the subtle offering of a final way out, while there was still time. But Marques wasn't easily spooked; he might have been even more fearless than Pedro. What's more, Marques's sense of loyalty whispered that it wouldn't be right of him to let his friend embark on that dangerous journey alone; Marques's total confidence in Pedro murmured that his friend knew exactly what he was doing; Marques's endless financial troubles, added to the news that Angélica was pregnant with their second child, hinted that he shouldn't pass up this opportunity to make money. All of which made Marques susceptible to the determination in Pedro's eyes, cementing his own desire to see things through.

"Alright, brother," he finally said. "Let's do it. If something goes wrong and we can't pay him back, then let the dude try and kill us. Death comes for us all. Life's shit and then you die. Except we ain't just rocks, are we? We got hands, we got legs, we can hustle. Let him try and come after us, we'll see who gets who first."

7

POPS

It really was impressive how quickly Marques ran out of patience. He knocked on the door twice and the lack of response was enough to make him frown, take a deep breath, cup his hands around his mouth, and holler at the top of his lungs:

"POPS!!!"

"Fuck's sake, I'm coming, I'm coming!" grumbled a gruff, sleepy voice inside the house. This was followed by the thud of something falling on the floor. "Goddammit! Fucking shit!"

It was still only ten A.M. on Wednesday, February 4, 2009, but the heat was so intense it felt like noon. The sun shone right over Marques as he waited at the closed door, sweat dripping down his forehead and the nape of his neck.

"Jesus! How can he sleep through this fucking heat?" he muttered to himself.

When the door finally swung open, a powerful smell of alcohol impregnated the air and a strange figure loomed in the doorway.

He was a robust man, body crisscrossed with wrinkles and skin the color of ripe wheat. His straight, grayish hair was disheveled and fell over his face, making him look equal parts wild and comical. He could have been anywhere between fifty and sixty years old, but something—maybe it was his posture or the brute strength implied by the girth of his arm—made him look younger. He was shirtless and wore a necklace with a handsome gold cross that was somehow less arresting than the two gruesome scars on his belly, likely the vestiges of a couple of gunshot wounds.

"Chwist, Marques. What the fuck d'you want, kid?" asked the Vila Lupicínio cartel boss.

Marques laughed. The fact that the man had trouble pronouncing a hard "r" tickled him.

"Chwist yourself, Pops! You gonna invite me in or what?"

The old man sighed and shook his head. He stepped back to let Marques through, then shut the door.

Marques looked around him. Like always, the house was neat as a pin, with the exception of a small, unusual mess in a corner of the living room. The couch was slightly off-kilter and the rug bunched up; on the coffee table were three glasses, one of them on its side next to an empty bottle of whiskey, a credit card, and a platter with a small mound of cocaine on it.

"Shit, man. What y'all get up to in here?"

"I'll tell you what I got up to," the old man said, throwing his head back so that his hair swished around him, then planting his hands on his hips. He paused for effect and wet his lips with his tongue. Then he explained: "The good times started out here"— he pointed at the couch with his index finger—"and ended in there." He pointed at the closed bedroom door with his thumb.

"Right, right, I feel you." Marques walked toward the room, cracked open the door, and peeked inside, where two naked women lay asleep on the bed. "Not bad!"

"Want a go?"

"Nah, thanks. Just came by to see if you were up for a game," Marques said, shutting the door again.

"I tell you you can have your banana peeled by one of these babes, and you want to play pool with this sad sack of flesh?"

"I . . . I'm just not hungry, y'know?"

"Ah . . . I see. Had bweakfast at home, huh? Angélica's a lucky charm. I mean it. What more can you want than a woman who wakes up wanting to swallow iron?"

"Listen, Pops. Cut the crap. You wanna play or what?"

"Marques, I got less than an hour's sleep!" he complained.

"Whatever, man. Remember that time you knocked on my door at midnight cause you wanted to play pool? I'd just gone to bed, but I still got up to hang with you."

"Yeah, but I was plastered, kid. You knew that if you didn't play pool with me, there was no way in hell I was letting you sleep." The old man smiled, apparently warmed by the memory. "Yeah, I weally wasn't gonna let you sleep! You made the wight choice. I'd have howled at you till the sun came out." He flashed a cheeky smile.

Marques raised his eyebrows and grinned. He sat down and draped both arms over the back of the sofa. He gazed at the old man in silence, shaking his head suggestively.

The old man got the message and grew suddenly serious. Then he sighed:

"I see. Y'ain't gonna let me sleep either. Not unless I come with you. That wight?"

"Just four games, man. I can't fuck around all day, for real. I gotta get to work. Then you can come home and sleep long as you want."

Pops walked across the living room shaking his head, then sat in the armchair across from Marques.

"Okay, I'll come with you. But know that what you're doing to me is wong, Marques. I'm an old man, fuck's sake!" He picked up the credit card on the table and cut up some cocaine on the platter. Meanwhile, Marques grabbed the calendar by the telephone and carefully tore off a piece of the page, rolled it into a straw and handed it to the old man, who used it to snort a line.

Pops went to his bedroom and woke the prostitutes, gave them some money, and told them to get dressed and leave. They did what he said. He went to the bathroom to splash some water on his face and brush his hair. Back in the bedroom, he threw on a shirt, leaving it part-way unbuttoned, as he often did, then looked at himself in the mirror. Satisfied, he left the bedroom and said:

"Let's bounce."

"About time, Bill!"

The old man's name wasn't Bill, though Marques called him that now and then; something about Pops reminded Marques of Bill from *Kill Bill*.

"Hold up. Better take this with me," Bill said, grabbing the platter of cocaine.

"Man, you gonna wind up dead one of these days!"

"No shit, Marques. We all are. The only thing that's twue in this world is the end, and we all know what that is. What we don't know is the path each of us taking to get there. You might go that way and I might go this way, but sooner or later we're all walking off the same cliff."

They stepped out into the sunny day. The old man casually carried the platter of cocaine down the alley, holding it near his shoulder like a waiter.

"All that's missing today is a nice breeze . . ." Marques joked.

"Jesus! Watch what you say, kid."

They went to the boteco where they usually played pool. The place was open practically 24/7 and rarely seen closed. The owner and his children took turns behind the bar. Sometimes the wife served customers too. Today, the man himself stood behind the counter.

Marques and Pops greeted the owner, who immediately collected tokens for the pool table, without either of them needing to ask. He dropped them into the old man's cupped hand and walked away, only to return with a large, ice-cold bottle of beer, the coldest in the house, and two glasses, which he set on the table beside theirs.

"Can I leave the blow here?" Bill asked, setting the platter of cocaine on the counter before the owner had a chance to respond.

"Sure thing."

"Help yourself to a bump if you want."

The owner of the bar didn't have to be asked twice.

Marques and the old man opened the ball trap and arranged the balls on the felt surface. They grabbed the pool cues and started playing.

As Pops took the break shot, Marques sipped his beer and asked:

"Hey, Pops, how come you don't sell weed round here?"

The question seemed to take the old man aback. He thought for a moment, then said:

"Weed's too . . . bulky."

"Bulky?" Marques hadn't expected that answer.

"Bulky."

"What d'you mean?"

"Chwist, Marques. Don't you know what 'bulky' means? When something's bulky, it's got too much bulk."

"So what if weed's too bulky?"

"So what? So what? I'll tell you so what. Okay, so picture I'm wolling into the hood with a twunk full of wock and dust. Behind me is another car. The guy dwiving this other car is some wandom dipshit like you. His twunk is full of weed. Which car is worth more money?"

"Yours, natch."

"How come?"

"Cause rock and dust are worth more than weed."

"Exactly. I could ship the same value in weed as the wock and dust in the twunk of my car. But then I'd need a twuck. Guess why."

Marques rolled his eyes.

"Yeah, yeah. Cause weed's bulky."

"That's it. And if I had a twuck, I'd just use it for more wock and dust, not weed."

They paused. It was Marques's turn, and he sank the two ball. On his second shot, he didn't sink anything. Then he said:

"But you used to sell weed."

"I did. But times have changed. Folks didn't want dust then the way they do now. And there wasn't as many Bwits in Porto back then."

The term "Brits" had nothing to do with Great Britain but with the fact that crack was sold as small rocks known as britas, which is why crackheads were called Brits.

The old man took his shot, then asked:

"Why you so interested in my business all of a sudden?"

"It ain't that. Thing is, I wanna sell weed in the neighborhood. You don't mind, do you?"

The old man turned to face Marques.

"Are you for weal?"

"Yeah, man. Of course. Why? What's the problem?"

"Nah, no pwoblem. Just that I've asked you to come and work for me a thousand times and you always turn me down. Cause you say you wanna keep hustling at that piece-of-shit supermarket."

"You're too wild, old man. That's why I never wanted to work for you."

"Me, wild?" he asked in shock, bringing his hand to his chest.

"Well, ain't you? Remember that time when you Swiss-cheesed a pig who came into the hood in full gear? It happened right outside this bar. You dragged the poor fucker outta here by the feet. Remember? If I worked for you and fucked up, I know for sure you'd do the same to me."

"I'd never do something like that to you, Marques. How many times I told you? You're like a son to me."

"You're always pissed when you say shit like that."

"Not pissed now though, am I? We're on our first cold one—"

"Yeah, right. Don't think I didn't see that empty bottle of whiskey at your crib."

"It was those hookers, man! The pair of them were like camels! I give you my word: it was them two that dwank it all. Camels, I swear to God!"

"You're one crazy son of a bitch, Bill!"

The two men broke into laughter.

"Real talk, though: I'm gonna sell weed in the neighborhood. Just weed. We wanna fly under the radar, you feel?" He illustrated this by swooping his hand across the air.

"What d'you mean 'fly under the wadar'?" the old man asked.

"You know, make money without drawing attention to ourselves. Without getting into trouble."

"Forget about it, Marques. Ain't no money in weed."

"I know. Cause it's too bulky, right?"

The old man laughed and then reassured him:

"You wanna sell weed? Go ahead. It's fine by me."

"We've got a good plan. You'll see."

"A good plan, hunh? You couldn't come up with a plan to stick up your own fwidge, man!"

"It's not my plan."

"Then who's the mowon in charge?"

"Pedro, a pal of mine from the supermarket. But he ain't a moron. For real, dude's a genius."

"Geniuses don't work in supermarkets."

"You know what he said to me about that? He told me it ain't true that folks who work crappy jobs only work them cause they're dumb. It's the opposite: it's the crappy jobs that turn people dumb, after a while."

"Then he's dumb either way. Cause according to his own logic, y'all's shitty-ass job made him dumb."

"That's what I said. And you know what he said to me?"

The old man was running out of patience.

"Beats me," he sighed and raised his eyebrows.

"He said it was . . . Shit, I can't remember the word now . . . It was fucking weird . . ." The term Marques couldn't think of was *paradox*. "Oh, fuck it. I can't remember. But the word's got to do with something that gets your ideas in a knot, yeah? Cause if his theory's right, he is dumb, but if he is dumb, then his theory's wrong, yeah? Anyway, he explained it better. But it was just a game he was playing, right? Then he laughed and said he didn't think he was dumb. That the truth was he's a . . . Fuck, I can't remember that word either . . ." The word was *anomaly*. "Like, he thinks something happened to him, something that doesn't usually happen to folks, like an accident, something that was never meant to be, and whatever it was, it made him smart, even though he's poor, even though he dropped outta school real early and been working crappy jobs his whole life. Then he said that he wished he wasn't smart. That it'd be better if he was dumb, cause at least that way he'd be happy, at least he'd be satisfied with his shitty little life."

"Marques, this dude sounds batshit."

Marques looked very serious.

"Listen, old man. I known Pedro a long time now and, honest, every time I talk to him I think the same thing you're thinking now: dude sounds fucking batshit. He talks and talks and talks, and after a while you realize his brain works different than yours cause he's always coming to these weird conclusions. You should see it, it's a trip. Except, I always listen to what he's got to say, and I swear to God: it makes a ton of sense. And that scares me, Pops. You know why?"

"Why?"

"Cause then I think maybe *I'm* the one that's batshit, not him."

They played a few games and drank a few more beers. Every so often, the old man went up to the platter of cocaine. He always offered the barman a line and the barman always accepted. When Marques said he had to leave to have lunch and shower before work, the old man told the owner to put the beers and tokens on his tab, then grabbed the empty platter and walked outside with Marques.

"Listen, Marques. Come by the house first, yeah? I got something I wanna give you."

Marques had no idea what Pops wanted to give him. I better watch my step with that crazy bastard, he thought to himself. He wouldn't have been surprised if the old man suddenly decided to kill him because he wanted to sell weed in Vila Lupicínio Rodrigues, even though he'd said it was all right.

When they got to Pops's house, Marques waited in the living room while the cartel boss fetched the "present" from his bedroom. When he saw Pops come back with a gun in his hand, his heart skipped a beat. Then he noticed that Pops was holding the weapon by the barrel, which meant he wasn't planning to shoot him.

"Take this piece of cwap," the old man ordered, holding the gun out to Marques. "Careful: it's loaded."

"Why you giving me this?"

"Cause one of these days, kid, you gonna need it."

8

KEEPING THE PEACE

Vila Viçosa and Vila Nova São Carlos were enjoying a peaceful spell. Of course, every now and then some poor bastard still died in the occasional bar fight, or over a woman, or because of debt, but it'd been a long time since the region's rival drug cartels had staged constant shootouts. The reason for this was that drug trafficking was so profitable now that the parties involved were happy with the status quo. Demand was high and there were plenty of addicts to go around: war had fallen out of fashion. The question was: until when? History repeats itself: truces come, truces go. Those with experience knew that every day of peace and quiet was just another step toward more turbulent times.

And it so happened that, by some unfortunate twist of fate, peace was once again at stake for these two neighborhoods. Driving a motorcycle, three sheets to the wind, a teenage boy had run over a five-year-old girl on Estrada João de Oliveira Remião, killing her instantly. And if that wasn't tragic enough, the girl's father—a drug dealer with the cartel operating in Nova São Carlos, a man named Jair, although he was better-known by the suggestive moniker of Belly-Ripper, after the Mexican sitcom *El Chapulín Colorado*—was with her at the exact moment of the accident, holding her hand and saying silly little things to her in a falsetto voice, as grown-ups often do with children, so that he didn't even see the motorcycle zip past him, quick as lightning, buzzing like a giant bee. Instead all the man saw was his daughter flying into the air like a ragdoll, right after he felt her little hand slip out of his. The teenager driving the motorcycle emerged unscathed from the accident, stumbling off the vehicle a few meters up the road and jumping to his feet as if nothing had happened. But he didn't survive the sixteen .40-caliber bullets that Belly-Ripper immediately pumped into him, all in the head. And, as incredible as it may sound, this episode could easily have been just another day in the neighborhood, with no cause for shock or concern—after all, it had happened in Lomba do Pinheiro, where it wasn't easy to cause shock or concern. And yet it quickly caused a big stink, because the teenager who'd been shot to death by the drug dealer of the Nova São Carlos cartel was the younger brother of Fernando, a.k.a. Bison, named after a character in *Street Fighter*, and Bison was a member of the rival cartel, the one operating in Vila Viçosa.

Pedro found out what happened when he got home from work that night. He had trouble falling asleep. "Fuck, man! Why now?" he thought, tossing and turning in bed.

If war broke out again in the region, and this looked likely to happen, Pedro would have problems. With daily shootings and weekly deaths, the police would rain down on Vila Viçosa and Vila Nova São Carlos, stopping and frisking everyone in the streets every five minutes. Not to mention that cops would presumably scale up their random searches, kicking down people's doors at any hour of the day or night, making a mess of everything and beating up anyone who dared say a word. All of this meant that Pedro would have to delay selling weed in the neighborhood, for the foreseeable future . . . No, they had to keep the peace. The police needed to stay away. But what could he do about it?

The next day, Thursday, February 5, 2009, Pedro woke up a little earlier than usual and went to pay a visit to the cartel boss of Vila Nova São Carlos, a man by the name of Valdir. Just as Marques had spoken with the old man in Lupicínio Rodrigues the day before, Pedro also wanted to inform the boss that he planned on selling weed at the bottom of the hill between Nova São Carlos and Viçosa, that is, in the future Vila Sapo. Then he would tell the Viçosa cartel boss the same thing.

Valdir's house was at the end of an alley, at the highest point of Nova São Carlos. A large, attractive home, it contrasted with the shacks around it. As Pedro advanced toward the house, he sensed some unusual activity in the area. Right at the entrance to the narrow street, he'd passed a few of his friends, all drug deal-ers; now he was passing some people he knew only by sight, though he could have sworn they didn't live in the area, as well as men he'd never seen before, all grim-faced and eyeing him with suspi-cion. And if that wasn't enough to make him feel ill at ease, halfway down the alley he started seeing weapons. When it wasn't a sub-machine gun in one guy's hand, it was a revolver in someone else's; when it wasn't a pistol in the waistband of some guy without a shirt on, it was a rifle cradled in a man's lap, or a shotgun propped against a wall.

From an open window in Valdir's house, a young man saw Pedro arrive and went to the patio gate to greet him. Though he had a silver pistol in his left hand, it was clear from the large smile on his face that he was happy to see Pedro.

"Sup, Pedro? Y'alright, man?"

"Yeah, chill. Hey, what the hell's going on, Lucas? The alley's looking like a fucking barrack."

"Stuff got weird after all the shit went down yesterday. Didn't you hear?"

"I did."

"Well, that's what's going on. Dad's on the alert, you know how it is. Bullets gonna start flying any minute, it's just a matter of time. Bison ain't letting Belly-Ripper off easy for what he did to that jerk-off brother of his, and we're all in it together. Belly-Ripper's one of ours and he was in the right."

"Where's your dad?"

"He's in the back. You wanna talk to him?"

"Yeah."

"C'min, I'll take you there."

Pedro walked into the patio and followed the young man around the house. The property dipped a little toward the back and then leveled out again a few meters later. There was a small gathering of people (men, women, children) and a barbecue underway. When he saw Belly-Ripper at the lighthearted get-together, laughing with a beer in his hand, Pedro felt shocked. What kind of monster got over the loss of their little girl the next day, he wondered, especially when it was such a tragic death.

"There's Dad; go ahead, Pedro." And yet, after taking the guest up to his father, Lucas hovered around them.

"How's things, Seu Valdir?" Pedro said.

Valdir sat in a beach chair at a slight distance from the others. Like everyone else, he was holding a can of beer. He was middle-aged, bald, with a goatee. He seemed puzzled by Pedro's visit, as though the young man beside him had zapped down from outer space.

"Good, good," he answered, beetle-browed.

Pedro wondered if the cartel boss thought his visit might have something to do with the tragic events of the previous day. Wanting to make it clear the two things were unrelated, he got straight to the point.

"Sir, I came here cause I'm gonna start selling weed down the hill, and I wanted to let you know ahead of time."

"You can go right ahead. I don't sell weed."

His answer was a bit dry, and this made Pedro nervous. Valdir seemed angry for some reason. What was going through his head? Did he think someone had sent Pedro to spy on him? That was the last thing he needed . . .

"I'm here outta respect."

"Sure."

This time, Valdir smiled ironically. His eyes lingered on the young man, who was beginning to feel scared.

"D'you . . . D'you have anything you want to say to me?"

"Do I have anything I want to say to you? Like what?"

"I dunno. You're . . . You're looking at me strange . . . Like you're not happy I showed up here, for some reason . . ."

"It's all in your head. I ain't got a fucking thing to say. If I did, I'd say it. And you? You got something to say to me?"

"I did, but I've said it. I'm gonna sell weed down the hill."

"And where are you going now, after you leave here?"

Pedro was certain of Valdir's suspicion now.

"Straight talk? I'm going to see Renato."

Renato was the cartel boss in Viçosa and Valdir's main rival. Bison, the brother of the teenager killed by Belly-Ripper, who was present at the barbecue, was part of Renato's crew.

"I see. You're going to talk to Renato?"

"Yeah. For the same reason I came here. To let him know I'm gonna sell weed down the hill."

Annoyed, Valdir tossed the can of beer on the ground, but remained seated. Pedro looked around him. He was relieved to find that no one was listening to their conversation. Except for Lucas, who stood beside his father.

"I should pump you full of lead, Pedro," said the cartel boss. "But you know what? I'm gonna let you go. Go on. I don't give a shit what you tell Renato. Go on. Tell him how many guys you saw up here armed to the teeth."

Pedro considered turning around and leaving but thought doing so would only confirm Valdir's suspicions. Instead he pulled up a beach chair and sat down, taking the man by surprise.

"Listen, Seu Valdir. Honest to God, I came here thinking I'd have a short conversation with you and then leave, but that's not gonna cut it. I can't leave here with you believing this crap. Renato didn't send me. I don't take sides, you know that. If he asked me to come here, I wouldn't, even for all the money in the world. Cause I don't make trouble, you know that. Fuck, you know that, you know me! I just came here to let you know I wanna sell weed down the hill. That's all. C'mon, what does this sinister mood have to do with me? Just think about it. Anybody who comes here without good reason is gonna seem suspicious to you, yeah? But look at me, Seu Valdir. It's me, Pedro, the guy who lives down the hill and never makes trouble."

Valdir listened with an ironic smile that only grew bigger as Pedro spoke. Then he leaned forward a little, scratched his nose, and said:

"Alright, Pedro. Alright. You've convinced me. I believe you. I . . . I'm sorry I've been so . . . paranoid!" A more sarcastic man had yet to see the light of day. Pedro, however, was under the impression he really had convinced the cartel boss of his innocence and chalked up the man's snide tone to pride. It mustn't be easy for a man like Valdir to admit he was wrong, least of all in front of his own son. "Either way," he went on, "you're going to speak to Renato now, right? Do me a favor while you're there. Tell him Bison is invited to our barbecue."

Pedro sighed.

"You know I can't do that. I'm not gonna provoke him for you. What I want is to convince Renato and Bison to forget this whole fucking business. Consider it a favor, sir. After all, if I pull it off, I'd be saving you a massive headache."

Valdir's smile fell.

"You think I'm scared, do you? Let them try and come at me!"

"No, I didn't say you were scared, sir. I know you're not scared. None of us are morons here. Even Renato knows you're not scared. To be honest, you're probably enjoying how sinister everything feels right now."

"Yeah. I sure do. I've missed it."

"Right. Trouble is you've got more to lose than you've got to gain. Same goes for Renato. When bullets start flying and bodies start falling, the cops are gonna take over the whole fucking place again. They'll confiscate weapons, drugs, money, and a bunch of guys will wind up behind bars."

"He's right about that, Dad." This was Lucas's first interjection; the young man obviously hadn't inherited his father's mettle.

"Shut your mouth, kid!"

"Listen, Seu Valdir," Pedro continued. "Think about it. Y'all are even, aren't you? At least that's how I see it. Y'all are even. So what's the problem?"

"What do you mean? I don't follow."

"Bison's brother ran over Belly-Ripper's little girl. And Belly-Ripper killed him. End of story. I don't think anybody would've behaved differently in his place. And that's that. The little girl's getting buried tomorrow, the boy's getting buried today, and we've gotta bury this shit once and for all. It's done. Case closed. Time to move on. Can't nobody complain. See what I mean, sir? I can say the same thing to Renato and Bison when I see them too. They don't even have to know I was here, for real. If they don't listen, hell, that's their problem. But you never know. Maybe they will.

Maybe they'll even let it go. If that happens, it'll be good for everybody: you, Renato, all of us. Even me."

Valdir frowned.

"You? What do you get out of all this?"

"If y'all don't start this stupid war, the cops will leave us alone and I can sell weed in peace."

All this said, Pedro knew his chances of convincing Bison were slim. If the poor bastard chose to avenge his brother's death, then Renato and the whole Viçosa cartel would back him. There were plenty of reasons for a war to break out. Things seemed to actually be moving slower than you would think, considering the fuse had been lit several hours ago.

Unlike Nova São Carlos, Vila Viçosa was not homogeneous. The founding families were concentrated in the southeast of the neighborhood, where the atmosphere was as friendly, quiet, and civilized as it had been since its inception in the 1970s. But the northeast—the product of a series of unregulated mass incursions that unfolded throughout several years—there was nothing friendly, quiet, or civilized about the northeast. This part of Viçosa, affectionately referred to as Vilinha, wasn't even recognized as such by the Neighborhood Association. Vilinha was made up of a sad assortment of houses crisscrossed by pitted dirt roads, narrow back alleys, and open gutters, all of them spilling chaotically down the hillside, from Estrada João de Oliveira Remião, at the very top, all the way to the future Vila Sapo, here at the bottom.

And it was to the unfriendly, unquiet, and uncivilized part of Vila Viçosa that Pedro set out now, his pace slow and brain working at full steam. Later, deep inside Vilinha, he bumped into Bison straddling a motorcycle and smoking weed as he chatted with another guy. Pedro greeted the two men, then said:

"Hey, Bison, I heard about your brother, man. Tragic."

Bison frowned and shook his head, eyes fixed on the ground.

"Where's Renato?" Pedro asked. "He at home?"

"Nah. He's at the Slum."

The young man nodded and started walking. Then he stopped in his tracks and turned around:

"Listen, Bison: I got a couple of things to discuss with Renato. You might wanna be there for one of them. C'mon, let's head over together."

"What's it about?"

"Belly-Ripper."

Slum was the name given to the part of Vilinha that edged the forest. The Viçosa cartel headquarters had been set up there for strategic reasons. Unlike the atmosphere at Valdir's, the Slum did not appear to be on the brink of war. At the end of the day, the Viçosa cartel was the one with motive to stage an attack, not the other way around.

What Pedro saw when he arrived at the Slum shocked him: Renato and four other men were beating someone up. The victim, Pedro would later realize, was a crackhead who lived, or at least used to live, in Serra Verde, a neighborhood on the other side of Estrada João de Oliveiro Remião. Pedro only knew the guy by sight. A while ago, he'd started buying crack in Viçosa because he owed too much money in Serra Verde and couldn't afford to settle his debt.

As Pedro waited to speak with Renato, another man strode into the room with a bag.

"Here it is, Renato. We're good to go!"

"Hand it over!"

Pedro wondered what was inside the bag, and soon enough he found out. Holding it by the handles, Renato swung the bag at the crackhead. The sound each blow made left no doubt as to its contents: It was filled with shards of glass.

The guy cried, sweated, drooled, and bled while begging for his life. He was so badly beaten he didn't even have the energy to shield himself or roll away from the bag, which struck him square in the back, the chest, the belly, anywhere Renato decided to hit him. With each blow, the man let out a hoarse, high-pitched, animal noise. His voice vanished completely when Renato struck him in the face with particular violence. He fell in a heap on the floor, unawake.

"Get this motherfucker outta here!" he ordered.

"Should we kill him?" asked one of the henchmen as he picked up the poor bastard.

"Don't bother. Just drop him somewhere far the fuck away from here."

Renato noticed Pedro standing there and looked uncomfortable. Pedro wondered if maybe he didn't like civilians seeing him behave that way, just as grown-ups don't like children seeing them naked.

"The kind of shit people make us do sometimes . . ." the cartel boss joked as he walked over to Pedro.

"Claims he's got something to say to you about Belly-Ripper," Bison informed him.

"Hmmm . . ." Renato said. "Cool. Let's talk at my crib."

The living room of the house was large, though the sheer amount of furniture, all in poor taste, made it seem small. Pedro sat in the armchair and Bison and Renato sat on the sofa across from him.

"Right . . ." Pedro started, then immediately stopped. Renato's teenage daughter had just come in from the kitchen groggily eating an apple.

"GO TO YOUR ROOM!!!" her father hollered.

The girl ran back to her room and slammed the door. Pedro continued, as if he hadn't been interrupted.

"Right. First off, Renato, I came here to let you know I'm gonna start selling weed down the hill. You don't sell weed, so it shouldn't be a problem. We good?"

"Well, buddy, that depends," Renato said, "on whether you'll be working for Seu Valdir . . ."

Pedro felt like laughing. It was funny to hear Renato say "Seu Valdir," with respect, as though he wouldn't have killed the man given the chance.

"I'm not gonna work for him. The weed's mine. I'm gonna be the one buying the stuff and selling it."

"Cool. But what's any of that got to do with Belly-Ripper?"

"Right, that's a separate issue. Listen, I was over there talking with Seu Valdir just now—"

"Was that piece-of-shit Belly-Ripper there?" Bison cut in.

Pedro turned to face Bison. He made no effort to hide his annoyance at the interruption.

"Yeah, yeah, he was there. Bison and the whole Flamengo fan club, if you wanna know. Armed to the teeth."

"What did you need to talk to Seu Valdir about?" Renato asked.

"The same thing I just told you. That I'm gonna start selling weed down the hill."

"And what'd he say?"

"He said it was cool, natch. He doesn't sell weed either. Just rock and dust, like you. But he told me to come and talk to you before I got started. Truth is, honest to God, I wasn't gonna come and see you at all. Cause the bottom of the hill is more his side than yours. Like, the square over there is his turf. Always been that way, yeah? Anyway, he said I better come and talk to you. That's why I'm here."

"Hunh?" Renato smiled in shock. "Seu Valdir told you to come and talk to me? For what?"

"Right. So he said to do it out of respect, yeah? I don't get it either. He said he's been in charge over there for a while, and you been in charge over here for a while, and since I'm just getting started, right in the middle of both turfs, I should show respect and stuff. Then he sent me over here."

"Fuck, are you for real?"

"Yeah, man."

"Damn. Looks like Seu Valdir has changed."

"Oh, he's an old-school gangster, Renato. He's all about tradition, you know? He just likes shit done right, that's all. Course, y'all been at war before, but look how far we've come. There's peace now, thank God. It's time to make money and take it easy."

Bison lost his patience.

"C'mon, Pedro, what is it you wanted to tell me about Belly-Ripper?"

Pedro groaned.

"Listen, if you let me get a word in . . . I was just about to start and then you went and interrupted me."

"Spit it the fuck out, then!"

"Cool, alright. Here's the deal, Bison: Seu Valdir knows you're pissed at Belly-Ripper. So he asked me to give Renato a message." Pedro turned to the cartel boss. "He wants to know if you're gonna keep Bison under control, Renato. He said stuff's good right now. Everybody's making a load of money and nobody's got shit to worry about. Things could just go on like this, if you want. It's up to you. If you keep Bison under control, things can stay the way they are. If you let Bison retaliate, well, then . . . You know."

Bison got up and started laughing, though he was clearly furious.

"Cool, Pedro. You gave us the message. Now leave and tell that sack of shit that I'm coming after Belly-Ripper. End of story."

Renato patted Bison twice on the knee.

"Take it easy, man! Sit the fuck down."

Bison sat down again, heaving.

"That motherfucker killed my brother, Renato!"

"I know, man, I know! But let's hear Pedro out."

Pedro saw then that Renato wanted to keep the peace. Now he just needed to imply, though more pointedly this time, that stopping Bison from retaliating was a small price to pay for maintaining the status quo. But how, when Bison was sitting right there, thirsting for revenge? Pedro regretted asking him to join the conversation. Yet, when he spoke, it was Bison he addressed:

"I got a message for you too, Bison. A message from Belly-Ripper. He asked me to tell you there's a whole lot at stake now, shit that's bigger than either of you, that it's time you accepted that. He said business is booming, on that side and this side, that everybody's on good terms, on that side and this side, and it's not right for you to wanna start a whole war just to even the score and make yourself feel better. Truth is, at the end of the day, killing him won't bring your brother back. Instead, shit will just snowball: if you kill him, then somebody's gonna want to kill you, and so on." Needless to say, Pedro was performing a cunning psychological ruse; even as his words were addressed to Bison, their message was meant for Renato. Suddenly, Pedro remembered Renato had a daughter (the teenager who'd walked out of the kitchen moments ago), and added: "Finally, Belly-Ripper asked you to remember how everything got started. Cause if you're pissed about losing your brother, know that losing a daughter, like he did, is a thousand times worse. He wants you to think about it. He wants you to put yourself in his shoes. He was holding his little girl's hand when your drunk brother ran her over with a motorcycle and sent her flying into the air. Anyway. He wants you to try and imagine how he felt right then."

Bison jumped to his feet again and yelled:

"You think I give a fuck what happened to his daughter? Fuck his daughter! You hear me? Fuck her! I'm not gonna listen to another word you say. You can go back to Belly-Ripper and tell him I'm gonna murder his fucking ass. You hear me? I'm gonna blow his goddamn brains out!" He rushed outside, slamming the door behind him. But he didn't make it far. You could still hear him muttering things like "That motherfucker!" or "He's not getting away from me!" or even "When I get my hands on that piece of shit!"

Seeing Renato deep in thought, Pedro laughed dryly and said:

"Some temper, hunh? You know what my grandma used to say? Lie down with dogs and you'll get up with fleas." He sighed and started to leave. "Right, well, I'm off. Thanks, Renato. I'll be seeing you."

The cartel boss held up his hand.

"Wait up, Pedro. I need you to do me a favor."

"Sure. Shoot."

"Here's the deal. You go back to Seu Valdir and Belly-Ripper and tell them there ain't gonna be a war. Tell them everything's gonna stay the way it is."

"Hunh? What d'you mean? Bison . . ."

"You let me worry about Bison. Just tell them what I said, yeah?"

"Okay. I'll head straight there."

"Cool. Don't shut the door when you leave."

Pedro did as he was told. He walked outside and left the door open behind him. He heard Renato's voice call out:

"Bison, get over here!"

But as Pedro left the building, Bison, who was busy trying to light a cigarette meters away from the door, pretended not to hear him.

Renato insisted:

"Bison, I said get the fuck over here!"

This time the man listened. He walked into the house, still trying to light his cigarette. Suddenly, there were two gunshots. Birds scattered from a nearby tree. Pedro, who may have been more frightened than the birds, turned around in time to see Bison stagger out the door, wounded and in despair. Renato followed him out and unloaded two more shots into his back. Bison dropped to the ground, face down, and started shaking.

"Dad?!" The person calling from inside the house was Renato's daughter.

"Everything's alright, sweetie!" the cartel boss answered. "Stay right where you are and don't come outside!" he ordered, calmly reloading his gun and firing several more shots into Bison's bullet-ridden body.

9

THE FIRST COUPLE OF KILOS

Hans, a.k.a. Jéferson Almeida de Carvalho. Hard to imagine a more suspicious-looking character. A 24-karat gold necklace hung around his neck and a pair of diamonds gleamed on his ears, accessories that did not mesh with his ghetto manners. Hans had a penchant for soccer jerseys. Tucked behind them were the tools of his trade: Ruth and Raquel, as he often referred to his 9mm pistols.

It was after nine, on the evening of Friday, February 6, 2009. Hans parked his motorcycle, dismounted, and took off his helmet outside a respectable home in a quiet neighborhood in the district of Canoas, in greater Porto Alegre. His calm white face glowed in the moonlight. The street, asphalted and edged with small trees and trimmed bushes, was deserted at that time of night. He pressed the button on the intercom by the front gate, identified himself, and walked straight into the house, its interior even more opulent than its façade. The man who answered the door, clearly the owner, asked Hans to wait in the lavishly furnished living room, then vanished for a few minutes, returning with two glasses of whiskey. There was an obvious intimacy between the two men: Hans even let himself slump down on the sofa, though only after dropping his helmet and backpack in a corner of the room. His wasn't the only backpack there: another backpack, which looked quite heavy, sat on the glass table.

Hans took the glass of whiskey, then asked:

"Last deliveries of the day, right, Fabrício?"

"Four, altogether," the man confirmed. "Two crack, one cocaine, one weed. The addresses are all here." He pulled a folded piece of paper out of his pocket and handed it to Hans. "There's ten-thousand reais' worth of drugs in there; that makes your cut five hundred. Add to that the money I owe you for the other deliveries you made today, and we get . . . let me see . . . five thousand and two hundred reais. Anyway, we'll settle up when you get back."

"Guess I should get going, then," said Hans, knocking back his whiskey in a single gulp. "I wanna hit a club tonight," he explained. He unfolded the piece of paper and scanned Fabrício's meticulous handwriting. All of a sudden, he frowned and asked: "Who's this dude Pedro?"

"New client. The weed's for him."

"Hmmm . . . You know I don't like new clients. What if the fucker has blood in his eyes? Or tries to run off with the product? This kind of shit always makes me trip."

Fabrício laughed.

"Isn't that what Ruth and Raquel are for? But don't sweat: he won't give you a hard time. Jorge connected us, says he can be trusted. It's all good."

"Alright, cool," said Hans, shrugging on the heavier backpack and picking up his helmet. He pointed at the empty pack he'd brought with him. "The cash for the last few deliveries is in there, back pocket. Fifteen stack. Want me to wait till you've counted?"

"No need. Get going. You're already running late. You'll see on the slip of paper I gave you that this Pedro character needs the weed by nine thirty."

"Yeah, I saw. I'm off. Later."

Hans walked out into the hot summer night, ready to make his four final deliveries. Once he finished, he'd be free to burn through the five thousand reais he'd made. It'd been a lucrative day. He wouldn't have to work again until Monday, unless an especially important delivery came up over the weekend. He was happy with his lot. Sadly, his dignity and self-esteem were significantly healthier than that of most honest workers in Brazil.

Twenty minutes later, Hans was riding into Porto Alegre along Avenida Castelo Branco. That is, along the avenue known as Castelo Branco back in 2009, in honor of Humberto de Alencar Castelo Branco, a historical figure whose life achievements were lauded by some and mourned by others. WWII veteran, fervent anti-communist, and facilitator of the 1964 military coup, Castelo Branco was also Brazil's first president in the Military Regime. A few years later, in 2014, following the approval of a law backed by two left-wing councilors, the avenue would be renamed Avenida da Legalidade e da Democracia, after Campanha da Legalidade, a movement whose purpose was to secure João Goulart's inauguration as president of the Republic, prior to the military coup of 1961. But by mid-2017, in an unexpected turn of events, Rio Grande do Sul's Court of Justice would vote in favor of an appeal co-signed by five right-wing councilors, rendering the previous decision null and void. By 2019, most of Porto Alegre's residents would have no idea what the avenue was officially called.

Either way, it was down this avenue that Hans rode into the capital and then sped along Avenida Mauá. On Avenida Loureiro da Silva, he rounded the Edel Trade Center and merged on to Avenida João Pessoa, then proceeded to the corner of Rua Doutor Sebastião Leão, where he drove onto the sidewalk, parked his motorcycle by a newsstand, dismounted, and took off his helmet. Then he crossed Avenida João Pessoa and walked along Avenida Jerônimo de Ornelas, gazing at the distant lights of Hospital de Clínicas.

Hans chose to leave the motorcycle far from the meeting place for a reason. Sure, Fabrício said Pedro wouldn't cause trouble; but when it came to new clients, it was better to play it safe. If, for whatever reason, he had to kill the guy, he didn't want any potential witnesses seeing him drive off on a motorcycle.

He shuffled past Boteco Imperial, which was busy with people, and crossed Rua Santana to the location written on the scrap of paper in his pocket. The square he stood in was large and dimly lit, and at first glance he couldn't make out the person he was meant to meet. This put him on the alert. There must be a high school in the area, he thought. Groups of students with backpacks gathered around several of the benches in the square. He felt calmer now: the place was far from ideal for an ambush. Besides, Pedro had no idea what he looked like, which meant he couldn't be taken by surprise.

The last thing Pedro wanted was to surprise Hans. He was just sitting on a bench next to Marques, waiting for the delivery guy to bring the weed.

"Asshole's running late," Marques said for the hundredth time, looking around impatiently.

"Yeah," Pedro agreed.

"How long we gotta wait?"

"Till ten. If he doesn't show up by then, I'll call Fabrício."

But before Pedro had finished his sentence, his phone started to ring.

"Hello?"

"Pedro?"

"Yeah. Who's this?"

"I have something for you. Just got to the square."

"Okay, cool. I'm sitting near the middle, outside the supermarket. Do you see me?"

"Hold up, lemme have a look . . . Yeah, I see you. You're with somebody."

Pedro understood the significance of this observation.

"Don't worry. That's just my partner."

"Cool, cool . . . You packing?"

"What? No, man! Course we ain't packing. What gave you that idea?"

"Alright, I'm headed your way," the man said, then hung up.

As Pedro slipped his phone back into his pocket, Marques whispered with some alarm:

"You shouldn't've told him we're not armed, Pedro. What if he kills us and takes our cash?"

"Calm the fuck down, Marques. You think it's good business for them to kill off their clients like that, during the first transaction, just for a bit of extra scratch? A thousand reais is peanuts to these guys." Right then, Pedro saw a man with a helmet beneath his arm and a backpack striding toward them along the edge of the square. "Look. That must be him."

And it was. The stranger's eyes remained fixed on them as he rounded the lawn bordered with an ankle-height chain fence and walked toward the bench where they sat.

"So, what'll it be?"

"Hey, dude. Y'alright? I'm Pedro. This is Marques."

"Hans," the man said, shaking their hands. "Two kilo of weed, yeah?"

"Yeah."

It all happened incredibly fast. In the blink of an eye, one of the kilos had found its way into Marques's backpack; the other, into Pedro's; and the thousand reais—the twenty fifty-real bills Catarina had given them—were now with Hans, who was counting them.

"What the fuck bullshit is this?" Hans exclaimed, eyebrows knit into a menacing vee.

"What d'you mean?"

"There's only a thousand reais here and there should be fourteen hundred. Seven hundred per kilo."

"Fabrício said we could pay a thousand now and four hundred down the line."

"How come nobody told me? Y'all trying to fuck with me?"

"No way, man—"

"How am I supposed to take one thousand reais back to the boss when he never said nothing about fronting you four hundred. Here's what we're gonna do: Seeing as you only got one thousand, y'all gimme back one kilo and I'll give you back the three hundred. Go on now, easy does it . . ." Hans's hand was already on the zipper of Pedro's backpack.

Marques lost his temper.

"Hey, hey, hey, fuck you think you're doing?" In one swift motion, Marques pulled out the gun given to him by his old friend in Vila Lupicínio Rodrigues and pointed it at Hans.

A thick silence fell over the three men. Pedro, whose wide eyes were glued to the gun, was so shocked he couldn't breathe. Hans, meanwhile, held up both hands, though he looked more irritated than scared, pursing his lips as his eyes darted from Marques to Pedro and Pedro to Marques. Marques kept the gun trained on Hans. He didn't move a muscle, not even to blink.

"The fuck is that?" Hans asked Pedro, after a minute. "You said you weren't packing, damnit!"

"I didn't know he had that shit on him!" Pedro scanned the square and saw that the Luciana de Abreu students were busy chatting animatedly around the benches, oblivious to the tension rising between him, Marques, and Hans. "Damn it, Marques! Put that fucking thing away."

"Hell no! You can bet your ass this motherfucker's packing too."

"I know he's armed, Marques. But he isn't gonna shoot us, so put your fucking piece away. Now!"

"What makes you think he won't shoot us?"

"Cause no one's here to kill anybody, man!"

Marques thought for a moment, then shook his head.

"Fuck!" he grumbled, slipping the gun back in his waistband. Then he pointed at Hans and said: "Watch how you to talk to us, man! You crazy? We're all adults here. What d'you think you're doing sticking your hand in Pedro's bag like that? That shit ain't cool. Here's what *you're* gonna do: Call Fabrício and ask if he said he'd front us the rest of the money."

Hans quietly took his phone out of his pocket and dialed Fabrício, all while shooting daggers at Marques.

"Hello? Listen, Fabrício, I'm standing here with Pedro and his hot-headed amigo. They're saying you told them they could hold the four hundred . . . Hmm . . . Word . . . Nah, nah; it's all good . . . Nah, nah; don't worry about it . . . Thanks; talk later."

Marques immediately confronted him, asking:

"So?"

"So Fabrício confirmed what you said," Hans explained. "He just forgot to tell me is all. Anyway, we're cool. Sorry about that." Whether genuine or not, Hans seemed extremely volatile. A second ago, he'd looked like the devil himself, capable of anything; now a broad smile sat below his pointed nose, showing two rows of rotten teeth.

"No worries. It was just a misunderstanding," Pedro said as Marques kept on glowering. "Let's just make sure it doesn't happen again, yeah? We don't want trouble. You don't want trouble. So if we all just stay out of fucking trouble, everything will be alright."

WHEN MARQUES AND Pedro got home that night, they were both faced with the same dreary task: sorting the weed into one-gram portions and wrapping them in plastic, each of which would be sold for one real.

Marques could count on Angélica's help. Not only did she know and approve of his new side gig, she had even stolen a precision scale from the pizzeria where she worked.

Pedro had a precision scale too, borrowed from a friend who ran a corner store on his way home from the bus. Unlike Marques and Angélica, though, Pedro's bedroom didn't have a door, which meant he had no privacy. If his mother even suspected him of sorting and bagging weed that night, she'd throw him out of the house. His only choice was to do exactly what he was doing: wait for her to go to bed.

His mother sat on the floor of the kitchen-cum-living-room surrounded by screwdrivers and tiny screws as she tried to fix the broken front-door lock. She'd been at it since Monday. The second she came home from work, she picked up her tools and spent hours on end bent over the busted lock. At this point, it had become something of a hobby. Pedro wasn't convinced she would succeed, which is why he was surprised when he heard her exclaim:

"Done! Come have a look!"

"You fixed the damn thing, ma?" he asked, walking up to her.

"Kind of. See this here? It's a double lock. The cylinder is split in two. Only the outside was broken. So I took apart the lock and built it in reverse. I'm going to install it in the door, that way we can lock up again when we go out. The only trouble is we can't lock the door from the inside." She smiled triumphantly at her son. "See what a bit of hard work can get you?"

Pedro loved his mother, of course he loved her, but there were times, like now, when her humility depressed him.

"Well done, ma! Congrats, for real. You know something, though? You and me, we work our butts off. We work all day long. Then, when the lock goes, a simple lock, we can't afford a new one . . . See what I'm saying? It's awesome that you fixed the lock, but . . . it's wrong too. Know what I mean?"

"What's wrong about it, honey?"

Pedro found it difficult to explain things to his mother.

"I dunno . . . I guess I just don't think it's right that we're so poor . . . I mean, damn, look at how hard we work . . . Don't you find it humiliating?"

"No."

"Damn it, ma. How can you not? Is this what our lives gonna be like forever? Always fixing and mending things. I'm sorry but I don't know how you can just stand there and take it. Why do we work at all? We do it so we don't starve to death! Doesn't that bother you?"

"Things will get better one day, Pedro. God willing."

Pedro had heard her say that for as long as he could remember, and things never got any better.

"Yeah, ma, sure they will . . ." Right then, Pedro's brown eyes gave off a soft glow. "You know what, I think things really are gonna get better. I can feel it in the air."

The woman didn't hear the enigmatic tone in her son's voice.

"Well, I hope God's listening," she said, clasping her hands in front of her chest and staring devotedly at the wood ceiling, which had been rotten through and riddled with holes for God knows how long.

10

THE WEED GUY

For weeks the heat had been unrelenting, and on Saturday, February 7, 2009, it was no different. There wasn't a single cloud in the Porto Alegre sky, and everyone did what they could to get out of the sun. Downtown, crowds elbowed each other below awnings, steering clear of the open street, as if fleeing a biblical rainstorm. But there was excitement in the air too; it was Saturday after all, and most people didn't work Sundays.

That was also the day Marques and Pedro were going to begin selling weed, and at a fairly uninspiring pace, it had to be said. As incredible as it may sound, even though they'd spent all week planning out every last detail, they had failed to account for one obvious factor: that they spent most of the day stuck in the supermarket, leaving them virtually no time to sell weed. When they clocked in around one that afternoon, Pedro had ten miserable reais in his pocket, or one-hundred percent of the money they'd made so far from their weed operation, possibly the only money they would make all day, seeing that neither of them could start selling until their shift ended at 9:20 P.M., and after a thirty-minute walk to Lupicínio Rodrigues, plus an hour-long bus ride to Lomba do Pinheiro.

Ten miserable reais. A pathetic amount in Marques's anxious opinion, especially given they owed four hundred to his sister and another four hundred to Fabrício, all due in a month's time. In Pedro's level-headed opinion, on the other hand, they shouldn't read too much into the figure, it being the result of a single, unplanned sale between Pedro's house and the bus stop, not of their ideal operating model.

Earlier that day, Pedro had bumped into a friend on a corner of Vila Nova São Carlos and heard him pointedly complain about how difficult it was to find decent weed. Remembering he had a few grams on him, Pedro pulled the grass out of his pocket and held it out in his cupped palm. Based on the powerful smell and firmness of the bud, his friend decided the stuff merited buying ten grams on the spot. As Pedro did the math now, he felt optimistic. He'd managed to sell ten grams in a matter of minutes: how long would it be before he sold the rest of the kilo, if he worked at it every day for several hours at a time?

Marques hadn't managed to sell a single gram, even though Lupicínio Rodrigues was as promising as Viçosa and Nova São Carlos put together, as he explained to Pedro. The neighborhood was actually small and the demand per capita middling, but its prime location meant people came through there every day looking for drugs. There were the hundreds and hundreds of playboyzinhos from surrounding neighborhoods who usually sourced their weed from other playboyzinhos—rebels without a cause known in the colleges and bars of Rua General Lima e Silva. Every now and then, whenever their official suppliers ran out, their little friends in Menino Deus and Cidade Baixa were left with no choice but to pay vagrants to check for weed in Lupicínio Rodrigues, too frightened to go anywhere near the neighborhood themselves. There was also the sea of people who streamed in from all corners of the city to the shrinking shores of Guaíba River, right next to Lupicínio Rodrigues, many of whom stopped at the neighborhood to buy weed before going out for a stroll, or a bike ride, or skateboarding, or on a date, or just to watch the sunset.

"We've got to stop working here so we have time to sell the product," Marques said as he helped Pedro organize the stockroom, which they did every Saturday.

"Nah, we can't stop working here, man," Pedro countered, yawning. He'd barely slept. His mother had turned in late, and he had to wait for her to go to bed before he could start trimming and packaging the weed, which kept him up until sunrise.

Marques, on the other hand, had it easy. With nothing to wait for, he got straight to work the second he walked through his front door. On top of that, he had help from Angélica. It took them no time at all to trim and package their half of the product, which meant he was able to get a good night's sleep.

"What d'you mean we can't stop working here?"

"We still need the money. We'll be needing it for a while, to be honest. See, to start, anything we make selling weed has to go toward buying more weed. It's gonna be a while before we can use it on ourselves. We've got to grow the operation first, until we can balance our offerings with the demands of the market."

"Grow," "balance," "offerings," "market": Marques wasn't really following.

"Hunh?"

"Let me . . ." Pedro yawned again. "Ahhh . . . Let me explain. We got the weed yesterday, on a Friday, yeah? Cool. Now let's pretend that, by some miracle, we manage to sell it all by Monday. The next delivery isn't until next Friday. Which means we'll be out of product for the rest of the week, hemorrhaging hypothetical cash. That's why we have to buy more weed, enough to last us all week. Every delivery we get has to keep us busy till Friday, in time for the next delivery. Once we're set up, once we're selling as much weed in a week as we can, *then* we can split whatever money's left over. After we pay for the next delivery, natch. Make sense? That'll be our profit."

"And how much d'you think we can sell in a week?"

"Pfft, beats me. What we got to figure out right now is how to move the product while we're on the job."

"Only way is to get someone to sell for us."

"And that's what we'll do. Tomorrow's Sunday, and the two of us still gonna be busy, even if we're not working here. Me slinging weed in my hood and you doing the same in yours. On top of that, we'll have to find a couple of folks we trust to start dealing for us starting Monday, while we're at work. I'll find a prosthetic limb for me and you'll find one for you. They can work the streets while we manage behind the scenes."

"They gonna be like our employees or something?" Marques laughed.

"No. Not employees. More like business partners."

Marques had a sinking feeling.

"Hold up, hold up. What d'you mean?"

"The two folks we tap to sell weed are gonna make the same as us, brother. We're gonna split the profit four ways."

"Jesus fucking Christ! I can't believe it. You're gonna screw everything up with your dumb-ass ideas!"

Pedro sighed.

"Shit, Marques. It's about more than just ideas, brother. Remember when you came and told me you wanted to sell weed? Well, what would you have thought if I said I'd be making more money than you? Fuck, man, I'm trying to make a better life for myself cause I got to, right, and you want a better life too. So, like, how could I offer you less money? How the hell do I justify something like that?"

"Well, I guess, if you wanted to make more money than me, that'd be cool and stuff, whatever, I wouldn't kick up a fuss. I just wouldn't take you up on it. Period."

"Right, so you're not willing to earn less than me, but you still want to pay somebody else less than you. And that's cool, yeah? Look, if something don't feel right to you, Marques, then don't expect it to feel right to somebody else. Imagine we find somebody interested in selling weed for us, and for less money. How much can we trust this person? Before you know it, they're selling us down the river, all because they want more money, and, honest to God, I wouldn't blame them. Pretty soon, we don't trust this person and they don't trust us, and fuck, man, that's when stuff gets ugly. *Trust*, dude. *Trust*. That shit's gold. Trusting that the other guy won't try and screw you over. That's how it's got to be. That's what we've got, you and me. Isn't it? Well. That's how it should be for everybody."

"Right, I see what you're saying. But wasn't the plan for us to make money? To have a better life and all that? Fuck if I want to get mixed up in this crap for chicken feed."

"Me neither, man! Yeah, the plan was to make good money. It still is. I'm telling you there's gonna be enough to go around. Believe in me, man. Trust. You never agreed to sell drugs in Tuca with your brother, your own flesh and blood, but here you are selling drugs with me, cause you know I do things right, you know I got good ideas. So relax, cuz, and let me do my thing. We're gonna make mad coin. You'll see. Don't worry about it."

"Cool. We'll do it your way, then. But don't forget, man. The money comes first. We're in it for the money."

"Trust . . ." Another yawn. "Ahhh . . . Trust, the money comes first. Yeah . . ."

All day, Pedro was so tired he felt soft like butter. As he dragged his body around the store, the only thing he could think about was his bed and lying in it. Every minute felt like an hour. He didn't even have the energy to pretend he liked his coworkers' stupid jokes. Worse than the terrible jokes were the cheerful customers who went out of their way to have long conversations with every employee, just so they could sleep at night without feeling like a bunch of snobs. *Bougie motherfuckers.* They could go to hell for all he cared, thought Pedro, smiling at them with pure contempt. He regretted not having one of those jobs where the boss walks over and magnanimously says: "Take the rest of the weekend off, man. Go home and get some rest. I'll see you Monday." Did jobs like that really exist, or did that only happen in movies? They must. There were probably even better jobs out there too, ones where people went ahead and gave themselves a break: "You know what? I think I'll take the rest of the weekend off. I'll start again on Monday." Unfortunately, neither situation applied to him. The best he could do was give Sr. Geraldo some attitude and go home early, as he had plenty of times before. The issue was that Sr. Geraldo docked every hour he didn't work from his paycheck, and he was already several hours short. So he put up with it. With the exhaustion and the backbreaking work, with the "funny" coworkers and chatty customers. When it was finally time for him to punch out and go home, he could hardly believe it.

As Pedro stood on the crowded bus and nodded off amid dozens of other tired workers, his mind drifted out of habit to the fact that tomorrow was Sunday; meaning, he could sleep in. But then he instantly remembered that tomorrow was actually going to be his first chance to sell weed; meaning, he couldn't sleep in. The sooner he woke up and got the ball rolling, the better. The thought of devoting all day to this task was comforting. It wouldn't be like working at the supermarket. No, it was the dawn of a journey that he could only hope led to money—*real money*. He wanted to get started right away and see how things panned out, so he could make predictions and plan, then reassess those plans . . .

As soon as Pedro stepped off the bus, he popped the usual cigarette in his mouth and lit it. It wouldn't be long now. He'd be home in ten minutes. In the bathroom in fifteen. In thirty, he'd be eating dinner. In forty, he'd be asleep. The streets of Nova São Carlos stretched darkly before him, busy with people walking around, children plopped on the curb, cats and dogs racing this way and that, and cars parked bumper to bumper outside bars. Front doors and windows were flung open, heaving a breath of fresh air. Now and then you might see someone making dinner in the kitchen, or watching TV in the living room, or brushing their hair in front of the bedroom mirror. Pedro greeted the occasional acquaintance as he walked. Then, turning a corner, he heard an alarming murmur rising ahead of him.

"Look, everybody, it's him!"

"Here he comes! What's up, Pedro?"

"Yo, it's the weed guy!"

"You got ten grams, man? I'll take ten."

"Me too."

Five men stood in an alley, just a few meters ahead. It was clear they'd been waiting for Pedro to get home.

Pedro walked up to the group, lips curled into a smile and brow knit. How did they know he was selling? The guy who'd bought ten grams from him earlier that afternoon must have said something . . . Yes, that had to be it; Pedro couldn't think of any other reason they would know. He was the only one who could have told them . . . No, that wasn't exactly right either . . . Valdir knew Pedro was selling pot in the neighborhood too, as did his son Lucas, and Renato. Any of those four men could have been responsible for spreading the news.

The culprit was someone else altogether. Apparently, the men had gotten his name from the friend who ran the corner store, the one who'd loaned him the precision scale the evening before.

Pedro sold the group forty grams of weed and then continued walking home, down Rua da Guaíba. From there, at the very top of Vila Nova São Carlos, Pedro had an excellent view of the area. Down the hill, in the future Vila Sapo, shacks upon shacks crowded together, and another jumble of huts lay farther ahead, in Vila Viçosa. There were houses aglow all over the neighborhood, countless lights that together seemed to want to make the stars jealous.

Pedro wasn't sleepy or tired anymore. Instead, he felt . . . *important* . . .

"Yo, it's the weed guy!"

It occurred to him that he was assuming a role dozens of people had been waiting for someone to step into for a long time, and it was a small boost to his self-esteem. Thanks to him, potheads across the region would no longer have to scour the city for weed. Though it may not be the cleanest situation Pedro had ever been in, at least this time he got to play the lead instead of a supporting role.

In that moment he didn't feel second-rate, unlike at the supermarket, where he killed himself taking down mountains of boxes, packages, and crates in the stockroom to get at the products that needed restocking, only to put back together the mountains of boxes, packages, and crates and slide the items onto their respective shelves, from which customers could comfortably retrieve them and toss them into their shopping carts, without giving any thought to the sweat spilled or the enormous amount of energy wasted just so every item would be there, at hand, and especially without giving a single thought to the obscenely low wages attached to that labor, which barely covered a person's basic needs, yet always ready to complain if a *single* price tag was out of place, if a *single* item was out of stock, while all he could do was lower his eyes, because, at the end of the day, the customer was always right.

No, in that moment, he didn't feel second-rate. In that moment, he wasn't even thinking about all the terrible things the supermarket represented. In that moment, he wasn't Pedro, the calloused, sweaty stock clerk who had no choice but to break his back. He was Pedro, the salesman, with a world of possibilities ahead of him, and a future that transcended the present. Right then, in that moment, he was Pedro, the weed guy.

11

THE GANG
IS FORMED

It was just before ten in the morning on Sunday, February 8, 2009 when Pedro woke up. He couldn't remember the last time he'd gotten up that early on a Sunday. He sat on the edge of his bed and lit a cigarette.

There he was, elbow propped on his leg, head propped on his hand, eyes resting in the middle-distance, burning his first smoke of the day, as he liked to say, and thinking about life, as he liked to do. If someone could have seen him then, hair disheveled and lethargy stamped on his creased face, they might have thought he was the picture of failure. Though maybe that was a compliment. Truth be told, he was less than a failure: he was a man who had never tried. And as this thought slid through his head that morning, Pedro promised himself he would change. He wanted to turn over a new leaf, to take a different stand in the world; maybe that meant being a little blinder, a little more ignorant, having a little more faith in himself, following through on the plans he made, steamrolling over *whatever* got in his way, steamrolling over *whoever* got in his way, and never doubting he was right. That was it. Because, if he thought about it, his problem was his constant overthinking. He was addicted to thinking. This kept him in a permanent state of doubt and prevented him from acting on a given plan. He'd taken the initiative to sell weed. He couldn't let that become an isolated event: it needed to be a watershed moment, the spark of a fire, the mother of a whole new way of being. He was declaring war against himself; he'd become *a doer*, once and for all leaving behind the aimless path of indecision.

Pedro had the same breakfast as always: black coffee and his second smoke of the day. Then he grabbed the brown paper bag with the weed in it, all trimmed and packaged into plastic baggies. Just as he was about to step outside, he heard his mother call, and abruptly shut the door.

"What is it, Ma?"

"Where you going?"

"To a buddy's place."

This wasn't strictly a lie. He really was going to his friend Guilherme's house. He left before she had a chance to ask him what was in the bag. Seconds later, he stopped again to have a chat with Roberto, his cousin's husband, who was standing outside his front door, covered in grease, plate of food in one hand and fork in the other, jaws working up and down and eyes fixed on the old motorcycle he used for his job as a courier. By the looks of it, he'd been messing with the bike since early that morning and had just stopped for lunch, even though it wasn't even noon yet.

"What's up with your wheels, Roberto?"

"That's what I'm trying to figure out, man. I can't get it to start."

"Take it to the shop."

"Looks like I won't have a choice. But if fixing this piece of trash costs more than fifty cents, I'm fucked."

"Man, that blows."

"Yeah, it fucking sucks."

Pedro didn't have Guilherme's phone number and worried he wouldn't be able to get ahold of him. The kid was a bit of a street rat, the kind who only went home to eat and sleep. If he wasn't at his place, it would be hard to narrow down exactly where he might be. As luck would have it, Guilherme was sitting right outside his own front patio, on the curb of Rua da Guaíba, eating some bread. He looked like he had just rolled out of bed.

Guilherme was short with a square face and dumbo ears. He jacked cars for a living. Like everyone, he had a story. His dad, whom he'd lived with in that same house, was sent to prison for fraud when Guilherme was fourteen, and stabbed to death just a few months later, inside the Porto Alegre Penitentiary. Even before his father was murdered, Guilherme already lived with his mother in Viamão, and God only knows what he put that poor woman through with his teenage rebellion. School was for Guilherme what Church was for the Devil: there wasn't a soul who could persuade him to go to class. He spent all day long smoking up on the various street corners of Avenida Martinica, constantly getting into fights or simply disappearing, only to show up at home three or four days later. The moment he laid eyes on his mother, he'd start tormenting her, pleading for "his own space," for independence, saying he wanted to go back to Lomba do Pinheiro and live on his own in the house he shared with his father before the man was locked up. The house had to be looked after or they'd end up with squatters, he reasoned. At first his mother thought it was ridiculous. But after giving the idea some more thought, she eventually came around to it. A bit of independence could be good for Guilherme: he'd see that life was hard and come to appreciate the value of discipline, or so his mother told herself, day in and day out, like a mantra, until she finally believed it and forgot that, deep down, what she really wanted was to be rid of the boy. Back at his old place, Guilherme got a job at a churrascaria with the help of a kind, concerned neighbor. But being constitutionally incapable of putting up with guff, Guilherme smacked a customer with a skewer of rare rump steak in his first week, promptly ending his career as a waiter. His mother still called now and then to ask how work was going. She could send him some money if things were tight, she said. But he didn't need any, everything was fine, he assured her. His mother still believes to this day that her son is a waiter at a churrascaria, when the truth is he chose a different career path a long time ago, after finding a .38-gauge among his father's belongings.

"Yo, Pedro. How's tricks?"

"Sup, Gui?"

"Not much. Where's the weed hiding?"

Guilherme was asking out of habit; he had no idea Pedro had started dealing.

"So, here's the deal, cuz. I got some weed on me right now." Pedro dropped the brown paper bag in front of his friend. "This stuff is killer," he promised. "Fifty/fifty."

"Fifty/fifty" meant "fifty grams for fifty reais." The buyer didn't necessarily have to purchase a whole fifty grams; it was just a way of pricing the product, like saying one gram cost one real.

"No way!" Guilherme exclaimed, opening the bag to peer inside. "Man, you're a fucking godsend. I was thinking of heading down to Conceição to buy a joint, but I've got like . . . I've got the lazy blues!" Apparently, he liked the expression he'd just come up with and said it again: *"The lazy blues!"*

"Go on, how much d'you want, you bum?" Pedro asked, laughing along with him.

"I'll take a hundo. C'mon, follow me to my crib."

"Sure thing."

Once they were inside his house, Pedro collapsed on the living room sofa and started counting out one hundred baggies. Guilherme went to his bedroom for the money. Moments later he was back, tossing two folded fifty-real notes at him.

"Here you go. Right, lemme see . . ." he grabbed one of the baggies and pressed it between his fingers to check the firmness of the bud, then brought it up to his nose and took a whiff. "Fuck, man. This is some good shit!"

Pedro smacked his lips.

"Natch, brother. What'd I tell you!" And seeing Guilherme pull his cell out of his pocket, he asked: "What're you doing?"

"I'm spreading the good news."

He called at least a dozen of his friends and told them Pedro was selling weed down the hill. Good weed, and cheap too. Some of them promised to come over right away to buy a couple of grams.

"You're the man, Guilherme," Pedro said, thanking him. "But listen. Whenever you tell somebody I'm dealing, make sure you let them know not to look for me at home. Say I'll be around the hood: in the square, in a field, at a corner . . . Though . . ."

"What?"

"Truth is I'm only selling today. After that, I'm gonna need somebody else to sell for me."

"Who's that?"

"Not sure yet. Could be you . . ."

Guilherme laughed.

"Sorry, but that ain't my bag. Don't worry: you'll find somebody. Plenty of fools out there interested in that line of work. A dime a dozen."

The problem, Pedro explained, was it couldn't be just anyone: it had to be someone he could trust, someone who wouldn't try to screw him over at the first chance. But, he added, it made sense to go by parts, like Jack the Ripper said. First he would sell as much weed as he could on his day off; then he would find a good dealer to take his place.

One by one, Guilherme's friends came to buy weed as promised, and he was at the square to meet them. Pedro off-loaded two hundred grams just on Guilherme's friends. Then he hung around the square until four in the afternoon, letting any potheads he saw walking down Rua Guaíba know he was selling weed. Some pulled out cash and bought a couple grams on the spot; others went home, then came back with money for their purchase. Then there were those who claimed they were strapped and kept asking to start a tab; in response, they always got a resounding "no," each firmer than the last, until eventually they walked away, grumbling under their breaths.

Then Pedro went to the soccer field, at the foot of Viçosa. A kickabout always started around that time and went until sundown. Pedro figured he could sell weed to the audience, which is exactly what he did, though he wasn't counting on the strange incident that followed: at some point, the game slowed to a stop as various players realized Pedro was selling dope and started leaving the match one by one to fetch money from home, before it ran out. And it did, it ran out surprisingly fast: less than an hour after he showed up at the field, Pedro had sold his last gram and was on his way back home, brown bag empty and pockets full.

He bumped into Roberto again in the patio. The motorcycle was gone, and he was no longer covered in grease.

"Yo, yo, yo, Roberto! What a day, hunh?" Pedro said, letting out all of his excitement.

"Yeah, yeah. Hey, I wanna talk to you about something."

"Sure thing. What's up?"

"Listen, there any jobs going at the supermarket? I'll do anything."

Pedro pursed his lips.

"Damn, I don't think so, man. Why? What's going on?"

"That fucking motorcycle, dude. RIP. And I can't work without it, y'know? So I'm officially unemployed. The mechanic wants three hundred reais to fix it. Money I don't got, obviously. I'm fucked. But I have a plan. I'm gonna sell the bike to tide us over for a little while. Maybe even to the mechanic. Dude said he was interested. Either way, I gotta find another gig, stat. The money I get from the bike won't last forever."

Pedro immediately had an idea.

"Roberto, is anybody else home?"

Though the question struck him as unusual, Roberto said:

"Nah. Your cousin took the kids to see Paula."

"Cool. Let's step inside, then."

As soon as they shut the door, Pedro sighed and said, in a low voice:

"Listen, man. Here's the deal: there's no jobs at the supermarket, but I might have another opportunity for you . . ." Pedro then invited Roberto to join the weed operation, explaining everything in detail. He said he'd had the idea because he wanted a better life. He told him about Marques, his friend from the supermarket who'd asked to go into business with him and was selling weed in Lupicínio Rodrigues as they spoke. Finally, he told him another dealer chosen by Marques would be joining them too. If he, Roberto, decided to take part, he'd be one of four, and all profit would be shared equally.

"I don't know, man . . . Can you even make money from weed?"

Pedro tilted his head and cocked his eyebrows.

"Hear me out, Roberto. It's like I said. For a while every bit of profit goes toward buying more weed. Then, once we're selling as much pot as we can move, we'll split the profit four ways. So let's run the numbers, yeah? Based on what I just saw, a kilo of weed sells in a day in our hood, no problem. Let's assume the same goes for Lupicínio. That means we'll be moving fourteen kilo a week, yeah? Each kilo—after it's been trimmed, packaged, and sold in one-gram baggies—each kilo gets us a grand. That means fourteen grand a week. Except we need to use that money to pay for next week's installment, right, another fourteen kilo. Each kilo costs seven hundred, which sets us back . . . hold up . . . gimme a sec . . . nine thousand and eight hundred reais. Cool, that's what we're spending a week. Subtract that from fourteen grand and you get four thousand and two hundred reais, split four ways. *A week.* That's more than a grand apiece, man. *A week.*"

"Damn. That's good money."

"No shit! If you wanted to make the same amount some other way, you'd have to waste years of your life on college or some bullshit like that. And it might not even pan out."

Roberto rubbed his chin, gave it some thought, then said.

"Cool, cool. Count me in."

"Hell, yeah! That's awesome, man. You won't regret it."

Pedro said goodbye and went home, singing under his breath. As he stood in the shower, he felt the last of his worries swirl down the drain with the water. "It's so easy!" he thought. "It's all so fucking easy. The first step is the only step you got to take. Then things just happen organically, easy as can be . . . What was the big deal? Why didn't I start sooner? What was I so scared of? It doesn't matter. Nothing matters now. Pretty soon, I'm gonna be rich!"

It felt amazing to catch a glimpse of the future and enjoy the view. The feeling Pedro had right then—the urge to march forward, the excitement for what lay ahead, the faith, no, the confidence that everything would work, the enormous gratitude for the way things were sure to go, making it possible for him to have a good life—now that was happiness: pure, unadulterated happiness. It felt familiar somehow, like he'd experienced it before . . . Had he been happy? He guessed he must have been, though he couldn't remember when.

He left the bathroom and checked the wall clock in the living room. It was still early, so he decided to go to Vila Campo da Tuca to pay Catarina back the four hundred reais. When he walked into the bar, he was surprised to find Marques there too, sitting at the counter. Like Pedro, Marques had also sold the entire kilo of weed and decided to immediately pay back Catarina.

"Who'd have thought? Y'all's crazy-ass scheme seems to be working," Catarina said with a smile.

"And we're just getting started," Pedro said.

"That's right," Marques agreed. "Before you know it, we'll be rolling in money."

The two men were drinking beer, courtesy of Catarina, a small prize for paying her back before the deadline.

"Now we've just got to call Fabrício," Pedro said, "and ask for another two kilo. Except this time he won't have to front us. Since two kilo costs fourteen hundred and we've settled with Catarina, we should have sixteen hundred, right? So we use the sixteen hundred to buy the next order and throw in the two hundred reais we got left toward the four hundred we owe him for the first order."

Marques cleared his throat.

"I have a better idea, Pedro. How about we pay back all four hundred reais, then buy another six kilo of weed."

"What? Nah, man, you're outta your mind. There's no way Fabrício would give us that much on credit."

"Who said anything about credit?"

Pedro turned toward his friend. He said nothing and waited for an explanation, which he got soon enough.

"Here's the thing. Next Wednesday, *I'm gonna be coming into three grand, man*," Marques revealed, slamming the bar with his hand. "Three fucking grand! Three grand, and I'm not woofing!

Listen, listen: I've done the math, brother. Add the three thousand I'm getting to the sixteen hundred we have and you get four thousand six hundred reais. We pay back the four hundred we owe Fabrício. That leaves us with forty-two hundred, right? Each kilo costs seven hundred. That means we can buy exactly six kilo. Go on, check my fucking math!" A huge smile distorted his features, the pitch of his voice rising with each word. The effort Marques made to curb his excitement was obvious.

But Pedro made an even greater effort as he tried not to get ahead of himself and be infected by his friend's excitement. All the same, he felt his features stretch into a dumb smile, as if a pair of invisible hands were tugging at his cheeks.

"Are you for real, Marques?"

"Hell yeah, I'm for real!"

"Fuck! Where'd you get the money from?"

"It's Angélica's severance. The pizzeria fired her last night and told her to collect the money on Wednesday. She's been trying to get them to fire her for a while, and yesterday she finally did it, thank God! And it couldn't've happened at a better time, man. She's just been offered a way better gig."

"Damn! Good news all round. What's the new job?"

"That's the best part!" By then Marques's voice had started to sound a bit like a rabeca fiddle, choked with laughter. "She's gonna be slinging weed in Lupicínio!"

Pedro couldn't help himself. He burst out laughing too.

"Damn, my man. You are one conniving son of a bitch."

"Watch what you say about my old lady, you little jerk-off!" Catarina teased, also laughing.

Marques took another sip of beer. Then, he asked:

"How about you, Pedro? Did you find somebody to sell in your hood?"

Pedro told him about Roberto.

"So you're throwing family into the mix too, hunh? Can't say shit about me then, can you? You're just as much of a son of a bitch as I am."

"But Roberto isn't related to me. Dude's married to my cousin. We're not blood relatives."

"If that's how it is, then Angélica ain't my blood relative either. Wouldn't have married her if she was!"

All three of them laughed again.

"Listen up, kids," said Catarina. "One more cold one on the house. For the laughs."

"Hear that, Marques? You don't even have to sell weed to get rich. Your jokes are more than enough to brighten somebody's day. If you charged by the kilo, you'd be a goddamn millionaire!"

12

EXPANSION

A deficit of small bills, the scourge of many a commercial establishment, was no longer a problem at a certain branch of Fênix supermarkets. On Monday, February 9, 2009, Marques and Pedro made the first of what would become many transactions, in ever-increasing quantities. They handed the supermarket cashiers sixteen hundred reais in small bills and change and received the same in return in notes of fifty and one hundred reais. The senior cashier had to open three drawers, one per cash register, to cobble together the total.

That week everything went as planned. Angélica collected her severance pay on Wednesday. On Thursday Pedro called Fabrício to put in an order for six kilos of weed and tell him they were ready to settle up the four hundred reais he had fronted them last time. Fabrício seemed happy with how things were going.

"This order's three times the size of the last one," he said. "On top of that, y'all are paying your tab. I get the feeling we're gonna get along just great, kid."

This time, Pedro asked for the weed to be delivered in the early afternoon, if possible. Fabrício said it wasn't a problem; even though they had other, more important orders to fill, no one wanted their deliveries turning up before nightfall. Also, Pedro continued, the drop-off address would be different this time: the weed should be delivered to a small boteco in Vila Lupicínio Rodrigues, if possible. No problem, said Fabrício. One more thing, Pedro added. He wouldn't be there to receive the weed, either. A woman called Angélica would meet the delivery guy instead. No problem, Fabrício repeated. Then, with everything squared away, they said goodbye and hung up.

On Friday of that week, February 13, at one in the afternoon, Angélica received six kilos of weed at the boteco where Marques played pool with Pops. Per Pedro's instructions, Roberto went to her house around two in the afternoon and collected half the weed. This time, the weed lasted until Monday the sixteenth; Roberto and Angélica had trimmed and packaged it all by Friday, but only started selling on Saturday, he in the future Vila Sapo, and she in Vila Lupicínio Rodrigues.

The following Tuesday, February 17, an employee of the same branch of Fênix supermarket and close friend of Marques and Pedro—Luan, the teenager formerly known as Chokito—lost his job as a bagger. He'd made the mistake of carrying on Operation Witchcraft despite the additional security and was caught lowering his loot (a plushy heart with the words "I LOVE YOU" written in English, a birthday gift for his mother) out of the locker-room window, ending up fired for just cause. The assignment with the loaned security guards concluded in exactly two weeks, and Sr. Geraldo informed them they could return to their former positions. The next day, he asked the head of produce, who used to work in construction, to properly secure the window with mortar.

As mentioned before, Luan was a close friend of Marques and Pedro, and the only other person in the supermarket who knew about the weed operation, besides Jorge, of course, who had connected them with Fabrício.

Even before losing his job, Luan had wanted to take part in the operation, but Pedro and Marques had turned him down. Two things led the duo to reconsider his request. First off, Luan had once told them that the reason he took the job at the supermarket was that his mother, whom he lived with, was unemployed and too old and sick to work, meaning his entire salary went to her. In other words, as the sole breadwinner, his dismissal from the supermarket had put the whole family under financial duress, something neither Marques nor Pedro could tolerate. Secondly, Roberto and Angélica had noted that if things went according to plan and the amount of weed bought and sold continued to grow, they wouldn't have time to trim and package it all on their own before going out to sell. They needed someone exclusively for that task.

Luan joined the gang as a trimmer and packager of weed. Though it wasn't easy, Pedro managed to persuade Roberto that Luan deserved an equal share of the proceeds, and Marques, who was already under the influence of his friend's socialist ideas (or at least resigned to them), worked on Angélica.

On Thursday, February 19, Pedro called Fabrício. He wanted to buy nine kilos of weed and, if possible, for Fabrício to front them three hundred reais. Fabrício let out a curt laugh: no worries; this time it was on him. Pedro thanked him and said the delivery should still be made in the early afternoon, but the drop-off would be at a house in Vila Planetário, if possible. No problem, said Fabrício. One more thing, Pedro explained, the person meeting the delivery guy would be a teenager called Luan. No problem, Fabrício repeated. Then, with everything squared away, they said goodbye and hung up.

The following week, the gang sold all nine kilos of weed for nine thousand reais. They ordered thirteen kilos of weed. They were short one hundred reais and Fabrício gave them another discount. Hans, the delivery guy, had to make two trips.

The gang's weekly sales capacity was fourteen kilos: seven in Vila Lupicínio Rodrigues and seven down the hill, between Vila Viçosa and Vila Nova São Carlos, that is, in the future Vila Sapo. Were it not for their unique operating model, they could have sold much more. Angélica and Roberto only sold enough weed to meet their daily one-kilo goal, then went home for the day. How long they spent selling weed was therefore contingent on sales: some days they worked five hours; others, eight. It was Pedro who came up with this modus operandi, devised so Angélica and Roberto wouldn't have to work all day long, indefinitely.

It was finally time to divvy up the profit. They'd sold thirteen kilos of weed for thirteen thousand reais. They used the money to order fourteen kilos of weed, costing them ninety-eight hundred reais. The remaining thirty-two hundred reais were split into five equal parts. Each member took home six-hundred and forty reais.

The following week, the gang sold one kilo more than the previous week, making an extra thousand reais; they each took home eight-hundred and forty reais.

Marques, Pedro, Roberto, Angélica, and Luan were making more than three thousand reais a month each.

Sr. Geraldo gave Pedro and Marques the fourth week of March off. Neither had been on vacation with real money before. Excited, they decided to invite their colleagues to a water park just outside Porto Alegre that coming Sunday. The get-together wasn't only meant to celebrate their success but also give them the chance to discuss an opportunity for growth. One that, according to Luan, could not be passed up.

On the morning of Sunday, March 29, 2009, the five drug dealers took over one of the rustic tables on the left side of the water park, beside the forest. Roberto, who used to work in a kitchen, prepped the meat for their lunch, and was busy dumping charcoal into a nearby grill; Angélica brought rice and salad from home. The atmosphere was cheerful; punctuated by laughter and sips of cold beer, their speech reflected the happiness money had afforded them. Birds twittered all over and the lazy morning sun filtered through the tree canopy, falling in diagonal beams of light that flitted in and out as the branches and leaves shuddered in the wind.

"Right. Let's get down to business, shall we?" Pedro suggested. He gestured for attention as the others went on talking and talking, holding several conversations at the same time. "People, people, please! We'll have plenty of time to talk and laugh in the pool later." When he finally managed to get everyone to pipe down, he nodded at Luan. "Tell us what's on your mind, Chokito."

"I'll show you a fucking Chokito, man!" the teenager said.

Pedro laughed.

"Thought I wouldn't remember what people used to call you, hunh, Chokito?"

"I see how it is!" Roberto admonished from the grill, where he was trying to get the fire to catch. "You make us shut up so you can clown around."

"Yeah, let the kid talk, damnit," Angélica said.

"Go on, tell us your idea, Luan," Marques said. "Don't pay any mind to Hangman over there," he added, laughing.

Even though he had just scolded Pedro for being disruptive, Roberto couldn't help himself when he heard Marques call Pedro Hangman, a nickname that required no explanation, given his scrawny build. He burst out laughing with his hand on his forehead, head thrown back, and strong shoulders juddering, which is how he nearly always laughed.

"Jesus Christ. Hangman!"

Pedro turned to face Roberto.

"So I can't fool around, but when Lumberjack here cracks a joke, you're all shits and giggles, hunh, Roberto? Laugh all you like, man. Meantime, I'll be telling our friends over here how you like to dance around to the Spice Girls in your wife's apron."

Angélica smacked Pedro lightly on the forehead.

"Yo, what you got against the Spice Girls? And what's this crap about my husband being a lumberjack?"

"Just look at his shirt," Pedro said. Marques had a weakness for checkered shirts—as a fan of S.C. Internacional, he especially liked red ones—which made him look like one of those lumber-jacks in Hollywood movies.

They were laughing and talking over each other again. Luan spoke up:

"Y'all are just a bunch of fucking clowns. Scratch that. A real clown wouldn't be caught dead with you bozos."

After a few more minutes of chatter, everyone calmed down and let Luan speak.

"Alright, this time it's for real. Go on, what's on your mind, Luan?"

Luan, who'd been leaning against a mulberry tree, walked back to the table, where he took a seat next to Angélica.

"Okay. Y'all know I live in Planetário," he started, "which is right next door to the main police precinct in town, yeah? Cool. So recently some guys from TV were in the hood doing a news report. They wanted to show their viewers that drugs are being sold right in the cops' backyard. They had these hidden cameras and filmed all them junkies waiting in line to buy rock. It aired last Monday."

"Yeah, yeah, I saw that shit," said Roberto, who was still trying to light the fire. He turned around so that he was standing in front of everyone. "That fat bastard's outta his goddamn mind!" he added, referring to the host of the sensational program that aired the show. Then he blew up his cheeks and started mimicking him: "Ridiculous! Absolutely ridiculous! There are bums crawling all over the cops' backyard, tchê! Ridiculous! Absolutely ridiculous! I won't stand for it. No sir, I will not stand for it!" He laughed. "His jowls were fucking jiggling!" he concluded.

"Two days after that news report," Luan continued, "the pigs decide to raid the joint. It was wild. Assholes confiscated guns, drugs, money, the whole lot. Threw everybody's asses in jail."

"Alright, okay. But what's that got to do with us?" asked Angélica.

"Relax, I'm getting to it," Luan said, holding up the palm of his hand. "Listen, two things killed the drug trade in Planetário: rock and dust. All those junkies standing in line were crackers and brits, yeah? Not potheads. And it was the lines that drew attention. The lines of junkies waiting to buy dope right next to the precinct . . . The news report didn't sit right with the pigs, so they went to town on the place."

"So what you're saying is they didn't sell weed in your hood . . ." Roberto probed. "Just rock and dust?"

"Here's the thing. They did sell weed in my hood. Just not to the folks that smoked it. These gangsters only sold by the kilo. To other gangsters. That's why there was never any potheads standing in line outside their base. Almost nobody bought weed there, and when they did, they bought, like, five or six kilo at once to sell somewhere else. Listen, selling weed in bulk for resale, now that shit was gold. They didn't have to deal with any broke-ass hopheads, and business went quick: dudes took the kilo, handed over the money, and bounced. What I'm getting at is the only reason the trade got fucked was cause of the junkies standing in line outside. But those gangsters moved weed too fast for any lines to form, so no one paid attention to them."

"Right, right. I see where you're going with this," Marques said. "What you want is for us to take over the weed trade in Planetário now that the other crew is in the slammer. You want us to sell weed the way they used to."

"Exactly," said Luan. "I can keep on trimming and packaging weed for Angélica and Roberto and, on the side, sell weed by the kilo to the same dealers that used to buy the stuff in Planetário. All on the down-low, without drawing attention to ourselves."

"How much did the other guys charge for the kilo?" Pedro asked.

"A stack," Luan said.

Marques was surprised.

"*A stack?* What d'you mean a stack?"

The teenager shrugged.

"A stack, man. Ten times a hundred. One thousand."

"Hunh. But that don't make any sense. Think about it: we pay Fabrício seven hundred a kilo, right? Then after trimming, packaging, and selling it, we take home a thou. So if the Planetário gangsters were charging one stack per kilo, that means the fools that bought it from them couldn't turn a profit."

Pedro knew what his friend was getting at.

"The reason you think that is you don't smoke weed, Marques. If you did, you'd know everybody's been selling the stuff for *fifty/one hundred*. Meaning fifty grams of weed costs a hundred reais, or a one-gram baggie of weed costs two reais. That's market rate, yeah? So the dudes that buy a kilo for a grand are making two grand on the kilo. The only reason we can sell our stuff *fifty/fifty* is cause Fabrício gets his shit from abroad and sells it to us for chump change."

Pedro's explanation only managed to confuse Marques even more.

"Fuck, but that means we're losing out," he said in alarm. "Why aren't we charging two reais like everybody else?"

"Cause low cost equals a high sales volume. What I mean is we're making more money than we would if we charged more."

The flea jumped, leaving Marques's ear and landing in Angélica's.

"Sure, but how d'you know we're making more money this way?" she asked.

"I don't know for sure," Pedro admitted. "It's an educated guess."

"He means a *guesstimate*."

"No, no; it's not too much or too little; not a sure thing or a guesstimate: an educated guess is exactly what it is. Listen. There was this guy who used to sell weed in my hood. One day, before we started our own little operation, I asked him why he'd stopped. He told me he stopped cause it wasn't worth it. The most he could move in a day was a hundred grams. He used to charge fifty/a hundred though. Now at fifty/fifty Roberto's selling a kilo a day, easy. So you could say Roberto's selling ten times more than this other dude, all cause he charges half the price. Now, let's do the math. Say we sell each baggie for two reais. We'd get two grand out of each kilo; each kilo costs us seven hundred so we'd be making thirteen hundred in profit. But then it'd take us ten days to move the whole kilo, cause we'd only be selling a hundred grams a day. On the other hand, by charging half the price, like we're doing now, we're getting one grand out of each kilo; subtract seven hundred and that leaves us with three hundred; except we can sell ten kilo in as many days; ten times three hundred gets us three thousand. Which means we're making three thousand in ten days instead of the thirteen hundred reais we'd be making if we charged market rate."

Angélica thought for a moment. Then, apparently satisfied with what Pedro was saying, she tried to steer the conversation back to Luan's idea.

"Cool, cool, cool. Say more, Luan. So, like, if you take over the weed trade in Planetário, how many kilos you think you could sell?"

"See for yourself." Luan pulled out a small notebook, folded in half to fit his pocket, and placed it in Angélica's hands.

"What's this?"

"It's a notebook, belonged to one of the former dealers. Sounds like one of the pushers tossed it in the scrapyard when the pigs raided their base. The owner, Skewer, found it and showed it to me. I took it off his hands."

Roberto stepped away from the grill to take a closer look at the notebook. The handwriting was tiny and the pages about half-full, with a horizontal line marking the cut-off of a period of time. Heading every three or four pages were words like "JANUARY," or "DECEMBER," or some other month, though the pattern didn't always hold. Sometimes a page would be covered from top to bottom with names, numbers, or random phrases that wouldn't have made sense to anyone but the person or people who had written them: "always always always be straight cause toe is wigging and pâté's a ghost," or "five P.M.'s a hairy time to fix dickhead." On the margins were snatches of simple arithmetic and crude drawings that betrayed the childishness of the previous owners.

"Look here," said Luan, pointing at some digits. Angélica was still flipping through the notebook and saw that the same digits showed up every few pages, sometimes circled.

"I've got it," she said. "Dude was moving forty kilo a month, give or take."

Roberto whistled suggestively as he walked back to the grill.

"Not bad! Not bad at all."

"Ten kilo a week," Pedro said. "That's seven grand of grass we could turn around for ten grand, and three grand in profit. That's pretty good business. Maybe."

"*Maybe*," Marques emphasized. "Well said, Pedro: *maybe*." He looked over at Luan. "You think you can sell that much weed? How you gonna find the dealers who used to buy in your hood and let them know you've taken over?"

"Angélica, show your husband the last page," Luan said with confidence, crossing his arms.

Angélica opened the notebook again, this time to the last page, where a series of names and phone numbers were headed by the words "HERB BROS."

"All I gotta do is call," said Luan.

"Damn, kid!" Marques smiled. "Way to bury the fucking lede. Bring on the pain! Ain't nothing left to talk about."

13

PROSPERITY

Pedro was walking through Vilinha, that is, through the part of Vila Viçosa that was neither friendly, quiet, nor civilized. He was on his way home from the bakery with some groceries for his mid-afternoon snack, things he wouldn't have been able to afford earlier that year: fresh bread, ham, cheese, croquettes, pastéis, a slice of savory pie, yogurt. His eyes became lost in the familiar landscape. In a way, it all seemed completely new, like something straight out of an oil painting: the sun setting behind the empty fields, people ambling up and down the dirt roads, workers stepping off a crowded bus, deadbeats chatting in alleyways, children playing in the streets, dogs barking and running around without leashes, the bars, the shacks, everything. His unprecedented financial security had given him a new perspective: it was as though everything were lyrical now, steeped in beauty and poetry. His soul felt unspeakably light, at last free from sadness, silent rage, and self-hatred. For the first time, he felt almost whole. At peace. Content, in a way.

Only, something niggled at him now and then, not so much a real concern as a faint idea that had been popping into his head more and more, with greater and greater urgency: that he ought to save money and invest it so he could keep up his lifestyle without having to sell weed or do anything illegal. But whenever this thought entered Pedro's mind, it took him less than a second to mount a defense, making it grind to a halt: it wasn't time yet to rein in the lavish spending that was so enriching his material life, making a once-arid desert flourish. He had years and years of poverty to make up for. He'd bought clothes, shoes and sneakers, earrings and chains, watches, instruments, stacks and stacks of books. He'd bought more stuff than he could keep track of, and it was always top shelf, always high end. His pastimes had also become increasingly refined: he went to the movies, strolled through Porto Alegre's downtown parks, smoked good cigarettes, good weed, drank good whiskey, ate good food. No: it wasn't time yet to rein in his spending. He had to tear down his house and build a new one—nice, spacious, safe from rats. He had to replace all the furniture and appliances. And there was also the small matter of a car. He needed a cool, sleek ride—one of those bad-boy mid-life-crisis sedans he'd been aching for all his life. Only after that, and maybe even a bit later, would he stop spending money like crazy and start thinking about the long-term. At least that's what he told himself.

Pedro's mother, who hadn't been in the best health for a while, didn't have to break her back cleaning houses anymore. She'd retired, a bit on the early side according to the National Labor Relations Act, and a bit on the late side according to common sense. She was finally free to watch her afternoon telenovelas while sipping chimarrão. Free to eat tangerines in the sun and gossip with the neighbors. Free to take it easy and live life; to take it easy and live life for herself; to take it easy and live life for her late parents; to take it easy and live life for all her ancestors who had died old and calloused without ever tasting the power of simply not working, of just taking it easy and getting on with their lives.

"Praise the Lord!" she whispered as she waited for Pedro to come home from the bakery.

She thought to herself that the Lord had been too good to them when he promoted her son to assistant manager of the Fênix supermarket branch where he worked. A promotion that happened to come with a generous raise—one that made her boy sunnier and less gloomy, that made it possible for her to quietly retire, that brought so much joy into their home . . .

Obviously, Pedro's promotion was just a cock-and-bull story: a bit of fake news he had fed to his mother and that she had naively believed. Even so, when has having all the facts ever made a person feel real joy? When has anyone felt happy, if not when they are told a complete lie or curated truth? When reality walks through the door, there isn't a single smile that doesn't fly out the window. A happy fool is first and foremost a fool.

TUESDAY, AUGUST 4, 2009

SWADDLED IN COMPLETE tranquility, oblivious to the world around them, eyes closed, soul untouched—now there was a crea-ture relishing the peak of their life. Shame it wouldn't leave a mark. Shame it wouldn't be remembered. Shame these memories would disappear forever, like leaves swept far away by the October wind and never to return to the branch from which they'd fallen. On second thought, wasn't that—the ability not to remember, the abil-ity not to ruminate, the ability to forget, to let things go—wasn't that the creature's greatest virtue? Yes. Their soul was immaculate:

today would be no more than a hazy dream tomorrow; even less the day after. A perfect existence, for sure: without anxiety, guilt, heartache, or longing. Only peace, in all its splendor.

Unfortunately, this perfect existence was coming to an end—just like that, suddenly and without warning. The first taste of fear would be the end of nothingness and the most peaceful comfort; the first taste of fear would be the beginning of everything, the beginning of the worst kind of misery. Poor creature. It was with bared teeth and drawn claws that the world greeted them. It was with the urge to bite them, chew them up, and swallow them whole that the world welcomed them in. Just like that, yet another soul slipped out of a set of pajamas they would never again wear; just like that, yet another soul squeezed into a suit of armor they would never again be free of; just like that, yet another soul stepped on to a battlefield, where they would give it their best shot, where they would fight for survival, where they would face an invincible enemy, knowing in the end that they would lose.

"Go on! Keep pushing. Here she comes. I've got her. She's here!" the obstetrician said, raising his voice over the war whoop that was the newborn's first cry. "If she isn't the sweetest baby I've ever seen!" he said, feigning a level of excitement that no longer came naturally after several years of delivering babies. "Congratulations, Dona Angélica!"

Angélica was pale and sweaty, and smiled weakly as the doctor cut the umbilical cord.

Outside the room, Marques waited and prayed to God everything was going smoothly. He was visibly nervous, though nowhere near as nervous as he had been when Daniel, their first son, was born. Back then, he wasn't sure what scared him more: his son dying in childbirth or else surviving. The thought that his son would have no choice but to endure a life of hardship and deprivation, all because Marques couldn't provide for him, filled him with despair.

But things were different now. Let little Lúcia come into the world! Let her in—this time, Marques knew he could give her a good life.

"Are you the father?"

"Yes . . ." Marques's voice came out as a sliver from underuse. He cleared his throat and tried again. "Yes."

"The delivery went smoothly. You can stop worrying now. Your daughter is perfect. Congratulations!"

MONDAY, OCTOBER 5, 2009

THE BUILDINGS FROM Avenida Ipiranga to Parque Farroupilha rose up high-and-mighty. Curiously, their residents seemed to have absorbed some of the buildings' personality: much like those steel-and-concrete structures, their flesh-and-bone residents looked down on everything. The streets in that area were quiet and genteel. They were clean too, thanks to the careful labor of the public works crews, who didn't just sweep any old street. The public nature of the works was more "thy will be done" than "thy kingdom come," which was reserved for the lucky few. Naturally, every resident of Porto Alegre, whether rich or poor, whether cafuzo or mameluco, had to pay taxes. The street sweepers' wages came out of this pot. Yet, only streets like that one, whose residents had pink skin, nasal accents, and pets with pedigree, were swept.

But a surprise awaited anyone unfamiliar with the neighborhood who happened to wander all the way down Rua Luiz Manoel, a street that came to an abrupt end on a surprisingly grungy, roundish cul-de-sac. From that point on, there were no more signs of the city's public works. There were no more tall buildings or pinkish residents. No more nasal accents or pets with pedigree. Instead, there were modest houses, spray-painted walls, trash strewn all over, mangy dogs, flea-ridden cats, horses exhausted from pulling carts, people with weathered skin, people in cheap clothes, people who looked beaten down by life, people with crass and careless tongues. And the only way forward was by foot, down narrow alleys that led straight into the depths of hell.

Thus emerged Vila Planetário, ugly and unwanted, right in the middle of an affluent neighborhood in Porto Alegre, like a lone zit on a beautiful woman's face.

Luan was in the Loop, which is what the locals called the cul-de-sac at the end of Rua Luiz Manoel. Seated in a beach chair, surrounded by women, he was trying to figure out his new tablet. A task that was proving difficult on account of the women hanging off him, no matter how often he reproached them, and occasionally dragging their curious fingers on the touch-sensitive screen.

"Leave it alone, Larissa! I told you already, damnit. And Suzana, back up! You're breathing right in my fucking face."

Among the various beautiful specimens around Luan were two women who looked about the same age as him. The rest were old enough to be his mother. All of them were glued to the teenager, as though life were only fun by his side. Like groupies around a musician, they couldn't help fawning over him and vying for his attention. They had no qualms about groping him in public either: groping that bordered on the obscene.

Living like a king for the past two months had had a radical effect on Luan's personality. All trace of Chokito's former shyness was gone. Now his eyes drank up everything around him with wild excitement, as though the whole world were an amusement park. Yet, somehow Luan had managed not to get too big for his boots, in part thanks to his mother, who was, and had always been, the official oracle of Vila Planetário.

"It's about humility, son," his mother used to say to him, with the air of somebody who knows things, her face set in a stony expression and a joint in the corner of her mouth. "Nobody's better than anybody else in this world, and don't you forget it: that's the only thing you got to learn in life. You do what you want, and don't let nobody stop you. Not even the police has the right to stop you. And if the cops try and get in the way of what you wanna do, don't let them. Don't let others decide what's right or wrong for you, son. *You* decide what's right and what's wrong, then do what you think in your heart is right. It's simple: you got to make your own rules."

Naturally, the woman knew all about her son's illegal activities. And if her face, which was always stern, hid how she really felt about them, it was safe to say it was more pride than disappointment. Sure, she'd tried to encourage him to live a so-called "honest life," to finish school and get a job, but her attempts had been tepid at best, like when someone prescribes regular exercise.

After the police operation in Planetário in late March, which ended with the whole gang behind bars, the dealers who used to buy weed from them in bulk and resell it across Porto Alegre were at loose ends. But it wasn't long before the tides changed: later that month, they all received an unexpected phone call informing them they would be able to continue buying weed in bulk in Planetário for the same price. On top of that, Luan explained, there was no danger of another police operation. They wouldn't be selling to users, so there would be no hopheads standing in line at the corner, or any strangers coming in and out of the neighborhood; to sum up, there was nothing for reporters to report on and no reason for the police to police. The customers were happy to pick up business where they'd left off, and even happier when they learned Luan's weed was significantly better than the weed they used to buy from the other crew.

"Fuck, man. This stuff is dope!" they all said whenever they came back for more.

The fact that Luan sold weed—and good weed—in bulk earned him a reputation in the drug-trafficking underworld of Porto

Alegre, and the small-time dealers who bought product from Luan started recommending him to third parties.

"Listen, if you're looking for weed to sell, go hit up my buddy Sheik in Planetário. His stuff's cheap, you'll see. It'll blow your fucking mind."

People called him Sheik because he was constantly surrounded by women.

Luan looked up from the tablet: a customer was coming his way.

"Sheik!" the man said, a big smile plastered on his slender face. As soon as Luan got up, the women started making a fuss.

"Leave the tablet with me, babe!"

"No, me!"

"No, leave it with me, honey!"

"No, I'll look after it!"

"Shush!" the young man ordered. "Larissa gets the tablet cause she ain't fucking high maintenance like the rest of you."

Larissa was Luan's favorite concubine because she was the only one who didn't make demands, or, to be more precise, the only one who didn't make a big deal out of his pubic hair; the rest were always complaining about it, saying how gross it was and nagging him to shave it off.

Luan shook the customer's hand, then walked him to the house. Moments later, the man was on his way out again, his backpack five-kilos heavier than before. After counting the five thousand reais, Luan stashed them in his bedroom. Then, as he cut through the living room on his way back outside, he saw his mother pull a face on the sofa, and stopped:

"What's up, Ma?"

"You're happy, aren't you, son?" she asked out of the blue.

"Yeah, I am," he said, smiling and a little confused.

"Good. May it last."

Smoke rose from the pans. They were new, just like the stove, and like the plates and silverware on the table, also new. Even the food, which was just about ready to be served, smelled fresh. No one in that house was used to the glut and variety of food that had graced their dinner table for the past few months. Yesterday, it was lasagna; today, steak and fries; tomorrow, grilled meat. These days, sitting down for a meal was a real source of pleasure for that family—pleasure that would have been unthinkable for someone with no choice but to satisfy their hunger with rice and beans, or, on a good day, with fried eggs and ground beef. But the food and kitchen implements weren't the only new things under that roof. The truth was they were living a whole, brand-new *life*. A much better one at that. The mother, who only had a ninth-grade education, had quit cleaning toilets and gone back to school, boldly hoping to become a lawyer. Now—and only now—did they finally have the money for her to study in peace. She could afford the commute, whether by bus or taxi; she could afford the best books instead of borrowing the used ones that the school set aside for students in need; she could afford college-level courses, and a tutor; she could buy it all, from the mandatory to the optional; they had enough money to cover everything. And she could have all this without sacrificing her precious eight hours of sleep, sometimes even ten; she could have all this without bending over backwards, without rushing around like a chicken with its head cut off, trying to pair school with the shattering need for a source of income. Their income was secure now—her husband had secured it. She could study in peace. She only looked up from her books to clean the house, make food, or mind the kids, responsibilities she viewed as exclusively her own.

"Listen, if you ask me, I think the way y'all are living is straight-up sexist," her cousin Pedro said to her once. "Just cause Roberto's the one bringing home the bread now don't mean you should be the only one looking after the kids and cleaning the house and shit. Put that lazy-ass motherfucker to work. It's not like you're hanging around with your legs in the air. You're back at school, studying to become a lawyer. Sure, you still got a long road ahead of you, but once you graduate, you'll be raking it in, and whatever money you make is gonna go to your house, right, and to your family. What I'm saying is, I think all the work you do deserves to be recognized now."

She couldn't care less about what her cousin had to say. She was grateful for the turn their lives had taken, and when people feel that way, when people are *genuinely grateful*, they don't usually see the flaws. Maybe Pedro was right. But things were so good, everyone was happy, what point was there in nagging her husband? For what? What mattered to her was that the house was clean and tidy now, unlike when she and her husband worked around the clock and didn't have the time or the energy to deal with that mess. Besides, the fact that she could be with the kids every day now, and not once in a blue moon, had worked wonders for their relationship. Both she and their schoolteachers could hardly believe how well-behaved the children had become. Now that she was holding the reins all the time, it was much easier for their lack of discipline to be shaped into obedience, their bad attitude into respect, their disinterest in school into a thirst for knowledge. And there was only one possible outcome: the little pests, who weren't even really pests anymore, had passed the school year with the highest grades in the whole class. As a reward they would get a next-generation video-game console for Christmas in six days.

The front door opened. It was Roberto, who'd spent all day out in the streets, slinging weed.

"Perfect timing, love," his wife said. The food had just finished cooking.

14

FEET, DON'T FAIL
ME NOW

To justify all the money he was bringing home, Pedro told his mother he'd been promoted at work and prayed she never discovered the truth. In the meantime, he enjoyed all the suspicious looks he and Marques received at the supermarket: everyone there knew the two stock clerks hadn't been promoted to anything, which made some of their behavior impossible to explain. Every day, on their breaks, Pedro and Marques dropped obscene amounts of money on snacks at the supermarket—potato chips, boxes of chocolate, candy bars, yogurt, soda, and energy drinks—and not only for themselves either, but for any staff that happened to be around, which only made their colleagues love them more. The sickening smell of new clothes wafted off the two men, and if you were the kind to notice that sort of thing, you'd realize that between late 2009 and the present day, in early 2010, Marques and Pedro almost never wore a single item of clothing or pair of sneakers that didn't look like it was fresh from the store. But the fishiest and most confounding thing of all was that they both showed up once a week with an abundance of coins and small bills to change at the cash register. They brought in so much money that not even every fifty and one-hundred-real bill in every supermarket register was enough to change the money in one go, forcing them to do it in parts throughout the day. They changed one part when they clocked in for work, another during their break, once the customers had filled the registers with larger bills, and the last part before clocking out. Even then, there were times when they couldn't change all of it.

"Where are they getting all that cash?" the employees asked each other in whispers.

Naturally, Jorge, the security guard who gave Pedro and Marques Fabrício's phone number the year before, knew where the money came from. What he didn't get was why they were still working at the supermarket.

When Jorge asked, the only answer he ever got from either of them was, "Work gives dignity to man."

What Jorge didn't know was that when Marques said those words, he was just echoing Pedro; not even he knew the truth behind why they still worked there. A few months earlier, when Marques mentioned wanting to resign, Pedro asked him to hold off, but never gave him a good reason. All he said was that he had a plan, and that for the plan to work, they needed to keep their jobs. Despite his curiosity, Marques did what his friend asked, assuming that before long they would put the plan in motion and he would finally find out what it was all about. Yet as time passed, nothing happened, which only piqued Marques's interest. And unsettled him, too. He didn't like the idea of Angélica slinging grass all day in Vila Lupicínio Rodrigues, running the risk of being caught, while he safely worked behind the scenes; he wanted to resign from the supermarket and take turns selling weed with his wife. Besides, now that he brought home real money, all the time he spent at Fênix made less and less sense. Which is why Marques began to regularly confront Pedro about his mysterious plan; in response, he was always asked for patience. But then, one hot, sunny Monday, on February 22, 2010, Marques's patience ran out.

"Spit it out, Pedro. Why are we still working here?" he asked, as soon as they were alone in the locker room, on their break, during yet another workday. "Tell me, or I swear I'll give my notice right this second. I mean it, man."

"Chill, Marques, I—"

"Don't even start, cuz. I mean it, don't even try. Just open your mouth and start talking."

Pedro sighed and shook his head. Marques had given him no choice but to let him in on the plan.

"Fucking alright. Jesus," he conceded reluctantly, pursing his lips. "I'll tell you everything. I was gonna have to, sooner or later. So . . ." He paused for a moment to consider the best approach. Then he said: "Lemme tell you a story, Marques. One day, a long time ago, I was headed to work. Soon as I got off the tram, I lit up a joint. Right outside Julinho. A couple of daddy's boys hanging out on the bandstand came up to me and asked if I was selling grass. I said I wasn't, but the assholes wouldn't let up. In the end, they offered me twenty reais for the stick I'd just lit. *Twenty*, man! Twenty for a joint I'd rolled with, like, a gram of bud."

"So what?"

"So, ever since, I been trying to figure out a way to, like . . . build a bridge—"

"A bridge?"

"A bridge."

"*A bridge?*"

"A bridge."

"Alright. Cool. A bridge. The fuck does that mean?"

With a half-smile on his lips and a gleam in his eye, Pedro looked like a dreamer. Even though he was talking to Marques, it was like he was staring right through him.

"Right, okay, here goes." He extended his left arm and opened his hand as if holding something. "On the one hand, you've got a shitload of playboyzinhos like the ones I told you about. Kids who are itching to get hold of some weed, but don't got a clue how, or don't have access to it, or whatever. For these kids, money ain't a problem—it's a solution!" He extended his right arm and opened his hand. "On the other hand, you got us. And what do we want, Marques? We want to sell weed. The more we sell it for, the better, natch. We're talking about twenty reais a gram, the same gram folks are buying for one real in Pinheiro and Lupícinio. For playboys, that's nothing. For us, it's everything. It's real simple, if you think about it: we got what they want, they got what we want." Pedro joined both hands, then entwined his fingers. "All we need is a bridge."

"Right, right, I see what you're saying. But I don't know, man . . . I don't know if there's that many folks out there ready to drop twenty reais on a gram of weed every day . . ."

"You reckon? It's been on my mind a lot lately, and you know what? I disagree. Sure, plenty of daddy's boys do all right on their own; they buy stuff from a friend or a friend of a friend of a friend, or whatever; they got it under control. But it's not them I'm thinking about. The guys I'm interested in are the ones that hear some fool talking about bud and decide they want in on it but don't know how. I'm interested in the dude that maybe smoked weed this one time, at one of them yuppy-ass parties, and is jonesing for more but can't be bothered to wait for another party before he gets to smoke up again. It's those morons, brother, who piss away money. Don't think they think of twenty reais the way *you* think of twenty reais. They think of twenty reais the way you think of five fucking cents. They've gone through life watching their parents slip a twenty to the delivery guy and another twenty to the pizza guy and another twenty to the doorman. Their monthly allowance is more than a month of our wages, and dudes don't even got bills to pay. It's all cool for them, brother. C'mon, you really think these guys wouldn't drop twenty on fast, easy access to weed, all so they can smoke in peace and show their little friends just how badass they are?"

"Yeah, I guess that makes sense . . ."

"You bet it does, man! Thing is, whatever bridge we build has to be sturdy, yeah? *They've* got to feel safe on that bridge, but *we've* got to feel safe too. Like, we can't just be slinging dope outside Julinho. We look just like the kinda dudes cops already got eyeballs on. If we spend all day hanging around the bandstand, we're gonna stick out like a pair of sore thumbs and wind up behind bars in no time. So, here's the deal, man, listen up: the place where we build the bridge between us and the playboyzinhos has got to be somewhere we can hang for hours without getting noticed; somewhere we go so much folks are tired of hearing about it; somewhere we're as good as invisible; somewhere nobody would think we were stupid or bold enough to push dope in." Pedro threw his arms open, as though introducing a brand-new friend. "Here, for example."

"Here?"

"Here."

"*Here?*"

"Here."

"Okay. Here. Cool, cool, cool."

"Hey, hold up, Marques. Where you going?" Pedro asked as Marques got ready to leave.

Marques squared his hands on his hips. Though he was smiling, he looked far from happy.

"Where am I going? To hand in my notice, brother. Cause if you're serious about all this, then you must be outta your goddamn mind. Man, I can't believe *that's* why you made me stick around this fucking joint. You know what? Fuck you."

"C'mon, dude. Where's this coming from?"

"You tell me! What's all this crap about selling dope in the store, hunh? Did somebody spike your water?"

Pedro looked very serious.

"Sounds to me like you're about to do something I ain't ever seen you do before, Marques," he said in a somber tone.

"Oh yeah? And what's that?"

"Sounds to me like you're about to rush to a conclusion. Worse still, that you're about to rush to a *definitive* conclusion about something I just started, something I'm not even done telling you about. I never ask you for nothing, brother. But do me a favor this time: would you cool the fuck down and let me finish? I've never been nothing but respectful to you. The least you can do is show me some respect and not leave me stranded, talking to myself. That wouldn't be fucking fair, would it? Do you think you can manage that? At the end of the day, if you don't wanna help me sell weed here, there's nothing I can do. I'm not gonna strong-arm you. How could I? But I'd appreciate it, I'd really, truly appreciate it, if you could at least talk this shit through with me. Okay? Let's talk like we always do."

Marques leaned against the lockers and immediately threw open his arms.

"I'm listening."

"Right. First off: You really think I'd try and fuck myself? If I say we should sell weed in the store, it's cause I know we can make a shitload of money and do it on the down-low, without nobody finding out, without no shit hitting any fans. You still believe I can hatch a decent plan, right?"

"Listen, Pedro, I don't doubt you got a good plan. But you're talking about selling weed in our place of work. Right in the middle of this bougie, pig-infested neighborhood. I don't care how good the plan is; it's not foolproof. You know what the difference is between you and me? You think it's worth the risk; I don't. Taking bigger and bigger risks may mean one thing to you, but it means something completely different to me. I got two kids, Pedro. I need to think about them. Every risk I take is a risk my kids take. You get that, right? Listen. Last year when I was going through some shit and could barely support Daniel, when Angélica was pregnant with Lúcia, last year, when I was at the end of my rope, maybe I'd have said yes. But things changed, man. Things good now. And I owe a lot of that to you; I don't want you thinking I'm not grateful. I just can't be taking that kind of risk no more, you know? Things good now. Besides, Angélica and me are trying to save up enough money to stop selling. Cause we worry, don't we? Things good now, better than good, but the weather could turn any second, like this." Marques snapped his fingers. "Then what? Who's gonna look after my kids? Everything could come crashing down in the blink of an eye. You know that. Remember that time you said how bad luck is more creative than good luck. 'You're more likely to step in shit than turn up a lucky coin,' you said. 'Fate never has time to help you out, but when it comes to screwing you over, it always finds a way,' you said. 'Life is feet, don't fail me now: us on the run, and bad luck on our heels,' you said. Or didn't you? So, right now, what I'm saying is: feet, don't fail me now. Angélica and me, we're gonna run while we still can. Before bad luck catches up to us. That's why we want out. We wanna save a chunk of money and buy a couple of investment properties, or maybe a fleet of taxis or something, I don't know, so we can keep living a good life but, like, without the nagging feeling that everything will come crashing down at any minute. See what I mean?"

Pedro was nodding in agreement before Marques had even finished his speech.

"You and Angélica are right, and I'm happy to hear you say that, I swear."

"Wait, really?"

"Yeah."

"Hmm . . ."

"I thought I was gonna have two jobs ahead of me. First, convincing you to help me sell weed in the store. Second, convincing you it's time to close up shop."

Marques was surprised.

"You want out too?"

"Definitely, man. Listen: You know when you've got the news on and you watch a whole crew get thrown in prison after twenty years of boosting cars, or robbing banks, or cheating on their taxes? Whenever I see that shit, I wonder: why the hell didn't they quit while they were ahead? Me, I'm not making the same mistake. To start, I never wanted to be a drug dealer. It's a weird thing to want, ain't it, if you think about it. What kind of person wants to risk getting arrested and spending years in the can? Never mind that there's more bad cops than good ones out there. Dudes that, given the chance, would beat you black and blue before taking you downtown. Dudes that might even kill you, if nobody's looking. And they'd do it like the snakes they are: when you're asleep at home with your guard down, that's when they put you through hell and chalk it up to self-defense. It's the law's word against nothing, silence; cause you're dead and nobody saw shit. So let me ask you: What kind of person actually wants that kind of life? Who actually wants to take those kinds of risks? Nah, I never wanted to be a drug dealer. But I didn't want the shitty-ass life I had shoved down my throat either. What I wanted was money. You know that. I wanted to live the way we live now. Trouble is the life we living now wasn't meant for guys like us. We broke the rules, Marques. We went and took something that should never have been ours to begin with. If we only worked the kinds of jobs folks wanted us to work, we'd never have this kind of life."

Marques sighed.

"You really think so? I wonder, sometimes, you know. There's loads of folks out there who manage to move up in the world without getting mixed up in this kind of thing."

"Yeah, but under what circumstances?"

"What d'you mean?"

"How do folks move up in the world? Do they grovel and degrade themselves like vermin? Do they kiss the boss's ass until they get promoted? Do they work like dogs? Do they rat out their coworkers until everybody hates them? Or do they get qualifications? Put themselves through school? Do they live like zombies and not sleep right till they graduate? Do they drop all their money on books and bus fares while their kids lick each other's ears at home for the salt, cause there ain't no food in the house? Picture you're in college. You know only bougie fuckers go to college, right? Now picture you're in college and your buddies invite you to the cafeteria. They can buy whatever the hell they want cause they got daddy's money. What about you? Your stomach's growling and you can't even buy a goddamn lollipop. Is that the kind of shit people put themselves through to move up in the world? Fuck no. And fuck anyone who thinks I need to do all that just so I can have a decent life! Alright, I got a question for you: When a plane crashes, what happens to the passengers?"

Marques, whose head had been lowered as he listened to Pedro, immediately looked up, surprised by the question.

"They die."

"All of them?"

"All of them. Most of the time, they all die. Sometimes, one or two folks survive."

"That's right. Sometimes, one or two folks survive. What d'you make of that?"

"What d'you mean?"

"In your opinion, what's more likely: that you'll die in a plane crash or that you'll survive? At the end of the day, sometimes a plane crashes and one or two folks survive, right? What does that mean? That all of them could've survived? What about the ones that died? Why'd they die? Is it cause they lacked determination? Is it cause they lacked, I don't know, the will to live?"

"Man, I'm not sure I follow . . . I guess I think people die in plane crashes cause they're way more likely to die than survive . . . It's about probability."

"That's exactly it, Marques! The same applies to poverty, which is just a different kind of tragedy. Show me a poor man who moved up in the world. Go on. Show me somebody who was born poor— our kind of poor, yeah?—and left that life behind without committing a crime or winning the lottery. Go on. Cause for every *one* bootstrapper you show me, I'll show you *a million* people who were born poor and died poor. You know why? It's about probability, like you said. People who are born poor are way more likely to die poor than they are to move up in the world, just like, in a plane crash, passengers are way more likely to die than they are to survive. When it comes to tragedy, whether it's poverty or a plane crash, determination's got nothing to do with it. The fact is all tragedy *needs to be* or *should be* avoided at all costs. A plane *should not* crash, Marques; we need to be doing everything in our power to stop that from happening. Poverty *should not* exist; we need to be doing everything in our power to stop it from existing. Or at least we should be doing everything." Pedro paused. He seemed lost in thought.

When he started again, his tone was reflective, as if he were speaking to himself. "One time, when I worked at another Fênix branch, I saw something I'll never forget. I must've been like eighteen years old. I was in the parking lot rounding up the shopping carts customers leave behind after loading their trunks and going home. All of a sudden, this set of wheels rolls up. A beautiful, imported sedan. The kind of sweet ride that reeks of a midlife crisis. I figured it was some old geezer's, natch. Wrong. The dude who stepped out of that car was young, my age. Eighteen; twenty, max. You should've seen what the asshole was wearing too. He looked smug as hell in his James Bond. And don't forget the Bond girl. The chick with him, man. She could make you come just by taking off her dress. A guy my age, dressed like that, with a ride like that, and a babe like that. Damn. Meanwhile, there I was, rounding up shopping carts. I'm gonna be straight with you, Marques: I was ready to murder the motherfucker. I was ready to hack him to pieces and feed the pieces to my dog. I didn't choose to feel that way. It just happened. What do you call that feeling, again? 'Envy,' yeah? Right, let's call it envy. But, you know, there's something even worse than envy, right? And that's the feeling you don't deserve what someone else has. If I'd seen that display of inequality and injustice, one where I played an important role, whether I liked it or not, if I'd seen that crap and thought everything was cool, if I'd seen that crap and thanked God for my sad-ass, minimum-wage job, and just let it be, then, brother, even a fly—one of those flies that's always buzzing round cow shit—even a fly would've deserved more respect than me. Fuck no! I know my worth. I'm a stand-up motherfucker! Ask me to do something, and I will do the shit out of it. I'm not just a hard worker, either. I'm also good at everything I set my mind to. So why the hell should I look at that preppy piece of shit and not think I deserve what he has? I bet there's nothing in this world I can't do better than him. Cause I'm a flower that grew in a goddamn trash heap. I'm badass! *We're* fucking badass. We're *hard to fucking perish*. We've lived our whole lives in a world where life seems impossible.

"For real, think about it for a minute: Ain't it a miracle we're here at all, having this conversation? How many of your friends have wound up in body bags, Marques? Sometimes it's a stray bullet; sometimes a guy gets mistaken for somebody else and pumped full of lead; sometimes dudes are found stabbed in back alleys and their murderers are never found. Then there's the folks that end up living on the street and drop off the map, or the ones who feel they got no choice but to live like dogs for the rest of their lives—kicked around, taking crap, begging their neighbors for bread—people with hellish lives that fall back on crack, cramming their lives into a pipe and waiting for it all to melt away, even their souls, until finally they give up the ghost in some random corner. How many people you seen go that way, Marques? A bunch of dudes you grew up with, I bet. Dudes who played marbles in the dirt with you, who were with you the first time you went clubbing. All of them good and dead. But *we're* here. I don't know how, but we are. Staying out of trouble. Against all odds. Keeping food on the table. Laughing when there's shit to laugh about. And the reason we're here isn't that we're made of mud or glass or wax or whatever; the reason we're here is that we're tough motherfuckers.

"The minute I saw that guy with his suit, his car, and his girl, the minute I saw him, I knew he didn't have a right to a life like that unless *I* could have one too. See what I mean? It was my dignity kicking and screaming. Cause if you get me and that dipshit to bake a cake, I promise you mine would be frosted before the other dude had even sifted the flour. But there he was, living his bougie little life while I rounded up shopping carts. What you got to say about that, hunh? How d'you reckon he managed such a good life when he was just a snotty teenager? Did he start where we did? Did he kiss his boss's ass? Did he put himself through school? Please. I bet he had everything handed to him. I bet he was born holding all the aces. Maybe the car was a present from his parents or an uncle living in Finland.

"Listen to what I'm saying, brother: the world's a straight-up fairy tale. Some dudes are born in castles and spend their whole lives surrounded by stacks and stacks of treasure. All their shit is top of the line and, far as they're concerned, life is hunky-fucking-dory. Their only bother is the scary monsters living way outside the castle walls—monsters like you and me. And they think the only reason we were born into the circumstances we were born into is that our parents were lazy, that the only reason we still live in those same circumstances today is that we're lazy too. We can't want what they have cause that's a little thing called envy, and we're only allowed in the castle to scrub the floors and trim the hedges. When we're done, we can crawl right back into the hole we climbed out of. But I could give a flying fuck what they think, Marques. I've got the keys to the castle; I may still be scrubbing floors and trimming hedges, just like they want me to and like I have my whole-ass life, but this time I'm selling their kids magic grass, too!"

Marques quietly reflected on everything Pedro had said. It always astonished him, the way his friend could bring up something patently absurd only to rearrange and reposition it *exactly* where it needed to so that it no longer seemed absurd at all but was just another fact of life. All the same, he wasn't willing to bend.

"Alright, dude. Well, you do you. Wanna sling weed in the store? Go ahead. But you're on your own this time. Sorry. I can't help."

Pedro cocked his head, curled his lips, and raised his eyebrows, as if doubting Marques's resolve.

"Right, maybe you really don't want to help me sell weed in the store. Like I said before, I can't twist your arm and I don't want to, either. Thing is, though, by the time I'm done, I think you're gonna want to help me."

"And what makes you say that?"

"Cause you and me, Marques, we're on the same wavelength. You said you and Angélica want out, right? But you know that leaving now, out of the blue, would be a huge mistake. You'd be back to square one. Back to the grind. The truth is that things are good now for one reason: the weed. So, what's next? You save up a chunk of money. You invest it in something that lets you live as comfortably as you do now, except without breaking the law. Cool. That means we both got the same goal. The only difference is I wanna get there one way and you wanna get there another. What we have is different strategies. Does that make sense? I don't wanna sell weed in the store for the fun of it. It's all part of a master plan. Pushing weed in here is gonna help us leave this shit behind once and for all."

Only then did Marques show interest in Pedro's idea.

"Alright. Tell me how it's gonna work."

"Cool. First thing's first. How much money do you and Angélica wanna set aside before you bow out? Better yet: How *long* do you think it'd take to save up enough money?"

"Fuck if I know! A while."

"Sure, okay, the exact timeline don't matter. Let's call it a year. Does that sound right? A year's worth of socking away money so you can move on to greener pastures. Now, what if I told you we could make that same money in four months. In *a third* of the time. How does that sound? You said you and Angélica were worried and stuff, right? How did you put it? 'The nagging feeling that everything will come crashing down at any minute.' Did I get it right? So, Marques, my question is: You wanna feel that way for X time, or for *a third* of X? You wanna feel that way for a year, or four months? For two years, or eight months?" Pedro smiled. "You don't have to tell me 'feet, don't fail me now,' Marques. I'm the one saying 'feet, don't fail me now!' Let's wash our hands of this shit. Let's get out of here stat. Here's the thing: the fastest route from A to B is selling weed in the store. And I'll tell you why. If we move our product here, we'll be bringing in three times more money."

Marques was now taking the idea into serious consideration.

"*Three times more?* Are you sure?"

"No, I'm not sure. It's an educated guess. Three times more money. I swear I'm not just saying that to convince you. But that's all it is. You still believe in my educated guesses?"

"Man, that's a lot of money . . ."

"It is. And that's exactly what I'm getting at: *money, lots of it.* Besides, the plan I've come up with couldn't be more airtight. It's like I said before: the bridge has got to be sturdy, and I've made sure it is." Seeing how contemplative his friend looked, lips pressed between thumb and index finger, Pedro opened his arms. "What's up, man? Are you ready to speed things up so we can leave all this behind ASAP? Feet, don't fail me now?"

Marques slowly nodded:

"Feet, don't fail me now."

"Très bien!"

"Très bien, my ass. Tell me the fucking plan already."

Pedro laughed, then immediately explained what he had in mind.

15

AT THE WATER
PARK, AGAIN

Sr. Geraldo gave Marques and Pedro a couple of days off, again. There was an opportunity for them to grow their business, again. The gang met at the water park in the outskirts of Porto Alegre, again. It was March 28, 2010, and the day unfolded in a persistent déjà vu.

This time Roberto brought his wife and kids, and Luan brought Larissa, his favorite concubine. Morning and lunch were reserved for fun and games. Then, once their hunger had been satisfied, and they'd enjoyed a few beers, several stories, and some laughs, it was finally time to get down to business. Roberto asked his wife to take the kids to play on the slides and Luan asked Larissa to go with them. The members of the gang sat on the edge of the pool with their feet in the water. Angélica pointed out that beer didn't mix with serious business, and everyone agreed, which is why they were drinking vodka caipirinhas. According to the water park rules, for the health and safety of the clientele, no alcohol was allowed near the pools, but Roberto found a work-around: he slipped five hundred reais to the individual tasked with roaming the park and telling people what they could and could not do.

Pedro quickly explained why they were all there that day. He and Marques were going to begin selling weed at the Fênix supermarket branch where they worked.

"Y'all gonna sling weed at the store?" Luan asked in alarm. He was the only one who seemed shocked. To the rest of them, the plan wasn't news. Pedro had already mentioned it to Roberto, and Marques had raised the issue with Angélica. "Y'all are outta your fucking minds!" Luan concluded.

"None of us is crazy," Pedro responded. "We got everything planned out."

"I still don't know how this is meant to work," Angélica said. "Marques only gave me a rough idea. He didn't say nothing about *how* y'all gonna do what y'all gonna do."

"Yeah, I don't know any of the details either," Roberto said.

"I'll get to that in a second," Pedro promised. "I wanna say something first." He sighed, shook his head, and stared into his caipirinha as though disillusioned by the crushed lime at the bottom of his glass. "Here's the deal, gang: it's time to stop. To let it all go. That's why me and Marques wanna sell weed at the store. Sure it'll be dangerous, like you wouldn't imagine. But it'll make us a lot of scratch too. A *shitload* of scratch. The idea is to set aside all the money we can, soon as we start selling there. Cause this is the final stage of our scheme."

"What d'you mean?" It was Luan again, still sounding alarmed. "You wanna shut down the operation?" He smiled, scanning the faces around him, but no one backed him up. "Dude, are you for real?" he insisted.

"Let Pedro say what he's gotta say, kid!" Roberto admonished.

Pedro nodded in thanks, but then stayed quiet a little longer: he looked genuinely upset about the crushed lime in his glass. Sighing again, he confessed:

"It won't be easy for me either, Luan. The honest truth is I'm *scared* of stopping. Even if I manage to pull together a chunk of money and invest it so I can live large without needing to sell pot, who's to say I won't end up in the same shitty situation as before all over again? What if I make a bad investment? What if the money runs out and I wind up broke again? I'm scared, man. But I can't let fear call the shots, yeah? I gotta do what I *know* needs doing. If I'd listened to my fear, I'd never have started selling weed in the first place. Before we did all this, I was scared. And here I am, scared again, cause I don't know what's gonna happen once I stop. But irregardless of my fears about the future, I *know* I've got to stop, Luan. Cause if I carry on like this, things can only end badly. I'm tired of knowing this kind of shit doesn't end well for guys who don't know when to call it quits. Get this through your head, kid: the game we're mixed up in is worse than roulette. Sure, roulette may not be good for folks who don't know when to stop, and keep on playing, over and over and over, but at least in roulette it's up to chance whether you win or lose. And chance doesn't want anybody getting screwed. Chance doesn't want. To chance, nothing matters: you can win, the dealer can win, it don't care. But it's different with the game we're playing. It's us against the world. The law says that people who do what we do get fucked. Cops are *paid* to find out what we're doing, then fuck us for doing it. Honest workers who want what we have but don't got the guts to do what we do, they wanna see us get fucked too. So if you add all that up, you'll see there's more forces against us than there are forces pulling for us to stay in the game. See what I mean? Think of all the money we already made, man! And we're gonna make a shitload more. But *we've got to quit* while we're ahead, before it's too late."

Luan wasn't convinced. He actually seemed more unsettled than before.

"Fuck me. Are you for real?" he asked again. He laughed dryly and shook his head, as though what Pedro had just said was the most ridiculous thing he had ever heard. "Listen up, let me tell y'all something my ma's always saying: I can't let others decide what's right and wrong. *I* get to decide what's right and what's wrong for me. And fuck if I think what I'm doing right now is wrong. That's why I don't wanna stop. Hear me out, Pedro: first off, dudes buy weed from us cause they want to. None of us is forcing nobody to buy our weed. Second, who said it ain't right to sell weed? Fuck anyone who thinks it's wrong! It's like I said: I get to decide what's right and wrong in my life, and since I don't see nothing wrong with selling weed, I'm gonna keep doing it. Sorry, man, but I think with my own head and nobody else's, so whatever thoughts you got or don't got about this, I don't give a damn."

Before Luan could finish, the others had already started weighing in, talking over each other in a confusing racket. But Angélica's voice rose above theirs, forcing the others to finally quiet down:

"Nah, now listen here, yes, yeah, sure, but listen, no, no, see, that's what I'm saying, come on, hear me out, listen to me, shut up, let me talk for fuck's sake! Now, Luan, this lesson your ma taught you, did she teach it to all them pigs out there too? I don't reckon she did. Cause they don't think with their own heads. Pigs are deaf and blind. You try and say everything you just told us to a pig and see if they care. Pigs think the law is right. They think everybody that moves drugs is a piece of shit, period. If a pig catches you selling weed, you think they'd give a fuck what your mama taught you? You'll be lucky if they cuff you and throw your ass in jail."

"You think I don't know that, Angélica?" Luan retorted. "I know this shit's crazy. But I didn't make the world, did I? If that's how the world works, then that's the world's problem, not mine."

"Damn straight it's your problem, kid!" Marques argued. "At the end of the day, it's you that gets fucked, not the world."

Luan smacked his lips.

"Alright, Marques, then answer me this: If this was slaveholding times—"

"Slaveholding times!" Roberto parroted. "Quit tripping, kid!"

"I mean it, Roberto! Are you saying that if this was slaveholding times I should've just laid down and accepted my lot, without kicking up a fuss or trying to escape, just cause the world was built that way? Fuck no! If I was born then, I'd be a marooning motherfucker! I'd run for the hills and murder an assload of white dudes! Or, maybe they'd murder me. Still, that's what I'd do, or try to do—run away and murder as many white motherfuckers as I can get my hands on."

"The two situations are completely different."

"Alright. What's the difference then, Pedro?"

"The difference, brother, is that in slaveholding times, if you didn't run, if you didn't fight back, if you lay down and accepted the world like it was, your life would've been hell. *Straight-up fire and brimstone.* The kind of hell you wouldn't believe. But that doesn't matter, Luan. Sure, in a way, by shutting down, we're giving in to the status quo, but before that happens, *each of us* is gonna have enough time to pull together three hundred, four hundred, five hundred K. Think of everything we could do with that kind of money. Think of the kind of lives we could build. We could start businesses or, like, invest the money some other way, and live quietly, comfortably, without having to bust our asses, without having to put up with anyone looking at us sideways. We could buy ourselves freedom and dignity. No way is that the same as accepting a lifetime of slavery. There's no comparison!"

"You can't make up your own mind, can you, man!" Luan said. "A second ago, you said you're scared of stopping in case you wind up back where you started, in a shitty situation; now you're saying that as soon as you stop, it'll be all sunshine and fucking rainbows!"

Pedro was surprised by Luan's acuity. He hadn't expected to be caught in an obvious contradiction. Without flinching, he explained:

"I *am* scared of stopping. After all, shit, I could wind up the same as I used to be: a fuck-up. Cool, I can admit that. But, when I stop, Luan, I'm gonna have something I never had before."

"What's that?"

"*A chance.* That's what. *A chance.* And not just a symbolic one either, the kind where they say 'this is your chance: grab your skateboard and go race those playboyzinhos in Tarumã in their souped-up wheels.' Nah, this is a *real* chance! I'm gonna have a souped-up car in the race too. And that's not nothing. Can things go wrong? Sure they can. But, hell, I gotta have some confidence in my ability to succeed, don't I? All my life I've complained about not having the money. I was always saying, 'Man, if I had money, ain't nothing and nobody could stop me.' Well, I've got the money. The money's right here. And I still have time to make more too. Now what? Now, all I want is to prove to the world, and to myself most of all, that I wasn't faking it. See what I'm saying? This is my chance to prove I was right all along. This is my chance to build a decent life for myself, within the law, cause this time I can pay for my ticket to respectability. This is my chance to *be somebody*, like my ma says. This is my chance to prove I'm capable. Right, cool, so hear me out: know what I'm gonna do when all this is over? I'm gonna take that money and use it to pay for school, buy myself the right to study in peace. The truth is I like learning. Here's the thing. I'm gonna go to school the way rich kids go to school. I'm gonna pay to study at the best college money can buy. And when I graduate, my dude, damn, you're not even ready for this. When I graduate I'm gonna get a job in Europe, in the United States, you name it. Folks are gonna call me Dr. Pedro. When I walk into a room, the whole place will go quiet, cause Big Daddy's in the house, and everybody's gonna rush over to suck my balls. But that's *my* dream, yeah? We each got our own dreams. And whatever your dream is, you can make it come true. You're gonna make the money you need to make it come true. Alright? Go on, tell me, what's your dream? How d'you feel about making money to do something you enjoy, shit you'd do for free? The sky's the limit with the kind of money we're gonna rake in! You could be a porn star if you wanted, get paid to tap ass all day. How does that sound? Don't tell me you're not interested in getting paid to blow your load?"

Pedro's speech had gone from serious to farcical at breakneck speed. Everyone, even Pedro, had been in hysterics from the moment he called himself Big Daddy. Luan had to make a concerted effort to stop laughing so he could say something.

"Nah, man. I mean it. I'm living my dream. For real, I don't wanna quit."

Realizing there would be no dissuading him, Pedro wound his arm around Luan's neck and pulled him close, in a quasi-rear naked choke hold.

"I love you like crazy, Chokito. Hold up, hold up, it's not Chokito anymore, is it? It's Sheik now, right? Yeah, Sheik, well. I love you like crazy, Sheik! I just wanted to give you a heads-up is all. Alright?" Pedro let go of Luan and patted him on the shoulder. "If you wanna keep at it, be my guest. I'll talk to Fabrício, put in a good word. But here's the deal: *I'm* bowing out soon as I've scraped together a nice chunk of bread, cause I got plans, I got wild dreams, and for the first time in my life, I feel like things could work out for me. Honest, I think you're on your own, man. I reckon the rest of the gang's with me. We all wanna jump ship . . ."

Angélica, Marques, and Roberto quickly corroborated Pedro's statement, all at the same time.

"That's right!"

"Damn straight!"

"No doubt!"

Luan shrugged indifferently.

"To each his own. What I want is for y'all to explode and for my dick to grow."

"Right, right, that's enough of that!" Angélica said, losing patience. "So, Pedro, when're you and Marques gonna start selling at the store?"

Pedro stopped laughing and pursed his lips.

"Now there, my friend, is the rub. I been racking my brain for a while, and I still can't figure out how to get started. There's a decent customer base out there ready to fork over twenty reais for a one-gram baggie of grass, that much I know; the issue is figuring out how to lure them in. We can't exactly run an ad in the paper."

"Good thing that problem ain't long-term," Roberto said.

"What d'you mean?" Marques asked.

"Well, soon as you find a way of getting weed into the hands of a couple of playboyzinhos, they'll spread the news to their little pals, who will tell their little pals, and so on. Your customer base is gonna multiply all on its own; the only real trouble is getting started."

Their glasses had been empty for a few minutes.

"Alright, who's gonna top us up?"

"Let's see if your ho can help us out," Pedro suggested, in reference to Luan's concubine.

"Listen here, dude. First off, your grandma's the ho," he retorted, and everyone laughed. "Second, I didn't invite Larissa here to wait on us."

"She won't mind," Angélica said. "She's a nice, obliging girl."

Marques had an idea.

"Why don't we see just how obliging she is, then? Here's what you do, Luan. Call her over and say you're gonna go top us up, then ask if she wants a top-up too. If she offers to get the caipirinhas instead, then you let her."

"Sure, but what if she doesn't?"

"Then you go yourself, man."

Everyone laughed again.

"Alright, let's give it a shot." Luan cupped his hands around his mouth. "Larissa! Larissa, come here a sec!"

Larissa was on the other side of the pool with Roberto's wife and kids; hearing her name, she jumped into the water and gracefully swam up to Luan.

"Sup, babe?" She smiled after surfacing at his feet, on the edge of the pool.

"I'm gonna go grab us some more caipirinhas. Want one?"

"Nah, thanks, though. It's hard to drink on the slides. But lemme grab them for you." Larissa got out of the pool, picked up the five empty plastic cups, and slinked away, hips swinging side to side. She had a peculiar, exaggerated sway when she walked, but it suited her.

"See how obliging she is?" Angélica said.

"Cool. Now, where were we?" Marques asked.

"Roberto was telling us about how the news of y'all selling weed in the store will spread like wildfire soon as you find your first playboyzinho," Luan reminded everyone. "Honest, if you ask me, that sounds more dangerous than helpful. What if some shithead decides to turn y'all in?"

"It ain't likely, if you think about it," Pedro said. "Y'all remember Operation Witchcraft? Everybody that knew about Operation Witchcraft wanted to keep stealing from the store in peace, right?

Nobody wanted Seu Geraldo finding out and putting an end to it. So, *all of us* were real careful about who we chose to tip off. We only told folks we knew for sure wouldn't spill. It's gonna be the same when we start selling grass in the store. Our daddy-boy clientele won't be the least bit inclined to share their little secret with anybody they think will run their mouth."

"Alright, now tell us about the plan," Angélica asked. "How's it supposed to go?"

"Right, yeah, sure," Pedro said, realizing he had yet to explain how the plan would work. "Honest, it's real simple. First off, we hide the weed in a corner of the stockroom—"

"Huh?" Roberto asked. "What if somebody finds it?"

"Don't worry, man, not gonna happen," Marques reassured him. "You never worked there, but the stockroom is crazy fucking huge. There's loads of places to stash weed. No way anybody would find it."

"That's right," Luan said.

"Second," Pedro continued, "we'll have a code. Our customers will come in and find Marques or me in one of the aisles and ask if there's any tea. In response, we'll say, 'Well, what kind of tea you want?' Then, if they say, 'The smoky kind,' we'll know they're really after weed."

"Why put them through all that?" Luan asked.

"Call it an abundance of caution. Like, say some player asks another employee that isn't me or Marques. Since they don't know a thing, they take the customer to the tea aisle, which is when the player realizes he asked the wrong guy."

"Clever," Angélica said in admiration.

Larissa was back with the beverages. She held her arm in an L-shape, all five cups nestled between her arm and torso. With her free hand, she deftly passed out the caipirinhas one by one. She must have worked at a bar, Pedro thought.

After responding to all of their thanks in the same way ("my plezh"), Larissa left to join Roberto's wife and two kids. Roberto took a sip of his caipirinha, then asked:

"Alright, Pedro, but what if, even though, like you said, it ain't likely, what if some fool turns y'all in anyway?"

Pedro shrugged.

"I guess we get thrown in jail."

Angélica looked frightened.

"And you're saying it just like that, like it's no big deal."

Pedro sighed.

"Angélica, what if the cops catch you selling weed in Lupicínio, or Roberto selling in Pinheiro, or Luan selling in Planetário? That could happen too, couldn't it? All three of you are putting your necks on the line. Now me and Marques will too. But chill, there's no reason to worry."

"Chill . . ." Roberto murmured. "When the cops investigate a gang and start arresting dudes right, left, and center, that's what they're usually doing: chilling. In fact, y'all ever considered they might be investigating us right now? Or better yet: y'all ever considered that a bunch of pigs could storm the water park right this minute and take us downtown?"

Everyone laughed.

"They wouldn't arrest Pedro or me cause we're not deadbeats," Marques joked. "We're the only ones here with full-time j-o-bs. You, Roberto, are slinging weed in Pinheiro; you, Luan, are slinging weed in Planetário; and you, my love, are selling that shit in Lupicínio. The three of y'all might get screwed, but Pedro and me? We're golden. We've got jobs and shit, our papers in order."

"You're right about that, Marques!" Pedro laughed. "I'd even psych them up: 'Take them away, Mr. Officer, go on, take them! They're all just a bunch of deadbeats anyway.'"

"Sure. Except then they'd want to know why you fools hanging out with three deadbeats like us," Luan observed.

"Now, Officer," said Marques, "we're just chilling, knocking back some caipiras, soaking up some of that sweet sunshine, cooling our feet in the water . . . Now who doesn't love a bit of that? But drug dealing? Never! I can even show you my signed work card if you want. I'm a motherfucking supermarket stocker, facilitating access to the merchandise."

Roberto smacked his lips.

"Bitch, please. Stocker, drug dealer, it's all the same at the end of the day. You organize products, we sling it. You stock shelves, we stock people. We're giving half the dopeheads in Porto Alegre access to our merchandise."

Everyone laughed again, and Angélica immediately raised her glass for a toast.

"To the stockers of Porto Alegre!"

16

THE RULE-BREAKERS

More than a month had passed since they'd met at the water park, and Pedro and Marques had not yet started selling weed at the supermarket. So, on the evening of Saturday, May 8, 2010, after another hard day's work behind those sliding doors, the two men clocked out and went into the street. It was mid-fall, which meant that a hot night like that one might be the last of the year, until summer came around again in December.

"I can't put up with another day in this shithouse," Marques said.

"Yeah, I'm not loving it either," Pedro said. "But things are gonna change, soon as we move our business in there. We just gotta find our first customer—" Pedro fell quiet and sniffed the air. "Hmmm, fragrant. You smell what I'm smelling?"

"No shit," Marques said, glancing around with a look of disgust on his face. "The stink's coming from over there."

Pedro turned to face the direction Marques was pointing. About ten to twenty meters from where they stood, beneath a couple of trees in the square, was a small, incandescent dot.

"Hmm!" Pedro said, pulling a crumpled pack of cigarettes from his pocket. "Looks like it's our lucky day, Marques. I've got one last cig left."

"Lucky? Why lucky?"

"Come with me, I'll show you."

They walked into the twilight. As they drew closer, their eyes adjusted to the darkness, allowing them to make out the scene: the incandescent dot was actually an ember glowing at the end of a joint nestled between the fingers of a young woman standing next to another young woman. The two were having an animated conversation by one of the chess tables in the square, but instead of sitting on a bench, they were each mounted on a bicycle. When they saw Pedro and Marques approaching, they fell quiet. With his last cigarette in his hand, Pedro crushed the packet, and tossed it out.

"Lemme borrow that cherry to light my cig."

Marques knew Pedro had a lighter in his pocket and almost laughed at how easily he pretended otherwise, but he managed to contain himself.

The woman with the joint wordlessly reached out her free hand and offered her lighter to Pedro, who in turn lit his cigarette, then returned the lighter and thanked her. Instead of leaving, he smiled shyly, nodded and stared at the woman a bit longer, clearly wanting to make conversation. Finally, he asked:

"What about that joint?"

"What about it," she said in a tone that was both serious and maybe a little bored.

"You gonna give us a toke or what?" Pedro asked.

The woman coldly turned to her friend, who was clearly struggling to keep a straight face. Then she looked back at Pedro, and started bargaining:

"Alright. Trade you for a cigarette."

Pedro cocked his eyebrows and smiled.

"Fair enough," he agreed, holding out the just-lit cigarette. "But it'll have to be this one; it's my last."

The woman rolled her eyes and smiled for the first time. It was a pretty sour smile. She grudgingly accepted the cigarette in exchange for the joint. Pedro took a drag and blew out smoke from his nostrils with an exaggerated sigh of satisfaction. Then he spoke to Marques, though he made sure the two women heard what he said:

"Wanna know what I think, cuz? I think our lady friend over here has her own cigarettes. Now let me walk you through my reasoning. *I bet* she only asked me for a smoke cause she saw me tossing out an empty pack. She knew the cigarette I'd just lit was my last and figured I'd back down if she asked me for it. Or, hell, maybe she wanted tit for tat. But what matters is that I'm pretty sure she's got her own cigs. And she *still* asked me for my last one, man."

This time the smile on the girl's face betrayed some amusement. She quietly pulled a pack of cigarettes out of her pocket and set it on the chess table, proving Pedro's point.

"Ladies and gentleman, I think that's a checkmate!" Pedro joked.

"Is that right, wise guy?" the young woman asked. Then she looked at her friend and said: "Want to know what I think, Nanda? I think this gentleman over here has his own lighter. Now let me walk you through my reasoning. See, I think he smelled the weed from all the way over there and then *pretended* he needed a light, just so he could be smooth and have a reason to come over. When all he really wanted was a toke."

Pedro laughed and looked over at Marques.

"Damn, cuz. She's good! Real good." He pulled a lighter from his pocket and set it on the table.

This time it was her turn to joke.

"Ladies and gentlemen, I think that's a checkmate!"

Pedro sat on one of the benches near the table; Marques sat on the other. They introduced themselves, shaking hands. Their names were Pâmela and Fernanda.

"Where'd you get that stick from?" Marques asked.

"Hunh?" Pâmela queried.

"Where y'all get it, who'd you buy it from?"

"Right, I see. Some guy in Parque Redenção sold it to us."

"And d'you always buy from the same guy?" Pedro asked.

"No. We don't even really know who he is," Fernanda answered. "He was the one who approached us. Asshole fleeced us too."

"How much?"

"Fifty."

Marques was shocked.

"*Fifty?*"

"That's right."

"For how much weed?"

"For the weed in that joint."

"Right. And y'all didn't complain or nothing?"

"Are you saying we should have stood there arguing with some drug dealer in the middle of the park? We know he ripped us off, we're not stupid. We just wanted to buy the weed and get out of there. Besides, fifty reais isn't, like, a fortune or anything."

Pedro and Marques glanced at each other in silence. Then, Pâmela asked:

"You guys work at the grocery store, right?"

"Yeah, you can relax," Marques said in a somewhat disdainful tone.

"What do you mean 'you can relax'?"

"I bet your folks warned you not to talk to strangers."

"Specially at night."

"But," Marques continued, "now that y'all know we work at the grocery store, you can relax. We're not thugs."

Fernanda let out a small, mischievous laugh.

"You think we give a damn what our parents say? If it was up to them, I'd never have gotten my first tattoo." She turned her head to show them a small rose on the side of her neck. "Let's just say we like to break the rules."

"Then it looks like we're four peas in a pod," Pedro said, passing her the joint.

"Looks like it," Pâmela agreed. "Our parents are always telling us that drugs are, like, bad for you or whatever, blah-blah, but look at us here smoking up together."

"Speak for yourselves. *I* ain't touching that crap," Marques said. "I can't even stand the fucking smell."

"Then maybe you shouldn't be here," Fernanda shot back.

Marques gave her a piercing look.

"No, actually. I think I'm exactly where I need to be."

The young woman smiled, a little embarrassed, while also appearing to enjoy the way he looked at her.

"I couldn't agree more, brother," Pedro said, trying the same tactic on Pâmela. "No place I'd rather be."

Pâmela wasn't as easy to win over as her friend.

"No shit, what better place than smoking other people's weed . . ."

Pedro's jaw dropped in shock.

"You didn't. Y'all, she didn't just say what I think she said, did she?"

The four of them laughed.

"Relax, she didn't mean anything by it," Fernanda said, coming to her friend's defense. "We just tell it like it is."

"It's cool to tell it like it is or whatever. The problem is your friend here's accusing me of being opportunistic when I'm not!"

"Please. You're only here because you wanted a toke on that joint," Pâmela insisted.

"Damn, girl. You're hurting my feelings. I'm not here cause of the joint, okay? Me and my buddy just wanted to come over for a chat, to get to know each other and see how we got on."

"Oh, sure, whatever."

"Alright, alright. What would you give me if I proved I'm not here for the weed?"

Pâmela laughed dryly.

"There's no way you can prove that!"

"If there's no way I can prove it, then there's no reason for you not to take the bet, right?"

She thought for a second, then asked her friend:

"What do you think, Nanda?"

Fernanda shrugged.

"He's right, Pam. If you don't think he can prove he isn't here for the weed, then you should take the bet."

"Hell of a friend you are!" Pâmela thought for a moment and then, having decided to take the gamble, turned to Pedro and said, "Okay: prove you didn't come all this way just to smoke our weed and me and Nanda will stick around and hang out with you guys a little. But if I'm not convinced, and I know I won't be, then we leave."

"You're on," Pedro said. He shook Pâmela's hand to seal the deal, then pulled a fistful of weed baggies from his pocket and dumped them on the chess table. "And that, ladies and gentlemen, is checkmate!"

"You asshole!" Pâmela said as she picked up one of the baggies and smelled it.

"That's right, beautiful. As you can see, I've got more grass than I need. Now does the lady still think we're only here to smoke y'all's joint?"

A few minutes ago, the giant smile dimpling Pâmela's cheeks would have seemed impossible.

"Alright, wise guy. You win. Happy now?"

"Yep. Damn straight I am. But only cause you're smiling so big. You're beautiful when you smile, you know that? Much prettier than when you're all . . ." Pedro copied her, holding his body stiff and upright as he jiggled his shoulders and scowled.

"You're such a clown! That's not what I look like."

As she said this, Pâmela gently slapped Pedro on the shoulder and let her fingers slide five centimeters or so down his arm. The gesture lasted somewhere between a half second and a whole second, just long enough that there was no way of telling if it had been accidental or premeditated. All the same, Pedro was inclined to think it'd been an accident; he'd misread women more times than he liked to remember, but somehow he doubted Pâmela, innocent as she seemed, was slick enough to pull off such a subtle move. This thought led him to ask a question that was more like a confirmation:

"You girls underage?"

Fernanda and Pâmela nodded.

"And your folks still let you ride round on your bikes this late at night?" Marques queried.

Pâmela was the one holding the joint now. Blowing out smoke, she said:

"No. They think we're at a friend's house."

Fernanda quickly elaborated.

"See, me and Pam live in the same building in Bom Fim. One of our neighbors moved to Cidade Baixa last year. Sometimes we sleep over at her new house. Other times we *pretend* to sleep over. When we *pretend*, what we actually do is go out on our bikes in the evening and just ride around."

Pedro was impressed.

"Wait, you're telling me you're gonna ride your bikes until *tomorrow morning* just so your folks think y'all sleeping over at your friend's place?"

Pâmela pursed her lips.

"Uh, no, duh! We always tell our parents that if we change our minds and decide we don't want to sleep at our friend's anymore, we'll come home. If it's dark out, we leave our bikes and take a cab back. See? That way we can bike around for a bit while our parents think we're safe and sound at our friend's place. Then we just go home and tell them we didn't feel like sleeping over."

Marques was confused.

"Hold up. What about the bikes? Far as anyone knows, y'all are at your friend's place, right? You decide not to sleep over, so you leave your bikes and take a cab. But *where* do the bikes go?"

"Our building has this underground bicycle garage," Fernanda explained. "So before we go up to our apartments, we leave the bikes down there. Our parents never check. Then the next day, or any day really, we tell them we're going out to get our bikes from our friend's and then kill time around town."

Pedro clapped.

"Damn, that's impressive! See, Marques, they really are rebels."

Marques laughed.

"Dunno, man. I still got my doubts . . ."

"How come?"

Marques shifted in his seat, clearly excited about what he was going to say.

"Let me ask you something. When y'all stay over at your friend's, like, for real, what time do you get home?"

"Depends . . . like, ten in the morning, give or take . . . But then sometimes we don't go home until the afternoon."

"Cool, cool. Well, seeing as y'all are *pretending* to be there tonight, why not go all the way?"

"What do you mean?"

"It's simple. 'Stead of going home tonight, y'all can *pretend* you slept over at your friend's place and go home tomorrow."

Pedro slapped his forehead.

"Now that's an idea!"

Pâmela was somewhere between excited and appalled, eyes wide open and mouth ajar.

"Are you guys inviting us to hang out with you tonight?"

"Yeah! Why the hell not?" Pedro asked. "We just gotta swing by your house and drop off the bikes. Then we can go out and have a good time, maybe hit a flea trap downtown. Bet y'all never been to one before."

"You're crazy!"

Marques smacked his lips.

"Well then don't act like you're rebellious and shit, if that's as rebellious as you're willing to get."

"A bit of reverse psychology, hunh? Nice try, asshole. It won't work on us."

"Nah. I'm just telling it like it is. That's some half-assed rebelliousness there."

"What're you two afraid of, for real?" Pedro insisted. "We're just gonna dance, drink, have a laugh. C'mon, it'll be dope!"

"No one here is afraid," Pâmela said. "It's a dumb idea, that's all. We're underage, or did you forget? I don't know what a flea trap is, but I doubt they'd let Nanda and me in."

Pedro sighed and looked at her dreamily, like a man picturing himself wandering through the most astonishing landscapes.

"Listen, if that's what y'all are really worried about, then don't worry. Relax, we'll get you in, no biggie. I give you my word. Okay? And I promise you this too: it's gonna be an awesome fucking time."

Pâmela and Fernanda went with them. Fun was had. Time flew by. The young women were surprised to discover that a flea trap was just a late-night dive, and there was nothing glamorous about it. But since glamour is too fine a detail to shine through the haze of alcohol, it wasn't long before they couldn't tell that hole in the wall from Buckingham Palace. Soon Marques and Pedro were as drunk as Pâmela and Fernanda, and just as blind to the particulars. They were surprised to find that the two women contained multitudes beyond the label of "spoiled princesses": they were *people*, with all the messiness that implied. This realization led Pedro to declare, slurring:

"That stupid poet was right all along: in a bar, everybody is equal!" Pedro raised his glass, proposing a toast: "To *Ressinaldo Rogi*!"

The following morning, when he got home, Marques thanked God that Angélica was still fast asleep. Though he knew he'd have to explain himself sooner or later, he wanted to get some rest first. If he slept on the couch instead of the bed, he could minimize any danger of waking up his wife. But this precaution turned out to be moot: woken by the sound of the shower, Angélica got out of bed and went straight to the bathroom, where she caught her husband soaping his underarms.

"You scared the hell out of me, Angélica. Fuck!" Marques exclaimed when he saw his wife planted in the doorway with her arms crossed over her chest and a grim look on her face.

"Where you been, Marques?"

Marques held up his hand.

"Relax, yeah? I was out with Hangman. That's all."

"That right? You, Hangman, and who else?"

"Us two and some players we met outside Fênix last night."

"Hmm . . . Why was your phone off?"

"Battery died."

"Hmm . . . You, Hangman, and a couple of players you met outside Fênix . . ."

"That's what I said."

"Hmm . . . You're not sleeping around on me, are you, you piece of shit?"

"Nah, babe! Come on. Quit tripping."

"You're not, hunh? Then how come your nuts all sad and droopy? Marques, Marques, Marques . . . That there is the ball sack of a guy who spent all night boning . . ."

As Marques justified the flaccidity of his testicles to his wife, Pâmela and Fernanda were in the back of a taxicab making their way home.

"That was totally crazy, Nanda!" Pâmela said, smiling. "My parents would kill me if they found out."

"Yours? What about mine! It would be so much worse than when I got that tattoo, and I'm still paying for it. You know what, though?" Fernanda grinned and shook her head. "I don't regret it."

"Me neither. It was so amazing. Did you see all that money they were throwing around?"

"Uh, duh! It cost them a grand just to bribe the bouncer to let us in."

The two young women paused. Then, careful not to be heard by the cabdriver, Pâmela whispered:

"So, like, Pedro told me how they made all that money . . ."

Also in a whisper, Fernanda said:

"Yeah, Marques told me too."

"Did he ask for your help as well?"

"Yeah."

They paused again.

"Cool. Are you going to do it?"

"I am. You?"

"Me too."

"Those guys are so crazy!"

"I mean, it's not, like, actually dangerous for them. Unless we talk to the wrong people . . ."

"True, true."

17

THE BEST-KEPT SECRET

Hey. Got any tea?"

"Depends on the tea."

"The smoky kind."

"How much?"

"Two baggies."

"Be right back. Meet me in the pasta aisle."

Some things only happen in Brazil, and the creativity of the Brazilian people knows no bounds. Newspapers and broadcasts are filled with priceless stories about crimes and criminals, and for every one of them, the police uncover hundreds of others that never make the news, either because there isn't enough print space or airtime. Sometimes, in this circus show, the magician isn't just another clown; sometimes, the trick actually works. What about the quiet citizen who grew up without a father and inherited no money, but still lives mysteriously well? There are plenty of questionable people and circumstances out there, something fishy stinking up every corner. It's more than the cops could look into even if they wanted. In Brazil, a magician of this sort turns up every five seconds: it could be the owner of the newsstand who was in financial distress just yesterday but managed to pull a car out of his thin air earlier today; or the salaried employee who gave his notice out of the blue and went to spend some time in Fernando de Noronha. We all scratch our heads at these kinds of people, and that's the only thing we can do, really. We know they have something up their sleeve. The question is what.

Pedro and Marques's own trick was firing on all cylinders. By the looks of it, Pâmela and Fernanda knew every pot-smoking daddy's boy in Porto Alegre, and dozens of kids had started showing up at the supermarket for tea. Everything was peachy; the clientele was satisfied; the quality of the weed received constant praise; and no one whined about the price. And since there was only enough weed in each baggie for a single joint, it wasn't long before the same customers came back for more. Many stopped by the supermarket three or four times a day, while others bought three or four baggies at once to avoid having to return so soon. And, on top of all that, there was the delivery service Pâmela and Fernanda had set up.

As previously mentioned, the two young women lived in the same building in Bom Fim. However, they each studied at different schools—both private, both renowned, both chock-a-block with girls and boys looking for a reason to spend their allowances. Both schools had their fair share of so-called "occasional fiends," kids who didn't have a clue where to buy weed but liked—loved even—sending smoke signals whenever they were invited to by someone in the bad crowd; there were also the so-called "virgin lungs," who were tired of feeling awkward in conversations at lunch and couldn't wait to suck on their first joint. The issue was that most of this bunch lived nowhere near the branch of Fênix supermarkets that Pâmela and Fernanda directed them to. One fine day, the two young women showed up at the grocery store with two thousand reais. Muffling their childish laughter, they explained they were there on behalf of some of their customers, who couldn't come in person. From that day on, they arrived at the supermarket with more and more money and left with more and more weed. In exchange for moving the drugs, they were given as much free weed as their lungs could handle, on top, needless to say, of the thrill of breaking the rules and living dangerously; it was just the adrenaline they needed in their safe, comfortable lives. It didn't take long for Pâmela to adopt the nickname Four-Twenty at her school; Fernanda, for her part, went by Fernandinha Beira-Mar. Meanwhile, teachers in both schools couldn't make heads or tails of why half the student body had suddenly lost the ability to focus in class and laughed hysterically at every little thing. It was as if an outbreak of collective stupidity had struck both establishments.

Between the baggies of weed they sold in the supermarket and the ones Pâmela and Fernanda smuggled into their respective schools, Marques and Pedro were moving approximately two hundred grams of weed, at twenty reais a gram, every single day. In other words, they were bringing home an average of *four thousand* reais a day. Factoring in that they didn't work on Sundays, this meant they brought home *twenty-four thousand* reais a week, or upwards of *ninety thousand* reais a month, which didn't even include the money Luan, Roberto, and Angélica were still making in Planetário, Pinheiro, and Lupicínio. The gang continued to split the profit five ways, bringing home more money at the end of the week than they had ever dreamed of making in a month, never mind every seven days.

Just as Pedro had predicted, the Fênix drug-selling operation had a positive impact on the mood and outlook of the two stock clerks. At the end of the day, no job is too brutal to dampen the spirits of someone pocketing the kind of money they were pocketing. Besides, the more time passed, the more confident and relaxed the two men became. Back when moving product at the store was just an idea and their plan was based on conjecture alone, Marques and Pedro had prepared for dangers and setbacks that never materialized in real life. One of their many unnecessary concerns was that the scheme would draw suspicion. But as soon as the first few buyers started trickling into the store to ask for tea—a small fraction of the supermarket's countless customers—it became clear just how unlikely it was that the scheme would ever call attention to itself. Even so, everything was shrouded in the utmost secrecy. Not even Jorge, who'd given them Fabrício's number more than a year ago, knew what the two men were getting up to, right there under everyone's noses.

As for Jorge, his days at Fênix supermarket were numbered. On Tuesday, July 13, 2010, he surprised everyone by walking into Sr. Geraldo's small office and giving his notice: he'd found a better job and needed to leave right away. Just like that, from one moment to the next, without so much as a warning, Jorge withdrew from the supermarket's security team and started earning his livelihood with a 12-gauge shotgun in an armored car, or so said the handful of staff members who had the chance to say goodbye.

Robson, the man who replaced Jorge, arrived at the supermarket like an Energizer Bunny, armed with a clear objective: to collect as many prizes and employee-of-the-month titles as he could. As was to be expected, he did not make many friends. With every passing day, Robson's herculean efforts to ensure Sr. Geraldo's large hands always had a reason to pat him on the back made it more and more difficult for the other employees to put up with him. And even though there was no love lost between the stock clerk and the new security guard, sometimes Pedro felt bad seeing Robson so isolated and tried making conversation with him.

"Why d'you give that jackass the time of day?" Marques asked.

"I put myself in his shoes," Pedro quickly answered. "I mean, shit, picture having to spend eight hours a day in a place where *nobody* likes you, man. Picture sitting down in the cafeteria and having everybody move as far away from you as they can get. I'd hate it if people treated me like that, for real. That's why I don't, even though I'm no fan of the dude either."

"Right, yeah, sorry. I forgot you like to play devil's advocate." Marques pursed his lips. "Get over it, man. Ain't none of us crazy. Ain't none of us start treating him like shit for no reason. Hell, it's like the fucker went and swallowed *Ass-Kissing for Dummies*! He's a douchebag." Marques held up his hands and started counting off Robson's flaws. "Phony, ass-kisser, rat, smug, always in the right. Have you ever met a bigger douchebag?"

All the same, the security guard did have some qualities, one of which was his acumen, as Marques would find out firsthand that Thursday, August 19, 2010.

After telling a young woman to wait in the pasta aisle while he fetched her two baggies of tea, Marques went to the stockroom. What he didn't know, nor could have imagined, was that Robson had seen him slip away to the stockroom multiple times that day and decided to keep a close eye on him, following Marques wherever he went, as though minding his own business. Thinking he was alone, Marques squeezed into the space under the stairs to the locker room, crouched, and slid his hand beneath a pallet of washing powder. The second he pulled out the half-full grocery bag, it was snatched from his hands.

"What have we got here!" the security guard said, untying the handles to look inside.

Marques reacted just as you would expect, given his explosive temper. Standing up, he opened his mouth to say something, only to abandon all words, snarl like a rabid animal, and punch the security guard in the corner of the mouth. Stunned by the blow,

Robson teetered from one leg to the other, then fell onto an empty pallet, dropping the bag of weed. Marques charged at him, then lifted his foot intending to bring it down on Robson's neck. But the security guard recoiled just in time, a knee-jerk reaction that saved him from a potentially fatal blow: grazing the security's head, Marques's foot wedged itself between the slats of the wood pallet. Realizing what happened, Robson grabbed the grocery bag, jumped to his feet, and fled.

"Get back here, you asshole! Fucking coward! When I get my hands on you!"

As soon as he managed to release his foot, Marques tore after the security guard. He barreled through the double doors and crashed right into Pedro, who was on his way into the stockroom, sending both of them onto the floor. The customers spoke in hushed voices and parked their shopping carts to rubberneck.

"What's up, Marques?"

Pedro had just crossed paths with Robson, and although he had no idea what had happened, he thought it best not to let Marques go after the security guard and finish what had clearly already begun, judging by the blood around the security guard's mouth. He grabbed Marques and dragged him back into the stockroom.

"Marques, what's up?" he asked. "What's going on, cuz?"

"That piece of shit . . ." Then, realizing he was speaking too loudly, Marques quickly lowered his voice. "That piece-of-shit Robson has our weed!"

"What!"

"You heard me! He's got our weed! You walked right past him, man. Didn't you see him with the bag?"

"Fuckfuckfuck! How'd he find it?"

"He followed me into the stockroom, then snatched the bag right out of my hands."

"And what were you doing with the fucking bag?"

"What do you think I was fucking doing? I was getting weed for a customer. I bet she's still waiting in the pasta aisle. But who gives a shit! Robson's probably ratting us out to Sr. Geraldo right this second. We're screwed!"

An icy feeling that could not be chalked up to the store's temperature took hold of them, hearts pounding with such force they seemed likely to burst through their chests. But Pedro had an idea.

"Alright, here's what we do. Follow me. C'mon, keep up. We're gonna tell the girl in the pasta aisle to come back later."

As they rushed to the pasta aisle, Marques asked:

"But what about Robson and Sr. Geraldo?"

"It's cool. Don't sweat it, everything's under control."

"Nothing's under fucking control, Pedro! Fuck. I don't think you realize how much shit we're in."

"What's your problem, Marques? You wanna bail now? I'm telling you everything's gonna be cool, so trust me. Stand tall, brother, we're gonna get out of this. Today's the day we lay our cards on the table, Marques, that's all. And you know what I think? I think the game's still on, and we're still in it."

"What the hell are you talking about?"

"Don't worry. It'll all become clear soon. What you need to know is that we're about to have a little face-to-face with Seu Geraldo: you, me, and him. You don't have to say nothing if you don't want. Leave it to me. Just trust, Marques, trust."

After asking the smoky-tea customer to come back later, Marques and Pedro started heading down the pasta aisle, only to come to a sudden stop. Further ahead, walking in the opposite direction, was Sr. Geraldo, scowling, the bag of weed in his hand. On his heels, Robson hunched to whisper something in the ear of the manager, who was considerably shorter. Suddenly, the security guard moved his arm as if punching something, perhaps informing Sr. Geraldo about the blow he had gotten to the mouth.

"I'm gonna murder that fucking asshole!" Marques swore with a malicious smile.

"Whoa there, Marques," Pedro said. "Everything's under control, remember? Cool it, yeah? Loosen up."

Sr. Geraldo whispered, then sent Robson away with a nod of the head. Ever the obedient employee, and subservient as a butler, the security guard turned on his heels and left. A few more steps and the manager was beside the stock clerks.

"Marques, could I have a word with you in my office?"

Pedro cleared his throat.

"I think I should come along too, if that's alright, Seu Geraldo," he said, inviting himself. Seeing the curious look on the manager's face, Pedro smiled and explained, "See, that bag you've got in your hands doesn't just belong to Marques; it belongs to me too."

Sr. Geraldo smiled as if he had just found the missing piece to the puzzle.

"Of course! It all makes sense. I don't know why I didn't think of it myself. I guess you should come along too then."

There were only two chairs in the manager's small office, so Sr. Geraldo told the stock clerks to sit down and hovered over them.

"Can one of you please explain what this bag of cannabis was doing under a pallet in my stockroom?" Sr. Geraldo dropped the bag on the desk, next to his computer monitor. The manager looked triumphant. The two reprobates had finally been exposed; he could barely contain his satisfaction. It wouldn't be long before they discovered what happens when you step out of line. At the same time, he was sorry he had to fire them—they stocked shelves better than anyone. At least it was winter, the best time of year to recruit new staff. He continued, a bit sadistically: "Now I know where all the money you spend at the store is coming from. I'm right, aren't I? Unbelievable. But there's one thing I haven't decided yet: if I should fire you both for just cause and call it a day, or turn you in to the police too?"

Pedro sighed.

"Listen, Seu Geraldo, I think you need to know something before you make any big decisions."

"Is that right?" the manager smiled. "And what is it you think I need to know? Go on, tell me."

"See, if I'm honest, sir, Marques and me don't really wanna stop working here. Let alone go to prison. You've figured out how we make our money. Now you don't have to be a genius to realize we can't let you end things, yeah? Not after everything we've sacrificed. Not without payback."

"Are you threatening me?"

Pedro, who had been leaning forward, threw his body back against the chair, placed his right arm on the table, and smiled.

"Am I threatening you, sir?" He grew serious again. "Here's the deal: we've got no intention of fucking you over, Sr. Geraldo, if that's what you're asking. Truth is we'd have nothing to gain. But, if there's one thing you can be sure of, sir, it's this: If you fuck with us, nothing would make us happier than to fuck you back big-time. It's only fair, don't you think?"

Sr. Geraldo remained impassive. He ignored Pedro's threat with British sangfroid and opened the door.

"Get out of my office, go home, and bring in your employment cards tomorrow." Pedro tried to say something, but Sr. Geraldo wouldn't hear another word. He just kept repeating, mechanically: "Get out of my office, go home, and bring in your employment cards tomorrow. Get out of my office, go home, and bring in your employment cards tomorrow. Get out of my office, go home, and bring in your employment cards tomorrow."

When Pedro finally had enough, he slammed his hand on the desk.

"Alright, show's over! Now shut the fucking door, you rotten piece of shit!"

Unlike Pedro, Marques wasn't skilled at psychological warfare, which is why he stayed quiet. But when it came to thickening the soup, he was your man. He leapt out of his seat and kicked the door shut, then grabbed the manager by the shirt collar and tossed him like a garbage bag into the empty chair.

Pedro enjoyed the effect this had on Sr. Geraldo. Quite a bit, to be honest. The glimmer of fear and madness in the manager's eyes, the fact that he didn't know where to look or what his two employees were capable of. Marques's actions had helped Pedro see the obvious: words were no longer enough. Wanting to ensure Sr. Geraldo's undivided attention, Pedro decided to take a page out of Marques's book and slap the manager around a little, using every bit of strength he could muster. Then, a second or so later, he said coolly:

"Believe me, you don't wanna play with us," Pedro said. "We don't play nice." That small office space was his. The whole supermarket was his. The world was his. Boundless power galloped through his veins. Colorless and unscented, the best-kept secret was his now too. A bracing realization swept through him, at once spicy and sweet: all he needed to get what we wanted was the right amount of cruelty. It was this realization that made him soar, certain he was the master of all: nothing was out of his reach because there was no amount of cruelty he wouldn't be willing to commit. He was finally free from his conscience.

Pedro's soul was beating, as though about to explode. He needed a smoke. He pulled out his pack of cigarettes, lit one, and offered it to the manager, who took it, perhaps out of fear of what might happen if he said no; then, he lit a cigarette for himself. "I get the sense you probably think I'm a bad person, all cause I knocked you around a bit. But if you turned me into the cops and the cops beat me black and blue, I reckon you wouldn't think you were a bad person, sir. Or would you? Who knows, maybe you'd even sleep more soundly feeling you'd done your duty. Ain't that wild? Well, turns out I can be that way too, I can be *just like you*. It wasn't easy, but I learned to, uh . . . you know, not be so hard on myself. I learned to forgive myself for everything. *Whatever it is*. Now I can turn a blind eye to the bad shit too. I'd have no problem killing and burying you somewhere nobody can find you. I'd even treat myself to lunch after, like it was nothing. I could end you, sir, then go to bed, convinced I'd done my duty." Pedro heaved a long sigh, smoke curling out of his nose. It was the best cigarette of his life. "So what I'm saying, sir, is this: If you decide to fuck with us, things are going to get ugly for you. You could have me locked up, Sr. Geraldo, and I'd still find a way to pay somebody on the outside to rape your wife, your children, and your dog. You got a dog? Never mind. See, now your house is on fire and everybody's inside it but you. You get to live. You get to live and spend *every last day* of your miserable life thinking about how your family was burned to a crisp when you could've stopped it. See what I'm saying? I got a load of money saved up and only I know where it's hidden. If I get locked up cause of you, nothing would make me happier than to spend all of it, *every last fucking cent*, to send a hurricane of misfortune through your life. Believe me: everything that could go wrong in your life will go wrong."

The manager opened his mouth, but no words came out. Pedro continued:

"Now wouldn't it be easier to just let sleeping dogs lie? All you'd have to do is pretend you ain't seen nothing, that nothing happened. That's it. Don't mess with us and we won't mess with you. Live and let live. How does that sound, hunh?"

"But there's no way . . ." Sr. Geraldo timidly replied. "Robson knows everything. He's the one who found the weed, remember?

I can't just stand idly by and pretend I don't know anything. If I don't do something, he'll go running to Amauri, which will just complicate matters."

Pedro laughed dryly.

"Ah, that's right! Good, old Robson. Don't worry about him, sir. In fact, you might wanna start looking for somebody to fill his position, cause starting tomorrow he won't be working at Fênix supermarkets no more." Following this mysterious pronouncement, Pedro took the bag of weed and stood up. "Let's bounce, Marques. I've said all I have to say to this prick. Let's give him some time to think about his life."

The stock clerks walked slowly and quietly out of the office, across the store, into the stock room, up the stairs, and into the locker room, where they sat across from one another in complete silence for approximately one minute. Then, they burst out laughing. They laughed harder and harder, and their laughter grew heartier and heartier as it bounced around the locker room, which was deserted at that time of day. Once they finally stopped, Pedro tossed the bag of weed at his friend and said:

"We gotta be more careful with this shit."

"Yeah," Marques frowned. "Hey, what was that stuff about Robson not coming back to work tomorrow?"

"Oh, right, thanks for the reminder! I almost forgot." Pedro pulled his phone out of his pocket. "Lemme make a quick call . . ."

When the supermarket closed that evening, Robson punched out and walked outside, arms wrapped around his torso to keep warm. As he crossed the street, wondering if his wife had remembered to pay the utility bill, he failed to see a man near the square straddling a motorcycle with his arm crossed over his chest, not far from where Robson stood. The man's eyes scanned the length of the security guard's body, as if sizing him up.

"Look who we have here!"

"Excuse me?"

"Robson?"

"Do I know you?"

"I don't think so. You can call me Hans. And these girls here . . ." The man pulled out two guns, kissing them one at a time, ". . . are Ruth and Raquel."

Hans did not kill Robson. Although he came close. When Hans finally tired of pummeling him, the poor guy was curled up in a fetal position, his labored breathing making it difficult for him to speak. Blood poured from his nose, eyes, and mouth, and a few of his teeth were missing.

"Happy now, pretty boy?" asked Hans, crouching down to the level of his victim. "That'll teach you to stick your nose where it don't belong. Now listen: show your face here again and I'll kill you. And, Robson, you best pray the cops don't find out what happens at this store. Cause if they do, I don't care if it was you who told them or not. You're the one I'm coming after, cause you're the one I know knows. Got it? Got it, you *goddamn snake*?"

It took Robson all the strength he had to painfully nod in agreement.

"Alright. Peace."

18

HORROR SHOW

The following Friday, August 20, 2010, Marques and Pedro went to work like normal; Robson unsurprisingly did not. At the cash register, in the bakery, in the butcher's, throughout the entire store, the staff only wanted to discuss one topic: the previous evening's events. What exactly happened the night before? Robson had been seen with a bloody mouth, holding a grocery bag, but when asked what was going on, refused to explain. One of the rumors flying around was that the security guard had caught someone trying to steal jelly beans.

"Jelly beans?"

"That's what I heard."

"Oh, come on!"

"I heard the guy had filled a whole bag with jelly beans by the time Robson saw him. That's when they started swinging at each other. Robson took one straight to the mouth."

"Right, and then the thief ran off, came back with a gun, waited for Robson to leave, jumped him, kicked the shit out of the bastard, practically killed the poor bastard—all over some *jelly beans?*"

"That's what they're saying."

"Please. That's the dumbest shit I ever heard."

Dumb or not, in the absence of a more coherent, or at least less preposterous alternative, this was the version of events that was swiftly becoming the majority opinion.

It'd been a while since Marques and Pedro had stopped having to hide away like rats to enjoy their stolen goods. As soon as they could afford to pay—and pay they did—for what they wanted from the store, they began to hold their feasts farther afield, outside the locker room. That brisk afternoon, for example, the two stock clerks bought a bagful of snacks, then went outside to sit under the sun on one of the benches in the square near the supermarket. They'd barely gotten comfortable when a low, powerful voice barked:

"Marques! Pedro!"

The two men turned their heads and looked across the street where Sr. Geraldo stood with his hands on his hips.

"We're on a break, Seu Geraldo!" an annoyed Pedro yelled in response.

"I know that, but it's important, tchê! Get over here. I need to talk to you."

Moments later, the three men were standing in the manager's office, just like they had the evening before. Both Marques and Pedro were anxious to hear what Sr. Geraldo was so determined to tell them. Whatever it was, they agreed it couldn't be good; they also seemed to agree that it wasn't reason enough to postpone their afternoon snack. They sat down, opened their treats, dumped them on the table, and dug into them right then and there, while waiting for the manager to start talking. Sr. Geraldo stood with his arms crossed and his back against the door. He heaved a long sigh.

"Amauri just called," he abruptly informed them.

With a piece of savory pie in his mouth, Pedro asked:

"What'd he want?"

"He wanted to know what happened to Robson."

"And how does Horse Face know something happened to Robson?" Marques asked, peeling the laminate covering off a cup of yogurt.

"He spoke with Ana before our conversation. He called to go over some HR stuff, and Ana filled him in on the gossip. Which is why he called me."

"And what'd you say to him?"

"I tried to brush it off. Said I wasn't exactly sure what happened, yada yada, but promised to look at the security footage and get to the bottom of it."

"And?" Pedro asked.

"He doesn't suspect anything. The problem is he wants to look at the footage himself. Said we have to take the issue seriously. He wants the guy who punched Robson thrown in jail. He told me he would look at the footage as soon as he had the time. Lucky for us, Amauri is always busy, so it'll be a few days before he has a chance to sit down with it. A week, two weeks, who knows. That's how long we have to do something about it."

"Did any of the cameras catch Robson getting beat up?"

"Yes. One of the cameras outside the building caught everything. You can even make out your friend's face. But that's not what's important, tchê! What's important is that, when Amauri looks at the footage, he's going to see that the two of you harassed me in my own goddamned office, and that I didn't do anything about it!" Sr. Geraldo glanced up: above him, in a corner, was a security camera.

"Shit!" Marques said, alarmed, though not enough to prevent him from scraping the inside of the cup of yogurt with his finger.

"You could wipe the security footage." Pedro suggested.

The manager shook his head.

"I can't. The footage isn't stored here. Everything caught on the stores' security cameras goes straight to the head office. And that's where it stays. I can access the footage from my computer, but all I can do is look. I can't erase it."

Now that they were aware of the situation, Pedro and Marques went quiet and seemed mildly concerned, although their mouths kept chewing. A couple of minutes later, when it looked like they were done thinking things through, Sr. Geraldo started pressuring them.

"Alright, tchê, what're you thinking? How am I going to make sure I don't embarrass myself? What do I do? What do *you* do? If Amauri finds out what happened yesterday, it'll be bad news for you too."

"Don't worry, we'll figure something out," Pedro promised.

Yet neither he nor Marques managed to come up with any solutions, not that day nor the next. Things only started looking up on Sunday, August 22, 2010, when Angélica asked her husband:

"What if you hired a private investigator?"

Marques was puzzled by his wife's suggestion.

"A PI? For what?"

"To look into this Horse Face character and dig up some dirt. Then, you and Hangman will have something to use against him."

Marques laughed with gusto.

"Babe, quit tripping. You been watching too many movies."

Angélica laughed along with him, but still insisted.

"C'mon, I'm being serious, man! Stop clowning around. I'm being serious, goddamnit!"

The more she insisted, the funnier he thought she was being, and the more the two of them laughed.

"C'mon, Angélica, that's crazy!"

Later that same day, Marques called Pedro to ask if he'd come up with a plan yet. When Pedro said no, he jokingly shared his wife's idea.

"Wait till you hear this: Angélica said we should hire a private fucking investigator."

At first Pedro had the same exact reaction as Marques.

"A PI? For what?"

Marques explained, still laughing:

"To dig up some dirt for us to use against Horse Face." The connection wasn't very stable, and after a good five seconds or so, when Marques didn't hear Pedro laugh like he'd expected him to, or react at all for that matter, he thought the call must have dropped.

"Hello? Earth calling Pedro."

Finally, Pedro spoke up:

"Dude, that's fucking genius!"

"What! Are you freaking serious? I swear to God, man, between you and Angélica—I mean, damn. That PI shit only happens in movies, brother. Get with it!"

Now that made Pedro laugh.

"Nah, man. You're the one who's gotta get with it. Even though you're rolling in money, you're still thinking like a broke mother-fucker. Poor folks always think shit only happens in movies. There are private investigators in real life too, and we can afford one. In fact, we can afford the ritziest motherfucking PI in town."

That Monday morning, August 23, 2010, Pedro went to the offices of the most expensive private investigator in Porto Alegre. When he first saw the man, Pedro had some doubts. Not because he looked like one of those sad, scruffy guys who reek of failure, but because of his elegant, classic hairdo, and the sophisticated way he had of readjusting his glasses, all of which gave him a gentlemanly air. Pale skin, pale eyes, pale hair—the private investigator looked so Germanic that when Pedro saw him initially, he wondered—a silly thought, he knew—if the man even spoke Portuguese.

As mentioned, Pedro had some doubts. The investigator was so polished that Pedro couldn't help but wonder if he was unscrupulous enough for that line of work; he found it very difficult to imagine a man like him doing anything remotely indiscreet. What finally convinced Pedro otherwise was the PI's exorbitant rate: there must be a reason his services were so expensive.

Pedro wasn't sorry. Less than a week later, the PI rang to say he'd gotten his hands on a piece of first-rate intel. The phone call took place in the small hours of August 28. On the evening of that same day, Pedro left the supermarket and met the investigator for dinner at a restaurant of his choice, at the top of Bela Vista.

That Saturday, Porto Alegre was experiencing the coldest temperatures of the decade. The wind howled, and a persistent, irritating drizzle lashed noisily at every surface. A good night to be tucked in bed, Pedro thought, running his thumb along the edge of the table and gazing absently through the restaurant window. It felt like the investigator would never get there . . . Had he died on his way to meet him? Whenever someone was late, the first thought that crossed Pedro's mind was that they had died. We all give up the ghost sooner or later. Pedro himself was moments away from starving to death. Hearing his stomach growl, he wondered if he shouldn't just order something already. Promising to meet someone for dinner only to eat before the other person arrived was probably unconscionable for a man like the investigator and his kind. Surely it was even more unconscionable to be as egregiously late as he was.

"Fuck it, I'm eating!"

Pedro opened the menu. He might as well have left it closed. He didn't recognize a single item in it and doubted he could pronounce any of the names. He called over the server and asked him to bring the restaurant's most popular dish. He may as well not have bothered. The dish was pasta topped with baby vomit and a sickly green sauce. He tried to eat it. He may as well not have bothered.

Annoyed, Pedro decided he would eat at home. He called back the server and asked him to take the food away; it was revolting, even the smell made him sick. The server asked if he'd like the check too. No. He would keep waiting for his appointment, who happened to walk into the restaurant that very minute.

"My apologies, Pedro!" the investigator said. He shook his hand, then sat across from him at the table. He was holding a black leather briefcase, which he placed next to his feet on the floor. "The traffic in this city is a nightmare, and it's only getting worse," he explained.

"It's alright, don't worry about it," Pedro reassured him, though the look on his face said otherwise.

"So? Would you like something to eat first, or . . . ?"

"Hell, no. Just show me what you've got. I can't wait to get home."

"Right, of course." The investigator bent over, opened the briefcase, and rummaged through it. He pulled out what he was looking for, then closed the briefcase again. "I think I found just what you were looking for. Here, have a gander." He ceremoniously handed a photograph to Pedro, then proceeded to readjust his glasses in that peculiar way of his, all the better to see the look of shock on his client's face. "What did I tell you?"

"Oh my God."

Pedro could hardly believe his eyes. Even though the photo was taken from a distance, Sr. Amauri was perfectly visible, his body framed by the window. The curtains had been pulled shut, but happened to be mid-flutter in the picture, meaning the photographer probably had no more than a second or two to capture the scene.

In that fugitive space between the two fluttering curtains was Sr. Amauri, the respectable supervisor of the Fênix supermarket chain, kneeling in profile with a penis in his mouth and two penises in his hands.

"How did you get this shot?" Pedro was having a hard time believing what was in front of him.

"Oh, it wasn't me. It was my photographer. The man's very competent, I have to say. A drunk, but extremely competent."

"Are you kidding? He's more than just competent!"

"Right, yes. Even better, or maybe worse: everyone in the photo, except for our friend of course, is underage. The oldest boy is seventeen. What I'm saying is: that there in your hands is evidence of a felony. Our friend is a pedophile."

Pedro laughed. His mood had changed.

"Damn, people are sick."

"Some, yes . . . On that subject, are you happy with the photo?"

Pedro didn't catch the sarcasm.

"Of course! It's exactly what I need."

"Right, yes. Well, consider it an appetizer."

"What do you mean?"

"Did you see the briefcase I was holding when I walked in? It's all yours. There are plenty of other photos like that one. Most of them courtesy of a computer wiz I work with, who hacked into our friend's computer. It's a real horror show in there, let me tell you. There are a few other documents too, information pertaining to some of our friend's victims: their full names, their parents' names, how old they are, where they live, their phone numbers, those kinds of details." The investigator took a pen drive out of his jacket pocket and handed it to Pedro. "And this is a digital copy of everything in the briefcase. If you were to misplace any of the hard copies, you could just print them all out again."

The private investigator's services were worth every last cent of the fortune they cost, thought Pedro, smiling widely and slipping the pen drive into the pocket of his slacks. He was so excited about the ammo against Sr. Amauri, he decided to give the food another shot. He put his trust in the investigator, who claimed to have been patronizing that restaurant for a long time and appeared to have good taste. He asked for a recommendation. He'd eat anything—so long as it was good, he said. The investigator took Pedro's request very seriously. He pursed his lips and carefully studied the menu while drumming his fingers. Finally, he pointed to one of the entrées and said, You can't go wrong with this one. Which is how Pedro wound up trying yet another one of the restaurant's specialties. He may as well not have bothered.

That following Sunday, August 29, 2010, a bright, metaphorical sun shone in the Porto Alegre sky, producing no heat. The persistent drizzle had tapered off in the middle of the night, but the strong winds from the previous evening still blew down the street, mussing everyone's hair.

"Why not just turn him in?" Angélica asked. "Wouldn't that be easier? All we'd have to do is hand this stuff over to the cops. They'd throw him in jail. End of story."

"That's what I said," Roberto replied. "But then Pedro said something that made a lot of sense. See, this kind of shit takes a while to clean up. There's reams of red tape. We gotta file a report with the police, then the police gotta send it to a judge, who's gotta analyze it, and judges are busy motherfuckers, and sometimes lazy motherfuckers too, and God only knows when they'd get around to issuing a warrant for his arrest . . . Anyway, it's a lot. We could report him, but he'd still have time to see the supermarket footage before getting his ass thrown in jail. Then Pedro and your husband would be up shit creek."

Angélica and Roberto strolled down the cobbled sidewalk of a quiet street blanketed in leaves and flanked by large houses, stopping now and then to complain about the cold or the wind. Eventually, Angélica pointed to one of the houses and said:

"Number 293. Look, it's over there."

They walked up to the house and rang the doorbell. Seconds later, a woman opened the door. She frowned when she saw them.

"How can I help you?"

"Hi. We're here to talk to Seu Amauri. Is this his address?"

"Yes . . . I'm his wife. Is there anything I can do for you?"

"I'm sorry, but we really need to talk directly to Seu Amauri."

"Right, okay . . . One minute, please." The woman shut the door again.

"Ugh, Roberto. Would you mind talking to the perv?"

"Leave it to me."

The next time the door opened, the person on the other side was a man with a crimson, horse-like face. He too frowned when he saw them.

"Yes?"

"Seu Amauri?"

"This is he. How can I help?"

Roberto handed the briefcase to Sr. Amauri.

"Here. This is for you, sir."

Intrigued, albeit still frowning, Sr. Amauri cracked open the briefcase and riffled through its contents. Soon he found a photo that left him visibly nervous. He slid the photo back into the briefcase, then closed it again, clenching his jaw.

"How did you get these?" He stepped onto the street and closed the door behind him, possibly concerned his wife would hear them. "Listen here, if you think you can just show up at my house and . . ."

Though Roberto hadn't intended to use violence, the man's menacing tone pushed him over the edge. He shoved Sr. Amauri, slamming him back-first against the front door.

"*You* listen here, you fucking creep! Who d'you think you are? Don't you see you're in no position to be talking to us like that? You're the last person who should be acting rude!"

Sr. Amauri wasn't a young man anymore, and his back took the brunt of the impact of the hard wooden door.

"What do you want from me?" he asked, face screwed in pain.

"A small favor. Listen carefully: You are no longer an employee of Fênix supermarkets. First thing tomorrow, you're going to hand in your notice. Got it? It's that or prison. You choose."

19

THE TRAGEDY

One of the hardest decisions to make in this world is, without a doubt, to stop earning money. A thousand, two thousand, three thousand: the more we earn, the more we want to earn. It's like marching into uncharted territory: the more we advance, the more central the idea of advancement becomes, and the more meaningless any notion of destiny.

Days, weeks, months. Almost an entire year had passed since Sr. Amauri's resignation without the gang experiencing a single setback. In the meantime, Pedro tore down his house and built another in its place; he got the driver's license he'd long been dreaming of, bought a brand-new sedan, and set aside another two-hundred thousand reais. Roberto followed a similar path: new house, license, factory-fresh car. He only didn't set aside as much money as Pedro because he chose to take advantage of a golden opportunity (or an indebted citizen in dire straits), acquiring a large piece of property for a bargain on Avenida Cavalhada, where he opened a respectable, lucrative restaurant. Marques and Angélica also got their driver's licenses. But unlike their colleagues, they bought a simple, used car for both of them to share. They didn't feel the need to build a whole new house either, content to remodel their current place of residence. On the other hand, they did invest nearly half a million reais in the construction of modest rental properties across the city.

The truth is that Pedro, Roberto, Marques, and Angélica were in a good position to leave the cannabis business and scamper over to the side of the law—to a clean, effortless existence, albeit this time with some guarantee of dignity and comfort. But as mentioned above, one of the hardest decisions to make in this world is, without a doubt, to stop earning money.

Unlike his four colleagues, Luan, who wasn't even remotely interested in a life outside drug-trafficking, carelessly burned through stacks upon stacks of money. One night, he even hosted a party to rival all others in the heart of Vila Planetário. Free drinks and food for anyone who attended! And the reason for the party was a good one too. Sr. Joaquim, a beloved neighbor, had found a buyer for his house; he and his granddaughter were moving away.

A week after the historic going-away party, the new owner showed up, along with the furniture. The following day, a few of his friends came to visit and looked as if they were there to stay. There were five men all told, including the first man who moved in.

Several days passed and still no one knew what those strangers did with their time. They woke up late every day and then went to a boteco around the corner, where they drank beer, snorted cocaine, and laughed until nightfall, after which they vanished, only to be seen again the next day. Yet they seemed to have no trouble at all making friends. Before long, they were saying hello to nearly everyone they passed in the neighborhood alleys, even though no one knew for sure what they were called, where they came from, or how they made enough money to support their cocaine habit. The general feeling was that whatever the men did when they disappeared, it couldn't be good.

As if a group of men living together for no apparent reason wasn't strange enough, soon two more houses in the neighborhood were sold, only for more men to move in: five in one house, five in the other, just as it had been with the first house. The strangest part was that the residents of the three households all seemed to be old acquaintances, judging by the degree of intimacy between them when all fifteen gathered at the boteco to drink, snort, and laugh.

Luan, like everyone else, was obviously intrigued by the rabble that had seemingly parachuted into Planetário. But right then a different mystery had his complete attention: the sudden disappearance of his favorite concubine, Larissa. No one had heard from her in two days, and he had a sinking feeling. So, around three P.M. on Sunday, July 3, 2011, he went to see Larissa's mother for the tenth time to ask if she'd heard anything. When he got there, she was elbow-deep in the laundry sink, washing clothes. All signs pointed to her remaining unconcerned.

"Oh boy, back to harass me, are you?"

"Still nothing, tia?"

"Luan, get this through your head: that little she-devil drops out of sight sometimes. She gets up to no good, then shows up a few days later half-starved and stinking of cum. Listen, you ever seen a cat when it coughs up hair balls? Well, son, that's exactly what she does: she shows up here coughing up pubes from all the cocks she sucks around town."

Luan got annoyed. He wanted to tell Larissa's mother that she had changed: now that she had him, she wouldn't have left his side. But worried he might come off as arrogant, or worse naïve, he said something else instead:

"Okay, tia. But if you see her, please tell her to come find me."

The woman laughed.

"I should be the one asking *you* that. I promise that when that filthy bitch comes back, she'll go crawling to you first. Don't say I didn't warn you."

Larissa's disappearance stirred up a mix of emotions in Luan—concern, frustration, sadness, helplessness. The longer she was gone, the more ridiculous his thoughts. At one point, he'd have sworn his other concubines had murdered Larissa out of jealousy, or that her own mother was keeping her tied up and gagged in her bedroom. But the most absurd thought of all came to him now in the form of a bitter question, one he couldn't answer: What point was there in money if Larissa wasn't there to spend it with him?

On his way home, as he headed down a long, narrow alley, Luan bumped into the fifteen mysterious men who had moved into Planetário. They were walking in the opposite direction, all talking at the same time—laughing, gesticulating, making a racket, blocking the way. They were all armed with handguns, machine guns, rifles. Luan felt understandably scared, and the only reason his fear didn't paralyze him was the knowledge that whatever beef those guys had, surely it had nothing to do with *him*, thank God, given that he'd never had problems with any of them. For a second, a small dose of relief quieted his alarm. "I feel bad for the fool who fucked with those guys!" he thought. However, by jumping to the conclusion that he was free from danger, Luan had made a serious mistake. He realized this almost instantly. The men didn't just brush past him, like he'd expected.

"Look who it is!"

"Sheik!"

"Don't run, cuz!"

"Give up, Sheik. It's over, brother!"

"You're done for, motherfucker!"

"It's all ours now, man—ours!"

One of the voices had a certain malice to it, which chilled Luan to the bone. Now—now he was petrified, and there was nothing he could do. A sudden movement and his body could end up shredded by bullets of various calibers.

"W-what's up, guys? W-what's all th-this about?" he stuttered, holding up his hands.

The men cackled mercilessly.

"What a sissy!"

"Look at the guy!"

"Careful you don't shit yourself, Sheik!"

"Any final words, dickwad?"

"It's now or never, dude!"

"C'mon, let's kill the fucker already!"

"Nah, nah. Chill. Don't shoot. Hold up. Quiet down!" boomed a man who appeared to be the ringleader. "This is what we do. We take him to the Loop and kill the motherfucker there. It's busier, so more folks will see. That way everybody knows this ain't no picnic."

There was a loud, animal murmur of approval.

Hands grabbing him by the arms, hands pulling him by the jacket, hands pounding his back, guns trained at him, guns prodding him—this is how Luan was dragged through the alleys of Planetário toward the site of his execution: the large cul-de-sac at the end of Rua Luiz Manoel. As the residents of Vila Planetário watched this display of idiocy, this savage mutiny, they could only widen their eyes, drop their jaws, and whisper—no one had the courage to intervene. Luan tried to talk, but the men drowned out his voice.

"Planetário's ours now, Sheik!"

"What's ours is ours, and what's yours is ours. Cause we gonna take it anyway! Just you wait."

"C'mon, c'mon, c'mon! It's time for Sheik to become Swiss cheese!"

"Nobody messes with the Balas!"

Luan only got them to listen by using all his strength to yell a single word again and again and again.

"Money! Money! Money!"

This immediately piqued the leader's interest. He screamed at everyone to shut up and then, gesturing like a maestro, got them to stop talking and quiet down. He looked Luan in the eyes, then asked:

"Money?"

"Yeah! I been saving up for a while."

"How much?"

"About a hundred stack. C'mon, dude, take my money. You don't gotta kill me. Fuck is that about? You don't gotta kill me. I'll leave the hood. I'm not crazy or nothing, I'll get outta here."

"Is it all in your crib?"

"Natch, man."

The leader thought for a moment, then nodded and smiled.

"Cool. Guess today's your lucky day, Sheik."

The gang objected noisily to the news. The tone of voice the leader used made it impossible to tell whether he was being serious or sarcastic:

"Oh, fuck off, you assholes—a hundred G's a hundred G! We'd have no idea if the kid hadn't told us. C'mon, he gave it to us for free. Don't you think he deserves a break? Let's leave the fool alone, let him disappear—what do we care?"

Moments later, Luan was leading the way to his house while desperately trying to hatch an escape plan that could be executed without him showing his hand. He didn't have a hundred thousand reais. Far from it. He'd be lucky if the money stashed in his room added up to fifteen thousand, maybe twenty. Still, he assumed the pretense was reciprocal; even if he'd had the full amount, he didn't believe for a second his life would've been spared just because he mentioned money. They wanted to toy with him before they murdered him.

When Luan's mother saw her son being escorted into her home by armed men, she was alarmed. But before she had the time to get up from the sofa or say anything, Luan quickly stopped her.

"Don't move, Ma! Just sit right there, okay? It's gonna be alright."

In spite of everything, the men still showed respect to the house and the woman inside it. No one stepped through the front door without first nodding in her direction and saying, "Excuse me, tia."

"There's a ton of weed in there," Luan said, pointing at the closet. "Take it, all of it. I'm gonna go grab the money." The next minute, he was alone in his room, standing at the open window. He felt his stomach sink, his heart expand, every hair on his body stand on end. The adrenaline was so powerful he lost all ability to register what was happening. Reality had become too dense for his senses to freely absorb, or perhaps his senses had contracted too much. The outside world and his own self-awareness came to him in dribs and drabs, punctuated by blackouts. At one point he heard his mother saying in the living room: "Are you police?" And then, without further ado, he saw himself far away from the house, running down an alley while looking over his shoulder. Then, he was somewhere else entirely, pleading hysterically with his friend to lend him his motorcycle. Finally, he regained self-control. By the time he came to, he was on the motorcycle, driving at full speed, with no clear idea where he was in the city, let alone where he was going. It was a while before he could recognize Avenida Bento Gonçalves.

Meanwhile, far away from the trials and tribulations Luan had just experienced, Pedro was spending a carefree Sunday afternoon playing soccer on the clay field near his house, at the foothills of

Vila Viçosa. At one point he kicked the ball, aiming for the goal, and missed. With a click of the tongue, he lamented his failure:

"Fuck!"

As the goalkeeper for the opposing team waded into the brush after the ball, Pedro took the opportunity to join a group of young men smoking on the sidelines.

"Give us a toke," he said, holding out his hand.

"Nice shot, dude," joked the man who passed him the joint.

"No kidding."

Pedro's phone, which he had left in the care of that group playing, began to ring. He picked it up and glanced at the screen: "CHOKITO," it read. He casually took a few puffs of the joint and handed it back. Only then did he answer the phone:

"Sup, man?" At first he couldn't make out anything Luan was regurgitating on the other end of the line. Whatever it was, it was bad, very bad. He asked Luan to slow down a few times, then told him to wait a second. Turning to the other end of the field, where several young guys waited to play, he yelled, "Hey!" then raised his arm and waved it around to get their attention. "Yo, one of you tag me out!" He walked off the field and leaned against the nearest palm tree, then spoke to Luan more calmly. To his surprise, Luan had come all the way to Lomba do Pinheiro. He was at Stop 2-A on Estrada João de Oliveiro Remião, in front of the Parque Jardim da Paz cemetery. He wanted to know how to get to Pedro. "Alright, cool. Here's what you do, kid. Drive to Rua 12, then take the first right. Head to the end of the street, hang a left and go down, down, down, all the way. I'm next to the soccer field at the bottom, standing under a palm tree."

Luan followed Pedro's instructions and arrived a few minutes later. He parked his motorcycle by the palm tree, got off, removed his helmet, and immediately started talking and gesturing nervously, filling Pedro in on what had happened. Pedro stood there sternly, bottom lip pinched between thumb and index finger, silently taking in what his friend told him. As Pedro listened to the story, he couldn't help thinking that Luan was overreacting. Even though he understood the gravity of what had happened, even though he realized Luan had narrowly escaped death, even though he knew, or at least assumed it mustn't be easy to stay calm after such an experience, even so, he couldn't help thinking that, when all was said and done, the whole thing was just a scare, one that had happened an hour ago, in fact, if not longer, which is why he didn't understand why Luan was still crying. Luan cried, sniffled, sobbed, and choked through the story. When he finally finished his account of the events, lowering his head to blow his nose on the hem of his jacket, the first thing Pedro did was try to calm him down. He placed his hand on his friend's shoulder and said in a fatherly tone, as if speaking with a very small child:

"Alright, man. It's over. C'mon. There's no need to cry about it, brother."

Pedro's attempt at consolation did not have the intended effect. Instead, Luan started bawling even harder. Something was up. There was something missing. Luan hadn't told him the worst part.

"My ma, Pedro!" Luan blubbered.

Pedro started.

"What about your ma?"

"When I was on my way here—" Luan interrupted himself and openly sobbed, face twisted in anguish. He did his best to pull himself together, shutting his eyes and taking several deep breaths, until he could finally continue. "A buddy of mine from the hood called when I was on my way here. I pulled over on Bento to answer. Then he told me. Fuck! The bastards killed my ma, Pedro! They shot her, man, right in front of everybody. Right in front of fucking everybody . . ." Luan started sobbing again, face buried in his hands, shoulders juddering.

Only after this did Luan's sorrow brim over and touch Pedro. His throat contracted, his nostrils burned—signs that his soul would soon spill through his eyes. The feelings entering the hole in his heart were none of them good, and Pedro didn't know which to start with, whether the tang of sorrow, the zing of fury, or the bitterness of abandonment. Then there was the putrid taste of remorse. Because, at the end of the day, hadn't *he* been the one to start all that, with his ridiculous dreams of getting rich? Now, Luan was an orphan. Never again would he feel his mother's warm embrace or hear the sweet sound of her voice. These things were gone. His mother was gone. She had died. No, she had done more than just die: she was executed in public. And no one would do a thing about it. There would be no outcry. Nor was there any point in holding out for one, because nobody cared. That kind of thing happened every day—every godforsaken day. Too poor to be remembered, too Black to be acknowledged, Luan's mother was banished from the world of the living; and even though she was brutally murdered, executed in broad daylight, even though she was shot to pieces in the street, slaughtered before everyone's eyes, even so—nothing. No one cared, nothing would be done, everything would stay the same. A human being who had come silently into the world, lived silently in the world, and vanished silently from the world. A human being created, and destroyed, out of the clay of utter indifference: it was as if she never existed. A human being whose life and death were muddled in the shades of absolute contempt.

God, what world were they living in? Everything was wrong: the world was wrong, the people in it were wrong. As he watched Luan cry and joined him in tears, Pedro shook off the chains of solidarity and let his spirit soar in unconditional empathy—small, breathless, but also limitless and free. This is how Pedro was able to achieve a sense of communion; not only achieve it but transcend it too. At first, he only communed with his friend, only admitted to himself that he and Luan were equals—men adrift in a cruel world absent of logic and justice. But then, all of a sudden, he felt something greater. He didn't know if he was delirious, and he didn't want to know. He could see it clearly now: he *was* Luan. Luan's pain was *his* pain. It wasn't someone else's mother but his own mother who had died. He gazed at the clay field, where a soccer game was still underway, then at the forest, where the trees swayed in the wind, then at the sky, where clouds drifted. He didn't know where to look; no matter where his eyes turned, he could find no answer, no matter where he looked, he could find no foothold. The only thing that made sense was the fire roaring deep inside him—the unrelenting thirst for revenge. He clung to it. He let it goad him. He stopped crying. He cleansed himself of every feeling but hatred. He took Luan's head in his hands and touched it to his, forehead to forehead. And just like this, eye to eye, he made his friend a promise, each word the blow of a hammer.

"We *will fix this!*"

20

THE PLOT

Pedro didn't have time to get used to his new house. He still woke every morning convinced he would see rotten wood, whether on the ceiling or walls. But his old shack was gone. When he opened his eyes every morning, it brought him untold joy to see the bright plaster finish, the beautifully laid brick walls; it brought him untold joy to be reminded of the wonderful home he now lived in, the wonderful life he now led.

But on the morning of Monday, July 4, 2011, when Pedro woke up and sat on the edge of his bed, the joyful memory of his achievements mixed with the wretched reminder of yesterday's tragic events. As he smoked his first cigarette of the day, he decided to stay there for a bit and watch Luan, who lay on a makeshift bed of blankets on Pedro's bedroom floor, still fast asleep. He considered waking him up, then remembered the sound of him quietly weeping late at night. Luan must have had a rough night, he thought, deciding to let him rest.

He finished his cigarette, got up, stretched, and walked out of his bedroom, shutting the door behind him. His mother was at the living room table eating breakfast and listening to the radio.

"Morning, Ma."

"Good morning, sweetie." His mother looked kind of anxious. "How's your friend?"

"Never better, for now, at least. He's fast asleep. But when he wakes up and has to deal with . . . you know, his problem. Then, I don't know."

"What happened, exactly? I still don't get it," she whispered.

Pedro also lowered his voice.

"He's just come into some trouble, Ma. But he doesn't want me talking to you about it, so I'm gonna respect his wishes, alright?"

"Right, right, I see. Of course. Gosh, I just felt so worried when I saw him come in yesterday, looking like the world had come to an end."

"Yeah. But you don't gotta worry. The worse is behind him. He'll be okay."

"How long is he staying?"

"I'm not sure. A few days. Don't go interrogating the kid, yeah? Leave him be, so he can feel at home."

"Oh, go on! I'm not the witch you're making me out to be. Course I won't interrogate the poor thing."

"Hmm . . . We'll see, I guess . . ." Pedro went to the bathroom, brushed his teeth, splashed water on his face, then returned to the living room. "You been outside yet, Ma?"

"Yeah."

"Is it cold out?"

"It's winter, honey."

"Cool, I'll throw on a jacket then."

"Where you going?"

"I gotta talk to a friend. Listen, if Luan wakes up while I'm out, tell him I'll be right back."

Dressed in a jacket and sneakers, Pedro set out to find the best carjacker he knew. He had to pound on the door and call Guilherme's name several times to get him to wake up and let him in. As soon as he was inside, Pedro turned around a chair and sat in it back to front while Guilherme brewed some coffee.

"I'm gonna need a set of wheels for some business, Gui."

"Some business?" Guilherme yawned in the kitchen. "Has the weed money dried up?"

"Nah, nah. When I say 'business,' I don't mean a stickup or nothing like that. I mean a hit."

"Right, right. I see. Just the one ride?"

"Yeah, but make it a good one. For Wednesday night."

Standing by the stovetop with his arms crossed, Guilherme quickly did the math, then cocked his head and said:

"Cool. Gimme five stack and I'll get you a dope set of wheels. Only cause it's you, though. I'd give it to anybody else for three!" He laughed hoarsely, biting his tongue.

Pedro also laughed.

"Alright, shithead. Alright."

"Could you get me some of it up front. Half, maybe even less? I'm dead broke."

"No sweat. I can front you the whole five K. I don't have it on me, though. I need to see this other dude about something first, then I'll grab the cash and meet you back here. Sound good?"

"Yeah, trust. I'm around all day. Come through whenever."

"One last thing: Try not to kill the driver, for God's sake. If shit goes sideways and my crew ends up behind bars, we can hack a grand theft auto, but ain't none of us interested in getting stuck with a murder charge."

"Wait, you're going in on the hit?" Guilherme was taken aback.

"Yeah, that's right."

"I figured you were just helping some guy out, as a side hustle or whatever."

"Nah, it's got nothing to do with money. I'm gonna be out there, front and center. This shit's personal, Gui. The Balas took over one of my guy's corners in Planetário, then executed the dude's mom. He's sleeping it off at my place."

"Oh, damn! The Balas are no joke."

"I know. But this time they're in for it."

Pedro left Guilherme's house and turned up Rua Guaíba toward Vila Nova São Carlos. As he walked leisurely along the street, he pulled out his phone and called Marques. He still needed to break the bad news to him.

"Sup, Pedro?"

"Hey, Marques. Listen, the worst shit happened last night." He told him about Luan's mother.

"Fuck!" Marques said once he heard the whole story, clicking his tongue. "That's tragic, man."

"You're telling me. I'm full of hate. You know what I was thinking, though? I feel bad saying this, but Luan's ma dying was just the reality check I needed."

"What d'you mean?"

"Luan didn't think something like this could happen, right? Whether he thought it or not, fact is it did. Cause that's the kind of life we're living, see? The kind of life where—bam! shit happens to you or your family when you least expect it. So, like, right now, I don't think anything bad could happen to me or my ma, or anyone in my family, yeah? But that doesn't mean it can't. See what I'm saying? So I thought to myself: What the fuck am I waiting for to get out?"

"You're quitting?"

"I already quit, dude. I'm washing my hands of this crap. You, Angélica, Roberto, even Luan, if you all want to keep at it, then be my guests, it's your funeral. But I'm cool. I got plenty of money set aside. I don't need nothing else. I'm done! It's time for me to look after the life I made. When I go to Fênix today, I'm handing in my notice and sayonara, nice knowing you, see you never. All I wanna do now is work toward my goals, and space the fuck out! I don't mean with drugs, either. I mean a full-on good time! Stuffing myself with yogurt, eating tons of chocolate-frosted corn cake, playing video games, playing soccer, hanging out with my ma, hanging out with my buddies, having a blast, laughing, banging women, forgetting once and for all that the world's a shit show and pretending I live in Disneyland, cause I can afford a good time now. The rest of it, man . . ." Pedro laughed dryly. "The rest is history. I don't even wanna hear about it. Try telling me about the rest and see what happens. I want the rest to explode and for my dick to grow! I've lived in the real world way too long. I've had to choose between being a thug and a slave way too long. I've been swimming against the current way too long. Enough is enough! It's time to kick back and let the good times roll, cause I'm one of God's children too."

"Yeah, man. I'm done as well. And you're right. If Luan's ma hadn't died, we might never have stopped, we might've been stuck doing this bullshit forever."

"Here's the deal, though. Before we go straight, I wanna hit the Balas, on Wednesday night. I just talked to a buddy of mine who says he can get us a set of wheels."

"What's the plan?"

"The plan is to kill every last one of those cocksuckers. You in? Honest, I wasn't even sure I should ask, since you got kids and all. So if you're not in, that's cool, I get it."

"Are you kidding me? Hell yeah I'm in! I'm full of hate too, man. You know I love that kid to death. You bet your ass I'm fucking in."

"Yes! My man . . . That's what I like to hear. I'm on my way to see a friend about some hardware. I'm thinking four pieces—for me, you, Luan, and Roberto, since I figure he's gonna want in too. What d'you think? Should I ask my buddy for four or five?"

"Who's the fifth one for?"

"Your wife."

"Now you've really fucking lost it."

Pedro laughed.

"Look . . . knowing Angélica, she'll wanna come with us . . ."

"She can keep wanting."

Pedro laughed again.

"Cool, man. Whatever you say. Four, then. I'm gonna hang up. Call you later, yeah?"

"Yeah. See you later, Pedro."

As soon as Marques set his phone down on the table, Angélica, who was sitting beside him eating breakfast and heard everything he said, calmly asked:

"What's got you so worked up, love? What happened?"

Marques seemed to have lost his appetite. He set aside the pães de queijo he'd been devouring just a moment ago and told her about Luan's mother while slowly sipping his coffee.

"My God!" she said.

"Yeah. After all that, Hangman said he thinks it's time for him to get out of the weed business. And I gotta say, I think we should too."

"Yeah, yeah, for sure," Angélica quickly agreed. "I'm done with this crap."

"My God," she said again, appalled, shaking her head. She was having a hard time believing what those men had done to Luan's mother.

As for the plan to hit the rival gang, Marques and Angélica seemed to be at an impasse. Just like Pedro had predicted, Angélica wanted at all costs to take part in the hit. Marques, meanwhile, did his best to dissuade her.

"Listen, Angélica! This shit ain't exactly like stealing candy from a baby!"

"Marques, honey. You think I don't know that? I won't chicken out, I swear. You don't believe I can hurt anyone, do you? Look at what those guys did to that woman. She wasn't even mixed up in this! I'm not gonna chicken out, love. When I have those pieces of trash in front of me—cause that's what they are, fucking trash—I'm gonna let it rip, you'll see!"

"I'm not saying you'd chicken out, babe. But we could all wind up in prison—or even dead. Then who'd look after Daniel and Lúcia? If shit goes sideways, I need to know you're gonna be home with the kids." This finally got Angélica to hesitate. Marques took advantage of this lull to reach over and stroke her cheek, wanting to end the discussion once and for all. "It's better this way, yeah?" In that moment, he seemed to have an idea. "I'm gonna go visit Pops!" he said, leaping out of his seat.

"For what?" Angélica asked.

"He's got a load of cop stuff: balaclavas, bullet-proof vests, shirts, even radios with earpieces and stuff. All in perfect condition. If he's game, we could hit the Balas dressed as five-os."

Given that it was ten A.M. and the Vila Lupicínio Rodrigues cartel boss never woke up before one P.M. in the winter, the front door was closed when Marques got there. Knocking had little effect. Knocking a second time even less so.

"POPS!!!"

"Fuck me. I'm coming, I'm coming!" said a gruff, sleepy voice from inside the house.

Moments later, Marques was sitting on the sofa with the TV on while Pops, dressed in a spotless white bathrobe and struggling to stay awake, threw open the shutters. Apparently, he responded no differently to sunlight than a vampire.

"Chwist!"

"Hey, Pops, you still got all that five-o gear you showed me last time? I came to ask you to do me a solid."

The old man was surprised by his request.

"For what?" he asked, sitting in the armchair across Marques.

"A hit."

"A hit?"

"That's right."

"But I thought you and your crew wanted to stay out of trouble. I thought y'all didn't make enemies."

"We didn't. But things change. Remember I told you we started selling weed by the kilo down in Planetário?"

"Yeah, so?"

"Yesterday the Balas ran off my buddy, the one heading the operation down there, and executed his ma. That's why we're going after them. Wednesday night."

"Wight, wight. I feel you. Don't sweat it. Happy to beat the dwum for my favorite homeboy. Leave it to me. I'll set you up with the best gear in town."

"Thanks, Bill. You're the man."

"I know I am. No need to keep telling me . . ."

Meanwhile, some distance away from Vila Lupicínio Rodrigues, Pedro was in Lomba do Pinheiro speaking with Valdir, the cartel boss of Vila Nova São Carlos, who greeted him in a wool hat, a thermos in one hand and a chimarrão gourd in the other.

"Let me see if I follow," he said with his usual acid smile. "You want me to lend you some hardware for the hit. That about right?"

"That's right, sir. That's exactly it," Pedro confirmed.

"And why the hell should I want to help you?"

"No reason."

"No reason?"

"Yeah, no reason. I got nothing to give you in return for your help. Would if I did. But I don't. I came here hoping I could count on your generosity."

"Generosity?"

"Generosity."

"Right. And what if I don't want to lend you anything?"

"Then I'd apologize for wasting your time and leave."

Valdir nodded, still smiling.

"I've got to say, I expected more from your powers of persuasion."

"I'm sorry to disappoint, sir."

Valdir left the thermos on the veranda banister, freeing one of his hands to stroke his goatee.

"Remember that time you left here saying you were going to talk to Renato? Things were tense. A war was about to break out because the late Bison, God rest his soul, wanted revenge. Anyway, you didn't want another war. You wanted to sell your weed in peace. So you went and talked to Renato, and then Renato killed Bison, his right hand. Problem solved: there was no war, just like you wanted. Listen, I still don't know what you said to Renato, but I've always been curious. So, how's this: You tell me what you told Renato that day and I'll lend you some heat."

Pedro pursed his lips and shook his head.

"I'm sorry, but I can't tell you what I said, sir."

"Why not?"

"Cause, if I did, then you'd have to kill your right hand, your son Lucas."

Valdir started laughing. Still laughing, he picked up the thermos and poured water into the gourd.

"Touché! Alright, alright. If you don't want to tell me, then don't. I'll help you anyway. After all, there's people out there who think I owe you one, and I don't want to seem ungrateful. Go on, then. What do you want?"

"Not much, really. Four guns and eight thirty-round magazines."

"Alright. Let me go and grab them for you."

Shortly after, Pedro was diving back into Vila Sapo along Rua Guaíba with a small backpack full of weapons. He spotted Luan standing in the square speaking with Roberto and walked up to the two men. Roberto, arms crossed, face clouded over, quickly said:

"Luan filled me in. He also said you told him we're not gonna let them get away with it. I just need to know one thing: When're we heading over there to get our own back?"

"Yeah, I figured you'd want in," Pedro said. "The hit's scheduled for Wednesday night."

"Cool. And the heat?"

Pedro responded by pointing his thumb over his shoulder at the backpack.

"What's in there?" Luan asked.

"Four guns," Pedro said. "One for me, one for you, one for Roberto, and another for Marques. We each get two thirty-round magazines."

"What about the ride?"

"I already talked to Gui."

"Cool, cool."

That same Monday, Pedro paid Guilherme the entire fee in advance, just as he said he would. He also kept his promise to hand in his notice at Fênix supermarket. Marques soon followed suit. That may have been the luckiest day in Sr. Geraldo's life, and the unluckiest day in the lives of the other employees, who had grown accustomed to stuffing themselves with treats, courtesy of the two stock clerks.

Speaking of bad luck, Tuesday, July 5, 2011, was off to a bumpy start for Marques. That morning when he woke up, he had the unfortunate idea of calling Fernanda to ask her and Pâmela to tell everyone that the supermarket weed operation was over. The issue was that Angélica seemed to have a sixth sense attuned to the detection of any and all extracurricular activities. She crept out of bed and tiptoed behind her husband, eavesdropping on his conversation. Hands planted on her hips, eyes half-closed, and lips curled, she demanded an explanation about the woman Marques had affectionately referred to as "Fê."

That afternoon, Roberto, who agreed it was time for them to stop selling weed, reminded Pedro to tell Fabrício that they would be ceasing their activities. Their phone conversation was a long one. Fabrício did everything in his power not to lose his clients, even discounting the product to five hundred reais a kilo. He only stopped pushing when Pedro told him about Luan's mother and how her death had made up their minds to quit the weed business. As soon as the hit they had orchestrated was carried out, they would be saying goodbye to their life of crime, and nothing and no one could persuade them otherwise. Fabrício sighed. If that was the case, he said, so be it. It'd been a pleasure doing business with them. He asked about the hit, out of a mix of curiosity and concern. When he heard the plan, he offered to help. He could loan them firearms and bulletproof vests. Pedro thanked him a few times and even kicked himself for not thinking to ask Fabrício in the first place; it was too late now, he explained, they had everything they needed.

Later that night, Guilherme entered the future Vila Sapo behind the wheel of a silver hatchback. Glowing in the moonlight, the car looked like it had come straight from the factory. Roberto, Luan, and Pedro were in the square going over the details of the hit, and instantly fell quiet at the sight of the beautiful vehicle driving down Rua Guaíba. Guilherme pulled over beside the three men and, with a smug smile, asked:

"Will this one do?"

21

A GRUESOME NIGHT

WEDNESDAY, JULY 6, 2011

Intense cold. Heavy clouds in the dark sky. Strong winds wailing menacingly in the bowels of the night. Scraps of paper and grocery bags whirling in the air. Something malevolent prowled the streets of Porto Alegre, floated in the Guaíba River, and peeked out from behind the trees of Farroupilha Park. You could feel it. Demons had ascended from hell to cheer on the events that were soon to unfold in that southern capital.

Marques and Angélica had left their children with Marques's sister Catarina in Vila Campo da Tuca. Back in Vila Lupicínio Rodrigues, they were waiting for Pedro, Luan, and Roberto to meet at their house. It wasn't long before they arrived. They parked the hatchback on a side street, climbed out of the car, shut the doors, and rang the doorbell. Marques opened the door in the uniform of a bona-fide police officer.

"How's it going, everybody? Come in, come in," he said, shaking everyone's hand.

Pedro tossed the small backpack with the firearms on the sofa.

"Hardware's in there."

"Something to drink?" Angélica asked. "We got coffee, whiskey . . ."

A glass of whiskey, the guests answered in unison.

"Not sure it's a good idea for us to be drunk," Marques said.

"Just a shot to get the blood flowing," Pedro responded. "Nobody's gonna overdo it. Besides, I brought some eight-balls to help keep us on our toes," he said, pulling a handful of cocaine capsules from his pocket and dropping them on the table.

"Oh, nice. Good idea," Marques said.

The guests drank the whiskey, then went to the master bedroom and shut the door. A little while later, they opened the door again and walked back into the living room dressed in the same gear as Marques, that is, looking like bona-fide police officers.

"So, Luan, how's things in Planetário?" Angélica inquired.

"I called my buddy there today and he said that no new guys have showed up since Sunday," Luan said. "Meaning, there's still fifteen of them."

"What else your buddy say?" Marques asked.

"Nothing important. That they started dealing on Monday. Everything from weed to blow to rock, even yuppy shit like LSD."

"They selling out of one of them houses they bought?"

"No. My buddy says their turf is the Loop. Look, I drew a map to help us get around." Luan pulled out a sheet of notebook paper from his pocket, unfolded it, and lay it out on the table.

"That over there says 'Santa Terezinha,'" he explained, pointing toward the top of the paper. "I ran outta space. And this question mark is a street I can't remember."

Angélica looked down at the map.

"And these notes?"

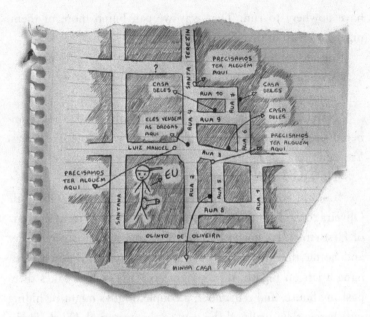

"Right, yeah. Let me explain." Luan pointed to different parts of the map as he talked. "The black dots are hot zones. The hottest is the one in the middle: the Loop. That's where they move their drugs and shit. The reason it's the hottest is that most of the crew is gonna be there, maybe even all of them. Other hot zones are their three houses, *here*, *here*, and *here*. There could be one or two guys in each. My house is *here*, see? I put my crib down as a hot zone cause they've probably taken over it by now. My buddy says they didn't, but you never know. I talked to him early in the day, around four. It's almost midnight now. They could've taken over my crib between now and then. We should play it safe."

"What about those white circles there?" Marques asked.

"Here's what I'm thinking. No point in all of us going to the same place, or we'd only get to wipe out two or three dudes before the rest of them scatter. What we need is to surround them. Those white circles are where we gotta be standing to trap the dudes in the Loop. If we set up in these three spots, they won't have nowhere to run. That way we can bump more of them, maybe even all of them."

Roberto ran his giant index finger along the sheet of paper.

"We can drive up this way and then turn here—"

Luan interrupted him:

"Nah nah nah, man. You can't drive into the hood. These numbered streets are streets in name only. They're more like alleys. You can't fit a car in there."

"How do we get in, then?"

"Look, I got a plan, so listen up. We drive up Dr. Olinto de Oliveira toward Santana, yeah? Two of us get out here, at the start of First street. It's got to be two cause this stretch is way longer and hotter than the other one. So, two guys head down First, hang a left on Eighth, then a right on Fifth—which takes them past my house, and remember, a couple of guys might be hiding out there—then walk all the way to the corner of Third. That's where they set up. It's got to be me and somebody else, cause I know the area. Right, so while those two are doing that, the car drives up Olinto de Oliveira, takes a right on Santana, and stops at the corner of Luiz Manoel. That's where the next guy gets out. He walks down Luiz Manoel and sets up as close to the Loop as he can without being seen. Then the last person in the car drives down Santana, hangs a right on the street with the name I can't remember, another right on Santa Terezinha, and parks all the way over here. This is where Santa Terezinha ends, and where Fourth and Fifth, which are actually alleys, start. The goal is to knock off everybody in the Loop. Then me and whoever's with me on the corner of Third and Fifth, plus the guy on his own on Luiz Manoel, cut across the Loop and take Fourth all the way to Santa Terezinha, which is where the last person is gonna be waiting. Then we all climb back in the car and get the fuck outta there." Luan looked up and scanned his colleagues' eyes, waiting for someone to say something.

Pedro smiled and nodded.

"Sounds good to me."

"Me too," Roberto agreed.

"Me three," Marques echoed.

"Just make sure y'all in position before you open fire," Angélica observed.

"That's right," Luan said. He glanced back down at the map, then continued: "A couple other points we gotta keep in mind. One: whoever's at the end of Luiz Manoel can't let *any*one down Second street. Cause if one of them gets through there, then he can take Eighth and come up behind me and my partner on Fifth. I'm gonna say it again: don't let *any*body slip down Second street, alright? Two: whoever sets up at the end of Santa Terezinha is gonna be in the best position to shoot anyone coming up Fourth street—whether they're running from the Loop to Fourth, or from Ninth to Fourth over here, see? You gotta watch out for Tenth too, cause one of their houses is right on Seventh. So look down that way every now and then, or you might get took by surprise. Three: me and the other guy on the corner of Third and Fifth are gonna have two tasks. To shoot at the fools in the Loop and keep an eye on their other house, over here on Third, case somebody comes out of there too."

"Cool, so who's going where?" Pedro asked.

The gang looked at each other for a second. Then Roberto volunteered:

"I can take Santa Terezinha."

"And I can take Luiz Manoel," said Marques.

"Cool. That leaves me and Pedro to take First."

"Sounds good," Pedro agreed.

Angélica stared at the map, picturing their strategy. As she visualized Marques walking down Luiz Manoel, she realized that unless he knew where the Balas were positioned, he'd be wide open. So she came up with a plan.

"Before y'all do anything, I could head down Luiz Manoel and cop an eight-ball from one of the Balas. They don't know me. It'll give me a chance to scope things out in the Loop."

Marques didn't like the idea.

"I dunno, Angélica . . ."

"Gimme a break, babe!" she said. "It's not dangerous. I just go in, buy the dust, and leave."

"It makes sense, Marques," Pedro said in support. "Knowing ahead of time how many guys there are in the Loop and where could make a big difference. Besides, like Angélica said, it's not dangerous."

Marques cocked his head and pursed his lips, making it clear he disagreed. Pedro, meanwhile, interpreted his physical response as a concession and said:

"Cool. Here's how we do it. Angélica sets out first, in her car; we follow in the hatchback. Me and Luan get off at First street. Angélica parks on the corner of Santa Terezinha and Luiz Manoel and walks to the Loop to cop an eight-ball. Roberto and Marques pull up behind her and wait. She comes back, passes on her intel to Marques and Roberto, and they radio it to us. Angélica gets back in her car and leaves. Then Marques climbs out of the hatchback and heads down Luiz Manoel. Finally, Roberto drives up to Santa Terezinha. Sound good?"

They all agreed in unison.

Right then, someone rang the doorbell. Whoever it was, patience was not their strong suit. Less than a second later, they were already pounding on the door. The air in the house grew thick. Roberto frowned and nodded at Marques as if to ask, "Who is it?" Marques shrugged and threw open his arms as if to say, "Not a clue."

"Who is it!" Angélica yelled.

A male voice yelled back:

"It's the police, goddamnit! Open the fucking door!"

Luan took a step back, ready to make a run for the kitchen; Roberto took a step forward, ready to throw himself on the officer if the door was battered down; Marques instinctively stepped in front of Angélica; Angélica took an empty whiskey glass from the table, ready to hurl it at the intruder; Pedro stepped behind the sofa and unzipped the backpack with the guns.

The man on the other side of the door burst out laughing and said:

"I'm kidding, I'm kidding. It's me, Hans! Open up!"

Seconds later, Hans was standing in the middle of the living room and being harshly rebuked for his off-color joke.

"Oh, fuck off!" he said, pulling up a chair and sitting down. "I'm the one should be pissed at you. Y'all throw a party and don't invite me? If Fabrício hadn't told me what y'all had planned for tonight, I wouldn't have found out. Good fucking friends you are. To make matters worse, I come over to offer you a boost, and this is how I'm treated? 'Wah wah wah, that shit's not funny, Hans. Wah wah wah.' Well, y'all can suck my dick. Here's what's up: I wanna look pretty too. Where my uniform at?"

Marques had to go ask the cartel boss of Vila Lupicínio Rodrigues for another police uniform. Meanwhile, the others filled Hans in on their plan.

"Cool, cool, cool. I got it," Hans said. "Where do I set up? Who's my partner?"

"There's already two guys on the corner of Third and Fifth: me and Luan," Pedro explained. "So you can partner up with Marques on Luiz Manoel or with Roberto on Santa Terezinha."

"Far as I can tell from this ratty map, it makes more sense for Hans to stick with Marques," Roberto weighed in. "That end of Luiz Manoel is closest to the Loop, where most of the Balas will be, maybe even all of them. If the map's right, that puts me farther from the Loop than the rest of you. Meaning I've got better cover too."

"The map's right," Luan agreed. "It's like you said: even though you got to keep one eye on Fourth and another on Tenth, you have the best cover, cause you're farther from the Loop than the rest of us."

"It's a plan," Pedro said. "Hans follows Marques on to Luiz Manoel."

As soon as Marques came back and Hans slipped into his uniform, it was time for action. They each snorted a generous line of cocaine, hooked their radios to their belts, slid in their earpieces, tested them to make sure they worked, loaded and holstered their firearms, and then finally left the house.

As discussed, Angélica set out first in her car, steering it down the streets of Porto Alegre, which were virtually deserted at that time of night; the rest of the gang followed in the stolen hatchback. Leaving the Menino Deus neighborhood, they drove through Cidade Baixa along Rua Dr. Sebastião Leão, then immediately crossed Avenida João Pessoa and took Avenida Jerônimo Ornelas straight into the Santana neighborhood. A bit further on, they turned right on Rua Jacinto Gomes, then continued south. It wasn't long before they were on the east side of Rua Dr. Olinto de Oliveira, which they took into Vila Planetário.

They stopped a few meters ahead, at the start of First street. Pedro and Luan pulled on their balaclavas, took out their guns, and exited the hatchback, shutting the doors behind them and scanning the area. There wasn't a soul around to see them.

The cars started up again, then turned right on the corner of Rua Dr. Olinto de Oliveira and Rua Santana. They reached the next corner in no time and pulled over again. It was Angélica's turn. She parked the car and walked down Luiz Manoel toward the Loop.

Roberto, who was behind the wheel of the hatchback, saw Marques looking anxious in the backseat next to Hans.

"Don't worry, Marques. She'll be back before you know it. Everything's gonna be alright."

"Man, I hope so," Marques answered.

"Y'all ever been in a shootout?" Hans asked. Marques and Roberto shook their heads, so he continued. "No matter what, don't ever turn your back on the enemy. Even if he shows up right in front of you, you swallow your fear and stand your ground."

"You mean we shouldn't run?"

"That's right. If you turn and run and shoot behind you, no way in hell are you hitting what you want to hit. If you come across a guy and decide to make a run for it in a panic, your chances of hitting him are nil, cause you're legging it and shooting behind you like a dumbass. The worst part is if the other dude stays in place and keeps calm. Then he can aim his gun right at your back, coolly pull the trigger, and bam."

"Alright. Then what do we do if we come across one of them?"

"You stay cool! Between you and him, the guy who stays the coolest has the highest chance of survival. If you bump into one of them, stay *right where you are*; get down and make yourself small, cause that way you're a harder target, then, take aim, be as straight as you can, and shoot. Got it? No matter how scared you are or how much you wanna run, you get down, take aim, shoot; get down, take aim, shoot; get down, take aim, shoot. Don't ever turn your back, brother. Just pretend the other guys are shooting blanks. If you can manage that, if you can pretend the bullets won't hit you, then you'll keep calm and do the right thing: get down, take aim, shoot."

Hans's explanation made sense to Roberto.

"Cool, thanks. Anything else?"

"Yeah . . ." Hans said, with a crazed smile. "Don't have mercy on them, for you shall receive none."

"Fuck off, Hans!" crackled Pedro's voice in everyone's ears. "That's from *The Lord of the Rings*!"

Roberto, Marques, and Hans laughed, and the sound filled the inside of the hatchback.

"Look, there she is," Roberto said, still laughing.

Angélica strolled down the sidewalk with her hood pulled over her head and her hands in her pockets. She went past her car, straight to the other vehicle. Roberto rolled down the window on the passenger side. Angélica hunched over and reached into the hatchback, opened the glove compartment and tossed in the eightball she had bought in Vila Planetário.

"So?" Hans asked.

"There's ten guys in the Loop. If we still think there's fifteen total, then I don't know where the rest of them are. Maybe in the houses Luan pointed out on the map. All ten guys are on the left side if you're coming out Luiz Manoel. They're listening to music, drinking, smoking pot. I couldn't tell if they were armed. They gotta be, though. But the plan should work. They're distracted, a bit stoned: I reckon y'all can clip about five of them before they know what hit them. Another thing: there's a car parked at the end of Luiz Manoel. Use it for cover."

"Thanks, love. Now get outta here," Marques said. "I'll be home soon."

"Okay. Be careful." Angélica turned on her heels and walked back to her car. Next minute, her vehicle was vanishing down Rua Santana.

"Pedro, Luan, y'all hear what Angélica said?" asked Roberto.

Both men said "no" on the radio at the same time.

"There's ten guys in the Loop. To the left if you're coming out Luiz Manoel. The other five are probably somewhere in the hood. So careful when you go past Luan's."

"Thanks, Roberto," Pedro said.

"Thanks, Roberto," Luan echoed.

Marques and Hans exited the hatchback and shut the door, balaclavas pulled over their heads. Then, Roberto started the engine and drove away.

Moments later, Hans pointed several meters ahead of him, at the corner of Luiz Manoel and Santana, and asked Marques:

"Ready to head in?"

"Not yet! I still gotta set up on Dona Terezinha."

No one thought of reminding Roberto that the street name was *Saint* Terezinha, not *Mrs.* Terezinha. Hans responded:

"We don't have to open fire on our way in. We can just close in on the guys and take cover while we wait for you all to set up. Then, when it's time, we go in together."

Luan cut in:

"That's a bad idea, Hans. The Balas could clock you and then you'd have to open fire before we're ready. Let Roberto set up first, since they can't see him on Santa Terezinha. Then me and Pedro will head over. You and Marques are last, cause y'all are wider open than the rest of us. We gotta make sure Pedro, Roberto, and me are in position before they see you."

"Okay, okay!" Hans said, clicking his tongue. He pulled out his guns with a flourish, then kissed them one at a time. "Have I introduced you to Ruth and Raquel?"

Wanting in on the fun, Marques pulled out the firearm Pedro borrowed from Valdir.

"And have I introduced you to . . ." Marques tried to come up with a good name, "Wanda?"

When Hans saw the gun, he scrunched his face in disgust.

"A thirty-round magazine? That's fucking gross, man!"

"How come?"

"Look at the size of that thing, the way it sticks out from the handle. It's fucking inelegant, dude, for real. That's not a classy weapon. That's some trailer-park shit there. If I was you, I'd be ashamed to be seen in public with that thing. It's like the fanny pack of firearms."

In the meanwhile, Roberto steered the hatchback to the right, leaving behind Rua Santana and entering the street labeled with a question mark on Luan's map. The street was Rua Laurindo, and it came to an end a bit further ahead on Santa Terezinha.

When Roberto read the sign and saw he was on the right street, it occurred to him that it might not be a good idea to drive into the neighborhood. Instead, he reversed onto Rua Laurindo and parked the car. He exited the vehicle, pulled on his balaclava, took out his gun, and walked to the end of Santa Terezinha. He glanced up Tenth street, to the left, and saw only darkness, but looking straight ahead, down Fourth street, which was just as dark, he saw the yellowish glow of a streetlamp over the Loop. He also heard voices and music coming from the direction of the light, though he couldn't make out any people: the ten men Angélica had seen were all on the other end of the alley, behind a wall on the right side.

"Pedro, Luan, I'm here," Roberto said.

"Cool, we're heading in," Pedro answered.

Pedro and Luan walked up First street, guns held out in front of them with both hands and fingers ready to pull the trigger at the first sign of danger. They turned left up ahead and skirted the houses on the right of Eighth street. At the corner of Fifth, they stopped and looked around.

"That's my crib," Luan said, nodding at a house sunken in darkness.

"Looks like nobody's home," Pedro said.

"Yeah, let's check it out."

They stayed low on their way to the house, then quietly opened the iron gate and stepped into the tiny patio. The front door was ajar. Luan carefully pushed it open and peered into the living room. It was so dark inside, he may as well have had both his eyes closed.

"If there was anyone home, the lights would be on."

"Yeah."

Even so, Pedro and Luan only relaxed after every last room had been checked. They did this without turning on a single light to avoid drawing the attention of any passersby.

"Is the house clear?" Marques asked on the radio.

"All clear," Luan confirmed. "Wait, we still gotta head over to the corner. Hold up."

Luan walked back onto Fifth and then slowly turned toward Third with Pedro on his heels.

"The fuck is that thing over there, Luan?"

Pedro pointed to several large trash bags sitting on the edge of the street propped against the side of a house.

"That's Skewer's junk shop. He recycles too. Those bags are filled with PET bottles."

The junk shop was near the corner of Fifth and Third. Across from the junk shop, on the right side of Fifth street, were a pair of trees that grew so close to each other that their crowns had fused into a single canopy. They paused behind them, their backs to the trunks. Luan pointed to a house on Third street and said:

"That's one of their houses. See how there's a light on? One of us should stay here. It's a good vantage point, in case we need to shoot any guys that come outta that house. The other guy can set up over there," he pointed to the other end of the alley, "so he can shoot at the fools in the Loop."

"Cool, I'll stay here," Pedro said. He cut across Fifth street, then took a couple of steps forward. Shoulder glued to the wall of the last house in the alley, Pedro carefully glanced left, down Third street: ten or twenty meters ahead, the Balas stood around an old portable radio, chatting under the yellow glow of the streetlamp. "I see them, I see them."

"Are you and Luan in position?" Hans asked.

"Yeah. You and Marques can head in now. They won't see you. They're not paying attention. And if they do, I'll open fire over here."

Marques and Hans walked cautiously down Rua Luiz Manoel. It wasn't long before they spotted the Balas in the cul-de-sac, thirty or so meters ahead of them, to the left. It was a tense moment—all it would take for Hans and Marques to be made was for one of the Balas to turn around. And yet, a few steps later, they were both crouching behind the car Angélica had told them about.

"Cool, we're in position too," Hans said. "Who's up first?"

"I can't see anybody from where I am," Roberto quickly explained.

"Y'all have to fire first, Hans," Pedro observed.

"Why us?" Marques asked.

"Cause if I shoot from here, they're gonna scatter toward you, and y'all are way too close. You might not have enough time to ice them all, and they could ice you instead. But if y'all shoot first, then they're gonna scatter toward Roberto, and we're in a good position to shoot them before they're anywhere near us. That way, we might even stand a chance of smoking the whole crew. If one or two of them survive, they're gonna run and hide in that corner there, where none of us can see them."

"Right, cool. Can we get started already?" Hans asked.

"Go strong, man. Blow their motherfucking brains out!" Pedro said, and then added, as if wishing them all luck: "God bless!"

And they all repeated:

"God bless!"

When Marques and Hans, dressed head-to-toe in black, rose behind the car to take aim at the enemy, it was as if they had been born from the very shadows of Rua Luiz Manoel. From one minute to the next, the stillness of the night was shattered by weapons spitting fire.

Three bodies piled on the floor. The rest of the men looked confused and, unsure of what to do next, they did everything at the same time: scanning the area for the shooter, retreating, ducking behind each other, unholstering weapons. In this instant of panicked indecision, another man was shot while pulling out his gun, and fell to the ground, howling in pain. Now that the Balas knew where the gunshots were coming from, the six men still standing sent back a salvo of gunfire. Their weapons were of varying calibers, and the sounds ranged from high-pitched to booming, from brief to long, with some shots coming in quick spurts of rat-tat-tat while others were more spread out. Marques and Hans were unharmed; the second the Balas started shooting, they ducked behind the car.

Even as they backed into Fourth street, the Balas never once stopped firing at Rua Luiz Manoel. Out of nowhere, one man collapsed from a shot to the back of the head; Roberto had opened fire from his position on Santa Terezinha. Another man yelped in surprised when a bullet struck his shoulder and made a mad dash for Third street. Realizing they weren't safe on Fourth, the rest of the Balas sprinted after him, only to freeze at the sight of his body jolting once, twice, three times, four, as if possessed by an evil spirit. Finally, he dropped to his knees and slumped to the ground, where he lay curled on his side like a fetus: Pedro had fired from the corner of Third and Fifth, hitting the man several times.

Four men were left standing. As Pedro had predicted, they all retreated to the corner of Fourth and Luiz Manoel, where—fenced in, desperate, perhaps even presaging their own deaths—they cowered. But they were safe in that corner, at least for now. Neither Marques, Hans, Roberto, Luan, or Pedro had a good view of them.

Now that the gunfire had ceased, they could hear dogs barking across the neighborhood.

"Anyone hit?" Luan asked.

"No."

"No."

"No."

"No."

Marques began to get up so he could look over the top of the car.

"You got a death wish, moron?" asked Hans, pulling him back down by the arm.

Marques wriggled free.

"Let go! We need to make sure none of them try and sneak up Second street."

"Fuck, you're right!"

The two men stood up and peered over the top of the car.

"Anybody see where they went?" Marques asked.

"Careful: They're pretty close to you," Pedro answered. "I can't see them at the moment, but I caught them running toward you earlier. I bet they're hiding out next to the building in front of you, in that corner I talked about."

"Marques, over there," Hans cocked his head and smiled.

Marques craned his neck and looked in the direction Hans had nodded. It was the man they'd hit at the start of the shootout while pulling out his gun. He was dragging himself forward in an attempt to discreetly join his friends in their hideout. Hans holstered Ruth, freeing him to hold Raquel with both hands. He stepped to the side, crouched, and coolly aimed his gun at the poor bastard. Finally, he fired. A single, perfect shot. The bullet hit the crown of his skull. He stopped moving. Blood pooled beneath his head.

"Who did that?"

"Relax, it was me."

Right then, the front door of the house being monitored by Luan swung open. Two men rushed into the street, slowing only to open the metal patio gate. Startled, Luan pointed his gun at them and pulled the trigger again and again, firing a total of ten shots, several of which struck the metal gate, judging by the sparks that briefly lit up that section of Third street. One man keeled over while the other rushed back into the house, not even stopping to close the door.

"Careful with the ammo, Luan," Pedro said. "Make sure you only fire when you got a good shot."

"O-okay," Luan stammered.

"Y'alright, man?"

"I'm cool, don't worry. Just shocked. Didn't expect nobody to come outta that fucking house."

An even greater shock followed. It was as if dozens of bombs were going off at the same time all over Planetário, as if dozens of cars were crashing into each and every house, as if dozens of thunderclaps were striking in quick succession in the very heart of the neighborhood: a powerful, unending volley of gunfire from a heavy automatic weapon aimed at Pedro and Luan. For a second Pedro was convinced he wouldn't survive that onslaught. He dropped to the ground and curled into a very small ball, shielding his head with his arms. He felt as if not only his life were about to end, but as if the whole world would soon be over, the noise so deafening it was as though the shots were being fired centimeters from his right ear.

While Pedro threw himself on the ground, an equally terrified Luan ducked for cover behind the bags of PET bottles. Peering through the gap between them, he located the source of the gunfire. Though he couldn't make out the shooter, he guessed from the bursts of light behind the tree canopy that the shots were coming from the top floor of the house on Third street, and that the shooter was likely the same man who'd been outside just moments ago and managed to flee back into the house. Neither Luan nor Pedro could see him from where they hid, and he couldn't see them from where he was either. An abundant tree canopy stood between them, leaving the shooter no choice but to fire blindly through the leaves.

Everything seemed to indicate that the shooter was squeezing the trigger until the magazine was empty. The moment the gunfire stopped, the whole gang radioed in at the same time, making a racket in their earpieces.

"Fuck!"

"What the hell was that?"

"What's going on?"

"Where's it coming from?"

"That was a machine gun, man!"

"Nah, it was an assault rifle!"

"Is everybody okay?"

"Pedro, get up and come over here! Get the fuck over here, Pedro!" It was Luan. It was clear Pedro couldn't hear him over the chatter, so Luan let out a long, aggressive *hist!* "Shut the hell up! Shut the fuck up already!" Once there was silence, he called out again: "Pedro! Hey! Get your ass over here!"

Pedro was still on the ground. Only when he looked behind him did he notice Luan wasn't where he thought he would be; the other thing he noticed, and couldn't understand at first, were the leaves falling from the tree canopy, slowly reeling in the dark of night. Pedro wasted no time. He stood up and ran over to Luan, just as the peppery smell of gunpowder overpowered the air.

The next second, there was the sound of five shots—"pah!," "pah!," "pah-pah-pah!"—their blasts less powerful than the ones that had ended moments ago.

"Who was that?" Luan asked.

"Me and Hans," Marques answered. "One of the dudes tried to leave their hideout and sneak down Second."

"Did you get him? Is he dead? Did you kill him?"

"He's dead."

"Good work!"

Luan pointed at Third street from behind the trash bags and told Pedro about the shooter on the top floor. But his voice was soon drowned out: the man in the house had finished reloading his weapon and started shooting again. This time he pulled the trigger in spurts, firing three to four rounds at a time. Luan used one of these pauses to finish what he was saying, adding:

"You stay here, Pedro. Stay here and keep shooting, okay? I'm gonna take First street and catch the motherfucker with his pants down."

"Alright, cool. I got this. Go ahead." Pedro fired four times through the tree canopy, then quickly ducked for cover, in response to a volley of gunshots he received in return.

As Luan rushed down Fifth street, the sound of blind gunfire faded behind him. He turned left on Eighth street and left again at the end of the block. Minutes later he was panting at the corner of First and Third. He paused to catch his breath, then stepped forward to get a better view.

His current position was much more dangerous than his previous one on the corner of the junk shop. There was nothing to stop the shooter from seeing Luan: all it would take was a look in his direction. The man in the house wasn't his only concern either. The Balas had taken over two other houses besides that one (one on Seventh and the other on Ninth), which meant there was a small chance one of them could decide to leave the house and surprise Luan by popping out of Sixth street. The longer he lingered, the more dangerous it was. He decided to keep moving. He creeped up Third street in search of the best angle to fire at the shooter.

The first thing he saw was the gun, muzzle smoking on the windowsill. Something about the way it was held, barrel pointing upward, took Luan aback, though it wasn't long before he figured out what was happening: the man on the second floor was reloading his weapon behind the wall. Assuming the shooter would have to expose himself to fire at Pedro, Luan stood in place and waited with his gun trained at the window. His stomach went cold. He nearly fired, then instantly changed his mind, realizing he'd be giving up his position if he missed. Instead, he decided to get one step closer at a time so that it would be easier for him to hit the target. He heard Hans's voice in his earpiece telling them to "get down, take aim, shoot; get down, take aim, shoot. Don't ever turn your back, brother." He got down, kept his weapon trained at the window, and stepped forward. He also decided not to turn his back or run away if he was seen (a terrifying prospect): he'd stay cool, stand his ground, and hit the target.

To Luan's despair, he was in fact seen by the shooter, who swiveled his gun toward him with alarming speed. They exchanged gunfire for three eternal seconds. Luan remembered to stay down as he sent shot after shot at the enemy. He heard the whiz of bullets and the whoosh of air displaced by projectiles that zipped past him like invisible bolts of lightning and remained perfectly still. Finally, the shooter let out a strange cry—like a belch cut short—and fell back into the house, dropping his gun out of the window and onto the roof above the front patio.

"I got him," Luan said, closing his eyes and breathing a sigh of relief.

"Good job, Chokito!" Pedro said. "You're the man! Now get over here. But take the back way again. I think the other guys can make you from their hideout."

"No, wait . . ."

"For what?"

"I'm gonna check on the asshole."

"You're going into the house?"

"Yeah." But Luan was already inside, which is why he was whispering.

"Are you insane, man?"

"Listen, I know I shot the guy and his gun fell out the window. What I don't know is if he's dead or not. What if I just clipped him? What if he's got another gun up there and, before we know it, he's shooting at us again? If he's still alive, then my coming all this way to get him won't make a difference."

"But what if there's more guys in there? Luan, listen to me. Get the fuck back here, man!"

"Stop bugging me, damn it! I can't answer. I'm already inside."

"Fuck!"

Pedro resumed his post on the corner of Fifth street so he could monitor the activity in the Loop. But his concern for Luan was so great that he could hardly pay attention to what was happening there. Next minute he heard a sudden, intense exchange of gunfire and went cold from head to toe. Amid the sound of multiple gunshots were several cries of hatred and pain.

"No, no, no!"

"You piece of shit!"

"Ow, ow, ow!"

Once the gunfire and yelling had died down, there was still the sound of a single, anguished voice screaming in a hoarse falsetto. Nothing about that voice seemed human. It was more like the devastating roar of a beast locked in battle, which gradually transformed into a shuddering cry of pain. A final gunshot followed, and the voice vanished for good.

At first Pedro assumed the shootout had something to do with Luan being in the Balas' house. It wasn't long before he realized the confrontation had actually taken place on Fourth street.

"Iced two guys on Fourth," Roberto said. "They came out of an alley up front—Ninth, if I'm not mistaken. There were three total, but one guy ran back into the alley."

"That was a lot of shooting, man!" Marques remarked.

"Yeah. Motherfuckers were clever. Came out the alley with two guys facing front and one facing back. Started shooting soon as I opened fire."

"Damn. You alright though, yeah?" Hans asked, more as a statement than a question.

"Yeah, yeah. My cover over here's real good. They fired a load of shots, but the bullets came nowhere near me. Man, the guy who got away though, the one who ran back into the alley, was packing a fucking monster of a piece. A 12-gauge, I think."

"Huh, I didn't hear any 12-gauge shots . . ." Marques remarked.

"Yeah, me neither . . ." Hans added.

"He didn't get the chance to shoot. He saw heads rolling on Fourth and ran back to Ninth or whatever that fucking street is. Didn't even try and shoot me."

"Keep your eyes peeled," Pedro warned. "He's clocked you now. Next thing you know, he could go around the back way and pop out of an alley right next to you."

"Don't worry. I'm on it."

By then Luan had checked every room on the ground floor and found no one. He was climbing the metal spiral staircase, as quietly as he could. Once he made it upstairs, he saw that the second floor was made up of two bedrooms and a small bathroom. All three accordion doors were open, and the only light source was in the hallway. Since the bathroom entrance was west-facing, Luan would only have to turn sideways and crane his neck to see if anyone was hiding there. The two bedroom entrances, on the other hand, were north-facing; the only way he could examine them was by walking down the hall and exposing himself.

He advanced slowly and in complete silence. Resting his head near the entrance of the first room, he glanced inside with one eye. Because of the acute angle, he could only make out a corner of the wardrobe on the left-hand side of the room. Careful not to breathe too loudly, he shifted his head little by little, expanding his field of view. Soon he could make out a single bed, headboard against the open window. The blankets were drenched in blood, which alarmed Luan. As far as he could tell, the shooter seemed to have collapsed on the bed after he was shot. And yet, the man was nowhere to be seen. As Luan took in more and more of the room, he saw part of his body: his legs were still on the bed. Judging by their position, Luan guessed the wounded shooter had tried to stand up, only to die (or faint) in the process, top half of his body on the floor and legs on the mattress.

Luan was correct, as he would find out once he had a view of the whole room. The other thing he discovered was the man was not alive: he lay there motionless—eyes wide open, mouth slack, left cheek pressed against the floor—with the petrified look of a person suddenly unable to breathe. There was an exit wound on the back of his neck; the sheer quantity of blood still gushing from that hole sent shivers through Luan's body.

It wasn't long before Luan forgot all about that body. As though drawn by a magnet, his eyes drifted to a backpack on the bedside table. It was clear why it was sitting there, by the window, just as it was clear why it was open: poking out from the backpack were a pair of magazines. Except it wasn't the ammo that caught Luan's attention. It was money. A lot of money. Rolls upon rolls of one-hundred-real notes fastened with yellow rubber bands.

Luan had the urge to grab the money and run. But he still had to scope out the second room, a process, he quickly determined, that would be far more dangerous than the first: the hallway light was positioned in such a way that it would cast his shadow directly into the bedroom as he advanced. This meant he couldn't use the same slow, cautious approach as before. Instead, he'd have to dive forward gun first and pray he was quicker on the draw than the man inside.

Luan closed his eyes, took a deep breath, and crossed himself. He lunged forward, spinning into the room gun first. What he saw shocked him. There was someone lying on the bed. It wasn't long before he realized he wasn't in danger: the body was curled on its side and looked dead. He groped around for the light switch, first on the right wall, then on the left. He flipped on the light, flooding the room with a white glow, only to get another shock, this one greater than the last.

"*Larissa!*"

Together, Pedro, Marques, Hans, and Roberto echoed: "Larissa?"

Luan was too stunned to listen to them. He holstered his weapon, leaped onto the bed, untied Larissa's hands, and tore the tape off her mouth.

"Hey, Larissa! Larissa! Wake up! Larissa!" he cried over and over, shaking her by the shoulders and slapping her face. "Larissa, come on! It's me, Luan!" He was surprised to see that tears were falling from his cheek onto her face. "Oh, Larissa. Fuck! Wake up, damn it! Larissa! Hey! Talk to me! Don't do this to me, please!" He held her body close, surrendering to the tears and hopelessness.

Strange how even when death is the most natural thing in the world, the one thing we can count on in life, strange how even then death remains unfathomable to the loved ones of the deceased. Larissa's body emitted no heat, but Luan couldn't help hoping she might not be dead. How could she, when his feelings for her were so unique, so beautiful and strong? How could she, when he hadn't yet told her how he felt? How could she, when he'd just hatched the perfect plan—to take the bag of cash from the other room, find her wherever she was, and run off together to live a quiet life in a peaceful corner of the city? He had lost his mother less than a week ago. How could he be losing Larissa too? It wasn't fair! But it was true. It didn't make sense! But it was true. It was a lie! But it was true.

And as unbelievable as it may sound to the reader of this wretched story, it remains true that, moments later, Luan himself would fall dead on the body of his beloved, a 12-gauge bullet taking off the top of his head.

"Luan!" Pedro cried after hearing the blast. "Luan!" he cried again and had the sinking feeling his cries would never be answered. "Luan!"

After the third call, he finally let himself plunge into the same heavy silence that had subsumed Marques, Hans, and Roberto. They remained like this for a while, absorbing that tragic turn of events. The first person to speak was Roberto:

"Shit . . ."

The next sound was not so much a voice as a series of hisses, crackles, small bursts of static. Someone was tinkering with Luan's radio.

The noises stopped. Pedro called out again:

"Luan?"

A gruff, male voice answered:

"Luan? Luan can't talk right now . . . Cat got his tongue. In fact, cat got his whole goddamn head."

"That right, asshole? Then wait there, stay right where you are, motherfucker, cause I got something to say to you."

Blind with rage and deaf to all the voices on the radio (including that of the man in the house), Pedro set off in the direction of the house. He didn't even remember to take First street like Luan had done and instead went straight down Third, where he briefly exposed himself to the men hiding out on the corner of Fourth and Luiz Manoel. They fired at Pedro three or four times and missed him every time.

In the meanwhile, the man was waiting for Pedro on the second floor. He switched off the light Luan had turned on as well as the light in the hallway. He spat out a flavorless lump of gum, perhaps assuming it would help him focus. He cracked his neck and back, like someone preparing to spend several hours in an uncomfortable position. Finally, he posted himself at the entrance of the first room with his shotgun at an oblique, upright angle, ready to fire his weapon at the first sight of a tuft of hair in the square in the floor. He hoped to shoot Pedro just as he had Luan—in the back of the head. Yet it was the back of his head that, moments later, took a bullet. Pedro never stepped foot through the door. Instead, he climbed onto the roof over the front patio and tiptoed to the open bedroom window. At first, as he peered into the dark of the bedroom, he saw nothing. He waited for his eyes to grow accustomed to the dim light. Once they had, he saw a man's silhouette at the bedroom door, just a few meters ahead, virtually indistinguishable in the dark, shotgun pointed away from the window. From his position on the roof, Pedro carefully aimed his weapon at the dark figure, then slowly pulled down on the trigger until his finger met resistance. He gave the trigger a brusque squeeze. There was a loud flash as blood sprayed the air and the man slumped to the floor, as if all of his bones had suddenly left his body.

"I got him! I killed him!"

Marques, Hans, and Roberto commemorated.

"Damn straight!"

"Die, motherfucker!"

"Have fun in hell, you piece of shit!"

In the rush of euphoria, they fired several shots into the sky.

"Hey, hey, hey. Cool it!" Pedro said. "That's enough, all right? Give it a rest. Let's bounce."

"But we didn't get all of them . . ." Hans objected.

"Fuck that! Forget about them. We shouldn't have come here in the first place. Luan's dead, man. Don't you get it? He's dead! It was fucking stupid to come here at all. Maybe we kill ten guys, twenty: What difference does it make? The kid's dead! He's dead."

"I'll grab the car," Roberto said. "Wait for me where I dropped you all off."

And it was a good thing they left, too. In the distance, there was the faint wailing of police sirens.

22

SOUP AND A
DECADE OF HELL

When Angélica opened the front door and saw everyone but Luan walk in, her first thought was to ask where he was. She did more than think the question too; she opened her mouth. In the end, there was no need. Her frightened eyes read the answer in the men's desolate looks. Holding her head in her hands, she collapsed onto the sofa.

Marques walked straight to the kitchen and came back with a bottle of whiskey. The others had already sat down. Instead of pulling out a chair by the table, he chose to sit on the sofa armrest next to his wife, where he drank whiskey straight from the bottle in silence. Tears were already streaming down Angélica's face. Her cries were painful but quiet, save for the occasional sniffle.

No one had the courage to speak. There was no room for words. Yet Hans didn't seem as rattled as the rest of the group. Every now and then he would sigh and shake his head with a grim look on his face, but it was as if he were more bored than anything else. At some point, he started flicking at a fern hanging by the window. Even though this annoyed the hell out of Pedro, he said nothing, instead censuring Hans with a hard look that had no effect on him whatsoever.

Pedro tried to ignore the repeated flicking and grabbed the bottle of whiskey Marques held out to him. He took a long swing and winced, then passed the bottle to Roberto, who lit a cigarette and said, smoke curling out of his nose:

"Man, I need a bump. Any of my coke left?"

"Nope," Marques responded with a shake of the head.

"Doubt they'll be selling that shit in Planetário anytime soon," Hans said with a smile.

For Pedro, this was a step too far.

"Look around, asshole. Does this look like a good time for a joke?"

"No point getting pissed at me, man," Hans said, still flicking at the fern. "To start, this shit wasn't my idea. I just came to help. It was your idea. The kid died. It happens. But if somebody's to blame, it ain't me."

Pedro cocked his eyebrows and curled his lips into a crazed smile, the way people do when they have several things to say but no idea where to start.

"Ah! Nah, you're right, you're right. My bad. It wasn't your fault. Course it wasn't. By the way, thanks for backing us, man. For real. I hadn't even got round to thanking you. Now, would you do me a favor?" His face suddenly clouded over. Pointing at the door, he yelled: "Get the fuck out of here before I shove that plant down your fucking throat!"

At first Hans seemed surprised he was being asked to leave, but since no one stepped in to defend him, not even the hosts, he pursed his lips and said:

"No problem, man. You're right, I best get going." He went to the master bedroom, where he changed out of the police uniform and into his own clothes. Then he cut back across the living room and walked out into the cold night without saying goodbye, shutting the door behind him.

After Hans left, no one said a word for almost an entire hour. It's hard to speak when your soul is clamoring, when all you want to do is listen. Water dripped from the faucet into the steel kitchen sink, competing with the living room wall clock, which never ceased its dissonant ticking. Outside, the wind kept blowing and the dogs barking. In spite of everything that happened that night, every single thing, the world, for whatever reason, refused to come to a stop or miss a single beat, even for a few seconds. The world remained indifferent, not only to Luan's death and those of the fallen members of the largest criminal organization in Porto Alegre—the Balas na Cara—but to every story of human suffering that occurred every day, across every nation. The world insisted on persevering, on thudding onward, as if nothing.

The bottle of whiskey had been passed from hand to hand until none was left and now lay abandoned at the foot of the sofa. Pedro missed the feel of the liquor burning his throat. As though waking from a trance, he sighed and asked:

"Any whiskey left?"

"No, but there's some vodka," Marques said, getting up to go to the kitchen.

"Angélica, what about that blow you copped in Planetário?" Pedro asked.

"It's in the hatchback's glove compartment," she answered.

"I'm gonna go grab it. Be right back."

Roberto took the vehicle's keys out of his pocket and tossed them to Pedro.

The hatchback was parked behind the Osmar Fortes Barcellos recreation center, better known as the Tesourinha recreation center. There were no tall buildings in that forgotten, melancholy corner of Menino Deus, and a strong, frigid wind blew in from the Guaíba River, hitting Pedro in full as he waded through the gloom of Rua Almirante Álvaro Alberto da Mota e Silva toward the stolen car, arms wrapped around him.

He opened the passenger door and slid into the seat, leaving his feet outside, then riffled through the glove compartment for the cocaine. But then his eyes fell on something else: Luan's map, which Roberto had left there, should they need it. It was an unexpected blow. Hard and unexpected. Pedro shut his eyes and bit his bottom lip but failed to stop the tears. It was almost pleasurable, or perhaps a relief, to be able to let his guard down, to let his tears flow openly and whimpers move freely up his throat, to let his shoulders shudder to the rhythm of his sobs. He was alone now; there was no one he needed to be smart for, nor firm in his convictions. He thought of what Hans had said and recognized a bitter kernel of truth: "But if somebody's to blame, it ain't me." Hans really wasn't to blame; it was Pedro's fault. Jesus, it was all his fault! The scrap of paper was a reminder of the guilt he'd carry for the rest of his life. The hands that just hours ago had drawn that map would never do anything else, and it was all because of him. Overwhelmed with regret, Pedro cried harder, and felt like he was losing his mind. Part of him wanted to believe—part of him did believe—that he was a monster; the other wanted desperately to be forgiven, but didn't know where to seek forgiveness, or from whom. Where was this forgiveness? Who could give it to him? His beliefs were in pieces; *he* was in pieces. He didn't have the faintest idea what was right and what was wrong. He didn't recognize himself. All he knew was he had gone too far. At some point, he wasn't sure when exactly, he'd crossed an invisible line that should never be crossed. Now he was lost and couldn't find his way back. Worse yet, he didn't even know if there was a way back. Oh, God. He had nothing to hold on to, no light to follow, and the truth was he didn't deserve a light or anything to hold on to. Which made him feel like he had nothing to live for. He wanted to gaze up at the stars for an answer, for a sign of forgiveness, but was convinced he'd even lost the right to raise his head, that he couldn't bear the shame of the clouds, of the recreation center, of the lamppost. At most, he could open his eyes. And what he saw shocked him. Bleary with tears, Pedro glimpsed a pair of legs in black slacks standing about a step away from him; the shoes, also black, indicated that the legs belonged to a man. Pedro stopped crying, took out his gun, and pointed it at the stranger.

"Get away from me! Get back, get back!"

"Hmm, hmm." The man's mouth was full, and he was holding a hot dog. He took a couple of steps back, quickly swallowed his bite, and said: "Point that shit someplace else!"

Despite everything, Pedro couldn't help wondering where the guy had managed to get hold of a hot dog so late at night. Instead, he asked:

"Why were you standing so close?"

"Well, you looked like you were having a hard time, and I wanted to make sure you were okay. I was gonna say hi, but my mouth was full."

Persuaded by this explanation, Pedro breathed a sigh of relief and put away his gun.

"You scared me."

Still eating his midnight snack, the man approached him again. As he chewed, he said:

"Hmm, my sweet mother, who kicked the bucket a long time ago, hmm, my sweet mother always said: 'Don't ever let them see you bleeding.' Hmm. Is that what you're doing? Bleeding where nobody can see you?"

Pedro said nothing. He just hung his head and sighed, staring down at the basalt pavement. The man continued:

"Sounds like the hit didn't go as planned. Did one of the cwew die? Hope it wasn't Marques. Hmmm, I like Marques. He's a good kid."

Pedro frowned and lifted his head, fixing the man with a curious look.

"Who are you?"

"Name's Avelino, but you can call me Pops. Hmm." The man pointed his index finger at Pedro and wagged it with a slight flourish. "I'm the one who loaned y'all that uniform you got on."

Pedro smiled.

"Right, yeah! Marques has told me a lot about you. Sorry for pointing the gun at you, sir. I didn't know who you were. Anyway, I'm Pedro."

They shook hands.

"I thought you might be."

"You did?"

"Yeah. Hmm. Marques has told me a lot about you too. One time he said you were so skinny you look like a clothes hanger." The old man was still eating, so he had to laugh through his nose. "That's how I wecognized you."

"I see . . ."

"But he also told me you're a smart guy. I was skeptical at first. But then, hmm, I had a change of heart."

"Oh, yeah?"

"Yeah. You know, thanks to that weed scheme of yours, things have got a lot better for Marques and his wife. Hmm, before that, they could barely feed their boy; I live in the neighborhood, so I know. Now they have another girl and plenty of food for the both of them. They got a car. Fixed up their house. Built loads of other houses to lease in the city. They got a nice bit of money coming in. Don't they? I bet things are better for you too. Anyway. Hmm. In this world, my fwiend, idiots don't make money. They don't! That's how I know you're no idiot. That little scheme of yours bwought in enough money to make life better for you and the other folks involved, the folks awound you. Hmm. There's not an idiot in this world can do that. When an idiot is born in the muck, he dies in the muck."

Tears welled up again in Pedro's eyes, but this time he quickly wiped them with the palm of his hand.

"You heard about the hit, so you know the Balas took Planetário from a buddy of mine. And, and, and, you know what they did? They went after this girl he was nuts about. Fuck knows why, but they took her. They must've asked her a load of questions: about my buddy's business, if he had any partners and stuff . . . God knows. But then they didn't just let her go. Nope. Negative. They didn't let her go. They kept her and waited for her to die of hunger, or of thirst, maybe they even strangled her. I don't know. Only God knows what they did to her. God alone. Maybe they raped her until they got bored. I, I, I, ah! I don't even wanna think about it. The thing is we found her dead today. And those pieces of shit shot my buddy's ma to death too, in public, where everybody could see. You probably know that part. You know that bit, don't you, sir? And after all that, after all that, the cherry on top of the fucking cake is my buddy died too, during the hit. So what I'm saying, sir, is count the bodies: first my buddy lost his ma the way he did, only to find out the girl he was nuts about died the way she did, and then, after all that, they go and kill him too! How does that sound to you, sir? All that happened cause of a crazy idea I got in my head. And, and, and, you know, I'm gonna have to live with it for the rest of my life. I can't erase it!"

Pops had finished the hot dog. He wiped his lips with a napkin and cleaned the inside of his mouth with his tongue, then shook his head and said:

"I know how it goes. You oversalted your soup."

"Hunh?"

"You oversalted your soup."

"I oversalted my soup?"

"That's what it sounds like. When I was a kid and used to take things too far, like the time I stabbed my older bwother and he ended up in the hospital, my sweet mother used to say: 'Careful you don't oversalt your soup, Avelino. Cause at the end of the day, you're the one who has to eat it.' Well, it took me a while to understand that lesson. Now I know she was talking about the stuff that spirals out of contwol and that you can't undo. It's like you said: You're gonna have to live with it for the west of your life. You oversalted your soup, and now you got to eat it. But if it's any comfort, my life used to be salty too. I know what you're going through. And I swear it's all gonna be okay. It'll pass."

"Nah, there's no way, it won't." Pedro shook his head vigorously and sniffled. "I don't mean to offend you, sir, but I'm not the kind of guy that forgets a thing like this. I'm going to think about it every day, and I won't ever forgive myself."

"Who said anything about forgetting? Who said anything about forgiveness? Look, my mother didn't tell me everything. I had to learn some stuff on my own too. One thing I learned on my own is that the soup is never finished. The soup is only weady to eat the day you die." Pops looked smug as he placed his hands on his hips and tossed back his head, smiling up at the stars. "Yeah, my mother forgot to teach me that . . . Maybe she didn't know. The twuth is you spend your whole life as soup. Life *is* the fucking soup! You tweak it and taste it, tweak it and taste it, tweak it and taste it." He looked back at Pedro. "What I'm saying, kid, is that if your soup's too salty wight now, the first thing you got to do is stop adding more salt. Stop adding more salt and add water instead. Chop up some potatoes and toss them in too. Add some cawots while you're at it. Some chayote, squash, noodles . . . Fuck if I know. Only put in things you like. If you add too much salt, that's it, you can't take it out. Just don't forget: the soup's only finished the day you die; until then, you got to make sure it tastes good, cause you don't want to spend the west of your life eating bad soup. Look, what I'm getting at is simple: if you're ashamed of the shit you done or the shit your actions caused, then spend the time you got left on this Earth doing whatever helps you weclaim some hope and dignity. Make sense?"

It did. It made sense. Yes, it made sense. A lot of it.

Strange how often these small, magical knuckle-cracks of good fortune, these unexpected and seemingly unimportant events, these precious moments we mine from the quarries of life, strange how often they seal a person's fate. If not for that fleeting encounter with the Vila Lupicínio cartel boss, Pedro may never have been able to reclaim some of his hope and dignity.

AND YET THE encounter happened. The encounter happened and Pedro clung to the soup analogy like it was a life raft. The encounter happened and not a day went by when Pedro didn't meditate on the soup analogy. The encounter happened and it was thanks to the soup analogy that Pedro managed to withstand the pain and the fear, the beatings and the death threats. The encounter happened and it was his focus on the soup analogy that helped Pedro not turn on his friends. The encounter happened, and it was in the soup analogy that Pedro found the strength to remain silent, even though he was sure his silence would end in his death at the hands of the police officers who arrested and tortured him for hours, determined to find out who else had taken part in the Vila Planetário shootout.

The encounter happened, and to this day the soup analogy has helped Pedro stomach nearly a decade of hell behind bars.

The answer to the question that may be plaguing the reader's mind is a four-letter word: Hans. Hans and his fury when he was shown the door that cold night in 2011. Hans and his cowardice. Hans and an anonymous tip. The events unfolded as follows. Midmorning the next day, Pedro's eyes flew open at the sound of the police battering down his front door. It was too late for him to regret having parked the stolen car outside his house when he should've made it disappear in the middle of the night; it was too late for him to regret that the weapons they'd used the evening before, and which he'd intended to return to Valdir first thing that morning, were still in his room. Then came the full extent of what police are capable of when they want to obtain information from someone against whom all abuse is permitted. Then came the fingerprints in the hatchback, the ballistics analysis, the trial, the sentence. Guilty. Seventy-two years.

As mentioned, Pedro never lost faith in the soup analogy. But it isn't always easy to find the right ingredients, especially in the cell of an overcrowded prison. It was some time before Pedro found the perfect addition to his life. It was early 2013, and he'd just had a visit from his mother.

"What's that, Gollum?" asked one of Pedro's cellmates when he saw him with a book in his hand.

"What does it look like? A book. My ma brought it for me, she knows I like reading and stuff."

"Whassit called?"

"*The Felons Come to Tea.*"

"Lessee, lessee. Handitover." He grabbed the book from Pedro's hands, examined it, then broke into a huge smile. "Looks dope! *The Felons Come to Tea,*" he read aloud. Then, a moment later, he said: "Whaddabout you, Gollum? Why don't you write something, brother? Ain't you supposed to be book-smart and shit?"

Pedro's face lit up. It was as if the curtains had been pulled back on the sun itself. How had he not thought of it before?

"Damn, Fenômeno. I gotta say, that idea's not half-bad."

"No shit. Ain't none of my ideas bad. Don't you know who you're talking to?"

With a glimmer in his eyes and a faint smile on his lips, Pedro started daydreaming. That was it. He'd write a book. Why not? It was just what his soup needed, no matter how grueling it might be. As a matter of fact, a few days later, when Pedro finally sat down to tackle that challenge, when he finally took up his pen with a great, yawning notebook page in front of him, he did wonder if it might be impossible to write an entire story from start to finish, at least for him. But he soon learned not to think of the book as a whole: best to take a slow, steady approach, step by step. Time wasn't an issue. With this in mind, he wrote the following words at the top of the page: "Pedro and Marques Take Stock."

AND IF YOU, dear reader, are reading this right now, *très bien*— that means Pedro wrote all that he hoped to.

ACKNOWLEDGMENTS

I'd like to thank my mother and father, Rita Helena Falero and José Carlos da Silva, who raised me as a dreamer. My sister, Caroline Falero, who is and will always be my role model. I'd like to thank my girlfriend, Dalva Maria Soares, who got me to leave the canoe. And my cousins, Douglas Falero and Hitalo Juliano, who read a first draft of *Pedro and Marques Take Stock* centuries ago and convinced me I was on the right track. To everyone who contributed, either directly or indirectly, to the making of this book, and of this writer.

Thank you.

PHOTO BY TOMAS EDSON SILVEIRA

ABOUT THE AUTHOR

José Falero lives in Porto Alegre, Brazil. He is the author of *Vila Sapo*, a story collection published by Todavia in 2019, and *Mas em que mundo tu vive?*, a collection of essays published by Todavia in 2021. The English translation of his story collection is forthcoming from Astra House. *Pedro and Marques Take Stock* is his first work to be translated into English.

ABOUT THE TRANSLATOR

Julia Sanches translates literature from Portuguese, Spanish, and Catalan into English.